The
Wallflower
Wager

Tessa Dare

The Wallflower Wager

GIRL MEETS DUKE

AVONBOOKS
An Imprint of HarperCollinsPublishers

THE WALLFLOWER WAGER. Copyright © 2019 by Eve Ortega. All rights reserved. Printed in the United States of America. No part of this book may be used or reproduced in any manner whatsoever without written permission except in the case of brief quotations embodied in critical articles and reviews. For information, address HarperCollins Publishers, 195 Broadway, New York, NY 10007.

First Avon Books mass market printing: September 2019
First Avon Books hardcover printing: August 2019

Print Edition ISBN: 978-0-06-295256-1
Digital Edition ISBN: 978-0-06-267215-5

Avon, Avon & logo, and Avon Books & logo are registered trademarks of HarperCollins Publishers in the United States of America and other countries.

HarperCollins is a registered trademark of HarperCollins Publishers in the United States of America and other countries.

FIRST EDITION

19 20 21 22 23 LSC 10 9 8 7 6 5 4 3 2 1

Because little girls don't stay little forever

Acknowledgments

My editor, Tessa Woodward, has my adoration. Best editor in the world. Yes, Tessa, I have compared you to a fictional dog. Unlike a certain hero, you are entirely deserving of the compliment. I can't possibly thank you enough. I'm out of words to express my indebtedness, and you know why.

Brenna Aubrey has my devotion. Every writer should be so lucky to have a friend who sneaks a life-size cutout of Chris Evans into her office while she's out of town.

Brittani DiMare has my gratitude for her heroic patience and my deepest apologies.

Kayleigh Webb and Elle Keck have my warmest appreciation for all they do.

Steve Axelrod, Lori, and Elsie have my admiration. Best in the business.

The Darelings, and the entire extended Dare family, have my undying love.

Mr. Dare has my heart.

Readers, you have my thanks. Always.

The
Wallflower
Wager

Chapter One

$\mathcal{O}$ver her years of caring for unwanted animals, Lady Penelope Campion had learned a few things.

Dogs barked; rabbits hopped.

Hedgehogs curled up into pincushions.

Cats plopped in the middle of the drawing room carpet and licked themselves in indelicate places.

Confused parrots flew out open windows and settled on ledges just out of reach. And Penny leaned over window sashes in her nightdress to rescue them—even if it meant risking her own neck.

She couldn't change her nature, any more than the lost, lonely, wounded, and abandoned creatures filling her house could change theirs.

Penny gripped the window casing with one hand and waved a treat with her other. "Come now, sweeting. This way. I've a biscuit for you."

Delilah cocked her plumed head and regarded the treat. But she didn't budge.

Penny sighed. She had no one to blame but herself, really. She'd forgotten to cover the birdcage completely at sundown, and she'd left a candle burning far too late while she finished a delicious novel. However, she'd never dreamed Delilah could be clever enough to reach between the bars with one talon and unlatch the little door.

Once the parrot had escaped her cage, out the window she flew.

Penny pursed her lips and whistled. "See, darling? It's a lovely biscuit, isn't it? A gingersnap."

"*Pretty girl,*" the parrot chirruped.

"Yes, dear. What a pretty, pretty girl you are."

Delilah made a tentative shuffle sideways. At last, progress. The bird came closer . . .

"That's it. Here you come, sweetheart."

Closer . . .

"Good girl."

Just a few more inches . . .

Drat.

Delilah snatched the biscuit from Penny's fingers, scuttled backward, and took a brief flight, coming to land on the window-sill of the next house.

"No. Please. No."

With a flutter, Delilah disappeared through the open window.

Drat and blast.

The old Wendleby residence had lain vacant for years, save for a few servants to watch over the place, but the property had recently changed hands. The mysterious new owner had yet to make an appearance, but he'd sent an architect and a regiment of laborers to make several noisy, dusty improvements. A house under construction was no place for a defenseless bird to be flying about in the dark.

Penny had to retrieve her.

She eyed the ledge connecting the two houses. If she kicked off her slippers, climbed out onto the ledge, clung to the narrow lip of mortar with her bare toes, and inched across it . . . the open window would be within reach. The distance was only a few feet.

Correction: It was only a few feet to the window. It was twenty-odd feet to the ground.

Penny believed in a great many things. She believed that education was important, books were vital, women ought to have the vote, and most people were good, deep down. She believed that every last one of God's creatures—human or otherwise—deserved love.

However, she was not fool enough to believe she could fly.

She tied her dressing gown about her waist, jammed her feet into slippers, and padded downstairs to the kitchen, where she eased open the top-left drawer of the spice cabinet. Just as she remembered, all the way at the back of the drawer, affixed to the wooden slat with a bit of candle wax, was a key.

A key that opened the Wendlebys' back door.

Penny removed the ancient finger of metal and flaked away the wax with her thumbnail. Her family and the Wendlebys had exchanged keys decades ago, as good neighbors were wont to do. One never knew if an urgent situation might arise. This counted as an urgent situation. At this hour, waking the staff would take too much time. Delilah could fly out the way she'd entered at any moment. Penny could only hope that this key still fit its proper lock.

Out into the night she went. In one hand, she carried Delilah's empty cage. With the other, she drew her dressing gown tight to keep out the chill.

Skulking past the front door of the house, she made her way down to the servants' entrance. There, obscured by shadows, she slid the key into the lock, coaxing it past the tumblers. Once she'd inserted it all the way, she gave the key a wrenching twist.

With a click, the lock turned. The door fell open.

She paused, breathless, waiting for someone inside to raise the alarm.

There was only silence, save for the thudding of her heart.

Here she was, a complete stranger to criminal activity, about to commit prowling, or trespassing, or perhaps even burglary—if not some combination of the three.

A faint whistle from above underscored the urgency of her mission.

Closing the door behind her, Penny set the birdcage down on the floor, dug into the pocket of her dressing gown, and withdrew the taper and flint she'd stashed there before leaving her house. She lit the slender candle, lifted Delilah's brass cage with the other, and continued into the house.

She made her way through the servants' hall and up a flight of stairs, emerging into the house's main corridor. Penny hadn't been in this house for several years now. At that time, what with the Wendlebys' reduced circumstances, the place had fallen into a state of genteel decay.

At last, she beheld the result of several months' construction.

If the new owner wanted a showplace, he had achieved one. A rather cold and soulless one, in her opinion. But then, she'd never been one for flash. And this house not only flashed—it blinded. The entrance hall was the visual equivalent of a twenty-four-trumpet fanfare. Gilded trim and mirrored panels caught the light from her candle, volleying the rays back and forth until they were amplified into a blaze.

"Delilah," she whispered, standing at the base of the main staircase. "Delilah, where are you?"

"Pretty girl."

Penny held her candle aloft and peered upward. Delilah perched on the banister on the second-floor landing.

Thank heaven.

The parrot shifted her weight from one foot to the other and cocked her head.

"Yes, darling." Penny took the stairs in smooth, unhurried steps. "You are a very, very pretty girl. I know you're grieving your mistress and missing your home. But this isn't your house, see? No biscuits here. I'll take you back home where it's warm and cozy, and you shall have all the gingersnaps you wish. If you'll only stay . . . right . . . th—"

Just as she came within an arm's reach, the bird flapped her wings and ascended to the next landing.

"Pretty girl."

Sacrificing quiet in favor of speed, Penny raced up the steps and arrived on the landing just in time to glimpse the parrot dart through an open doorway. She was sufficiently familiar with the house's arrangement to know that direction would be a blind end.

She entered the room—a bedchamber with walls recently covered in lush silk damask and anchored by a massive four-poster bed. The bed was large enough to be a room unto itself, and cocooned by emerald velvet hangings.

Penny quietly shut the door behind her.

Delilah, I have you cornered now.

Cornered, perhaps, but not yet captured.

The bird led her on a chase about the room, flitting from bed-post to wardrobe to bedpost to mantel to bedpost—heavens, why were there so many bedposts?

Between racing up the stairs and chasing about the room, Penny was out of breath. If she weren't so dedicated to saving abandoned creatures . . .

Delilah alighted on the washstand, and Penny dove to res-cue the basin and ewer before they could crash to the floor. As she replaced them, she noticed several other objects on the marble table. A cake of soap, a keen-edged razor, a toothbrush and tooth powder. Evidence of recent occupation.

Male occupation.

Penny needed to catch that parrot and flee.

Instead of perching on a bedpost, Delilah had made the mis-take of flying beneath the canopy. Now she found her escape stymied by the voluminous draperies.

Penny rushed toward the bed, took a flying leap, and man-aged to grasp the parrot by one tiny, taloned foot.

There. I've got you.

Catching the parrot would have been a triumph to celebrate. However, as her luck would have it, Penny immediately found herself caught, too.

The chamber's connecting door swung open. A candle threw

light into the room. She lost her grip on Delilah's leg, and the bird flapped out of reach once again—leaving Penny sprawled across a stranger's bed in her nightclothes, birdless.

As she turned her head toward the figure in the doorway, she sent up a prayer.

Please be a maid.

Of course she could not be so fortunate. A man stood in the connecting room doorway. He was holding a candle, and wearing nothing at all.

Well, he wasn't truly naked, she corrected. He was clothed in *something*. That "something" was a damp scrap of linen clinging so precariously to his hips that it could slide to the floor at any moment—but it qualified as clothing of a sort.

And everyone was naked beneath their clothing, weren't they? This wasn't so different. Why be missish about it? After all, he didn't look embarrassed. Not in the least.

No, he looked magnificent. Magnificently irate.

"Where the hell did you come from?"

His tone of voice was understandably angry. It was also knee-erasing.

Penny scrambled out from the bed hangings and all but tumbled to the floor. "I'm from next door. Where I live. In my house."

"Well, I own this house."

"I didn't realize the new owner was in residence."

"As of this evening, I am."

"Yes. So I see."

She saw a great deal. Far more than was proper. Yet she couldn't tear her gaze away.

Lord, but he was a big, beautiful beast of a man.

There was just so much of him. Tall, broad, powerfully muscled. And utterly bare, save for that thin bit of toweling and his thick, dark hair. He had a great deal of hair. Not only plastered in damp curls on his head, but defining the hard line of his jaw. And lightly furring his chest.

He had nipples. Two of them.

Eyes, Penny. He has two of those, too. Focus on the eyes.

Sadly, that strategy didn't help. His eyes were chips of onyx. Chips of onyx dipped in ink, then encased in obsidian, then daubed with pitch, then thrown into a fathomless pit. At midnight.

"Who *are* you?" she breathed.

"I'm Gabriel Duke."

Gabriel Duke.

The Gabriel Duke?

"Pleased to make your acquaintance," she said out of habit, if only because she could hear her mother tut-tutting all the way from India.

"You shouldn't be pleased. No one else is."

No, they weren't. The papers had exhausted an ocean of ink on this man, who came from unknown origins and now possessed untold influence. Ruthless, said some. Shameless, said others. Sinfully wealthy, they all agreed.

They called him the Duke of Ruin.

From somewhere above, Delilah gave a cheeky, almost salacious whistle. The parrot swooped out from beneath the bed hangings and flew all the way across the room, alighting on an unused candle sconce on the opposite wall. Placing herself directly behind Penny's new, impressively virile neighbor.

Oh, you traitorous bird.

He flinched and ducked as the parrot swept overhead. "What the devil was that?"

"I can explain."

I just don't particularly want to.

"It's a parrot," she said. "My parrot."

"Right. And who are you, again?"

"I . . . erm . . ." Her hands couldn't decide where to be. They merely displayed the panicked desire to be anywhere else.

Water dripped from some hard, slick part of his body, counting out the beats of her mortification.

Drip. Drip. Drip.

"I'm Lady Penelope Campion."

LADY PENELOPE CAMPION.

The Lady Penelope Campion?

Gabe tilted his head to one side, shaking the last bit of bathwater from his ear. He could not have heard her correctly. Surely she meant to say she was a *servant* in the house of Lady Penelope Campion.

"You can't be Lady Penelope."

"I can't?"

"No. Lady Penelope is a spinster who lives alone with dozens of cats."

"Not *dozens*," she said. "A touch over *one* dozen at the moment, but that's only because it's springtime. Kitten season, you know."

No, he didn't know. None of this made any sense whatsoever.

Lady Penelope Campion was the main reason he'd acquired this property. New-money families would pay outrageous amounts to live next door to a lady, even if said lady was an unappealing spinster.

How on earth was *this* woman a spinster? She was an earl's daughter, surely possessed of a large dowry. If none of the title-hungry, debt-ridden layabouts in Mayfair had seen fit to propose marriage, simple logic dictated there must be something remarkably off-putting about her. An unbearably grating voice, perhaps. A snaggletooth, or poor personal hygiene.

But she displayed none of those features. She was young and pretty, with no detectable odor. Her teeth were a string of pearls, and she had a voice like sunshine. There was nothing off-putting about her whatsoever. She was . . . on-putting, in every way.

Good God, he was going to sell this house for a bloody fortune.

Assuming the lady wasn't ruined, of course.

At her level of society, being ruined didn't take much. Strictly as a random example, she could be ruined by being found alone and scarcely clothed in the bedchamber of the aristocracy's most detested, and currently most naked, villain.

"You need to leave," he said. "At once."

"I can't. Not before retrieving—"

"Wait here. I'm going to dress, and then I'll see you home. Discreetly."

"But—"

"No argument," he growled.

Gabe had clawed and climbed his way out of the gutters, using the ruined aristocrats of London as stepping-stones along his way. But he hadn't forgotten where he came from. He'd learned how to talk and walk among people who would think themselves his betters. But that lowborn street urchin still lived within him—including the rough cutpurse voice that had genteel ladies clutching their reticules. When he chose to use that voice, it seldom went unheeded.

Lady Penelope Campion wasn't paying attention at all.

Her gaze was focused on something behind him, over his shoulder. He instinctively began to turn his head.

"Stop," she said with perfect calm. "Don't move."

He heard a strange flutter, and in the next moment it happened.

A bird landed on his shoulder. A parrot, she'd said? The creature's toes prickled along his skin. His muscle twitched with the urge to shrug it off.

"No, don't," she said. "I'll come for her."

Usually, Gabe would balk at taking orders from a lady—or from anyone else. However, this was a decidedly unusual situation.

"*Pretty girl,*" the bird squawked.

Gabe set his jaw. *Do you think I haven't noticed that, you cursed pigeon with pretensions?*

She crept toward him, padding noiselessly over the carpet,

step by silent step. And as she came, sweet words fell from her lips like drops of raw honey.

"That's it, darling," she murmured.

The fine hairs on the back of his neck lifted.

"Stay . . . right . . . there."

The hairs on his arms lifted, too.

"Yes," she breathed. "Just like that."

Now she had the hairs on his calves involved. Damn it, he had too many hairs. By the end of this they would all be standing at attention.

Along with other parts of him.

"Don't stir," she said.

He couldn't speak for the parrot, but Gabe was doing some stirring. One part of him had a mind of its own, especially when it came to beautiful women in translucent chemises. He hadn't lain with a woman in some time, but his body hadn't forgotten how.

He couldn't help himself. He stole a glance at her face. Just a half-second's view. Not long enough to pore over every detail of her features. In fact, he didn't get any further than her lips. Lips as lush as petals, painted in soft, tender pink.

She was so close now. Near enough that when he breathed, he inhaled a lungful of her scent. She smelled delicious. A faint hunger rose in his chest.

"I know you're feeling lost. And not a little frightened. You miss her terribly, don't you? But I'm here, darling. I'm here."

Her words sent a strange ache spreading from his teeth to his toes. A painful awareness of all his hollow, empty places.

"Come home with me," she whispered. "And we'll sort out the rest together."

He couldn't take any more of this. "For God's sake, get the damned thing off me."

At last, she collected the feathered beast. "There we are." Cradling it in her arms, she carried the parrot to its birdcage and tucked it within.

Gabe exhaled with relief.

"She'd settle more if I covered her cage," his beautiful intruder said. "I don't suppose you have a towel?"

He glanced at the linen slung about his hips. "How badly do you want it?"

Her cheeks flushed. "Never mind. I'll be going."

"I'm going to walk you."

"Truly, you needn't do that. It's only next door. No more than twenty paces down the street."

"That's twenty paces too many."

Gabe might not operate by polite society's rules, but he understood them sufficiently to know this situation violated at least seventeen of them. And anything that damaged her reputation would decrease the profit he stood to collect on this house.

Until he sold this property, her worth was intertwined with his.

"You're no doubt accustomed to having your way, Your Ladyship. But I've ruined enough lords, baronets, knights, and gentlemen to fill the whole of Bloom Square." He arched an eyebrow. "Believe me when I say, you've met your match."

Chapter Two

$\mathcal{P}$enny watched in silence as *the* Gabriel Duke turned and stalked to his dressing room.

Then she melted into a quivering pool on the floor.

Heavens.

He'd left the door ajar. As his towel dropped to the floor, she caught a glimpse of taut, muscled backside before tearing her gaze away.

Oh Lord oh Lord oh Lord.

Once she'd latched and relatched Delilah's cage for good measure, Penny stood and attempted to piece herself back together.

She glanced at her dressing gown. The faded toile print was years behind the fashion, and the ends of the sash were hopelessly frayed—the casualty of many a playful kitten's swipe. And her hair . . . Oh, she could only imagine the state of her hair after this adventure.

She peered into the dressing-table mirror. Worse than she'd feared. Her plait made Delilah's ruffled crest look sleek. Penny quickly unknotted the bit of muslin around her braid and combed her hair with her fingers before rebraiding it and tying off the end.

She squinted into the mirror again. Better, she judged. Not a great deal better. But better.

"Pretty girl!"

From the dressing room, Mr. Duke gave an annoyed groan.

"I'm so sorry for the imposition," she called. "Delilah only came to live in Bloom Square a few weeks ago. Her mistress passed away. Parrots are loyal and intelligent, and they often outlive their human companions. So she's not only been uprooted from her home, she's in mourning."

"I must say, she doesn't sound particularly aggrieved to me."

"She does say the most amusing things, doesn't she? 'Pretty girl,' and 'yes,' and—Do you hear that one? 'Fancy a . . .' what? I never can catch what she's saying at the end. It's certainly not biscuit. 'Fancy a cuppa,' perhaps? But who gives a parrot tea? It sounds a great deal like 'fancy a foxglove,' but that makes even less sense. I don't mind saying the mystery is driving me a bit mad."

"Fuck."

She froze. "I'm not *that* upset about it."

He returned to the bedchamber, now clothed in a pair of trousers and an unbuttoned shirt. "It's what the parrot's saying. 'Fancy a fuck, love.' That bird came from a whorehouse."

She spent a few moments in scandalized silence. No one had ever spoken to her in such a manner—but that wasn't the disturbing part. The disturbing part was how much she liked it.

"That can't be," she said. "She belonged to a little old lady. That's what I was told."

"Bawds turn into little old ladies, too."

"*Pretty girl.*" Delilah gave a cheeky whistle. "*Fancy a f—*"

Penny pressed a hand to her mouth. "Oh, no."

"*Yes! Yes! Ooh! Yes!*"

Mr. Duke sat to pull on his boots. "Please tell me I don't need to translate *that* for you."

Penny couldn't think of anything she might say to make this exchange less horrifying. She couldn't have said anything at all. It wasn't that she'd lost her tongue. Her tongue had curled up and died.

Boots donned, he strode to the door and held it open for her. Penny gratefully lifted the birdcage and hurried to escape.

"I know how fragile a lady's reputation can be," he said. "Just so it's understood—no one can ever know you were here."

"Lady Penelope?"

Penny jumped in her skin.

The housekeeper, Mrs. Burns, stood in the corridor. Her eyes slid to her employer. "Mr. Duke."

Mr. Duke cursed under his breath. If she were the sort to use profanity, Penny would have cursed, too.

Mrs. Burns had managed the Wendleby house for as long as Penny could remember. When she was a girl, the housekeeper had terrified her.

Little had changed in that regard. The woman was even more frightening now, clad in black from head to toe with her hair parted severely down the center. The candle she held threw macabre shadows across her face.

"Is there some way I can be of service?" she solemnly intoned.

"My parrot flew in through the window and I came over to retrieve her," Penny hastily explained. "Mr. Duke was kind enough to help. Mrs. Burns, perhaps you'd be so good as to accompany me home?"

"That would be prudent." The housekeeper gave her a disapproving look. "In the future, my lady, might I suggest you wake a servant to let you in the house."

"Oh, this won't happen again." Penny slid a glance toward Mr. Duke as she moved to leave. "I can promise you that."

In fact, Penny had formed a simple plan to cope with this situation.

Thank the man for his help . . .

Calmly make her retreat . . .

And then never, ever leave her house again.

As THE OWNER of properties all over Britain—hotels, town houses, mines, factories, country estates—Gabe was accustomed to awakening in unfamiliar rooms. Three things, however, never altered.

He always woke with the dawn.

He always woke hungry.

And he always woke up alone.

He had a set of rules when it came to sexual congress—he didn't pay for it, he wouldn't beg for it, and he damned well wasn't going to wed for it. When based in London, he found casual lovers with no difficulty, but lately he'd been moving from place to place so often he simply couldn't find the time.

On this particular morning, he sat up in the bed, gave himself a shake, and familiarized himself with his surroundings. Mayfair. Bloom Square. The house that ought to bring a satisfying profit, once it was finally ready to be sold.

The house next door to *her*. Lady Penelope Campion—the aging, frazzled, unsightly spinster who . . .

Who wasn't any of those things. Not by a mile. As fortune would have it, Lady Penelope Campion turned out to be a fair-haired, blue-eyed beauty.

In his mind's eye, he could still see her sprawled across this bed in her dressing gown. Like an all-grown-up Goldilocks, having crept into his house uninvited to test the mattress. Too soft, too hard . . . ?

He didn't know her opinion, but Gabe's reaction was the latter. His cock was in its usual morning prime, standing at full mast.

He scrubbed his face with one hand and stumbled to the bathroom.

He'd been too weary from travel to inspect the new fixtures yesterday, but all looked to be in order this morning. Tiled marble floor and an immense copper tub, complete with taps for running water—both hot and cold.

Last night he'd settled for a quick, cold dousing. Today, he meant to have a hot bath. He settled into the tub and turned the tap marked with an H. The tap shivered, but refused to give up any water. Gabe gave it a gentle shake, then a firm slap. Nothing.

In all his life, he'd never backed down from a fight, but this had to be his most inane confrontation yet: fisticuffs with a water tap.

He banged on the pipe, and it finally gave way with a rattle and groan. A blast of cold water sprayed him in the face. Needles of ice speared him in the eyes, the mouth. Bloody hell, even up his nose.

Round one to the water tap.

Blocking the spray with one hand, he closed the H tap with the other. Annoyed, he reached for the one marked with a C. A cold bath did have its benefits. After a few minutes of scrubbing in the bollocks-shrinking bathwater, he'd rinsed his mind of his neighbor's soft, pink lips.

Mostly.

The remainder of his morning toilette was simple. He brushed his teeth, shaved, combed back his stubborn shock of hair, and dressed.

Before leaving the room, he reached for the dull silver coin on the dressing table—a single shilling, rubbed smooth—and tucked it in the pocket of his waistcoat. Over the years, a shilling had become his talisman. A reminder of where he'd come from, and how far he'd climbed. Gabe never went anywhere without one.

He opened the door and bellowed. "Hammond!"

His architect appeared a minute later, huffing from the climb up the stairs. "Good morning, Mr. Duke."

"It might be a good morning, if the hot water taps I paid hundreds to install were functioning." He shook his head. "This house should have been complete months ago."

"I know that was your hope, sir."

"It was my expectation," Gabe corrected. "I spent three years wrangling in Chancery to gain possession of the place. I'm spending thousands to bring it up to modern standards. But I can't turn a profit until I sell it."

"As I indicated in my correspondence, Mr. Duke, there have been a few obstacles."

"You call them obstacles. To me, they sound like excuses." He gestured at the water basin. "You told me this is the latest innovation. Hot running water."

"It *is* the latest innovation. It's so new, in fact, that this is only the second boiler of its kind in England. There's only one man on this side of the Channel who knows how to perform repairs."

"So get that man in here to repair the cursed thing."

"Yes, well, here we come to the obstacle." Hammond pushed both hands through his silver hair. "That particular man is dead."

Gabe swore. "Get the other one on a ship, then."

"Already under way."

As they strode down the corridor, Gabe stopped to peer through the open doors, surveying the progress in each chamber. No wallpaper in this one, unfinished molding in another . . .

Unacceptable.

"So tell me about these other 'obstacles' you've encountered."

Hammond stared down the staircase and lowered his voice, speaking through unmoving lips. "I'm looking at one of them now."

Gabe peered in the same direction. "The housekeeper?"

"Oh, good," he muttered. "You see her, too."

"Should I not?"

"I don't know. I'm not certain she's human. Sometimes I think she's a ghost who's been haunting the place for centuries."

Gabe gave his architect a worried look. Maybe Hammond needed a holiday. The man *was* getting on in years.

He assessed the housekeeper in the light of day. The woman carried herself with a strict demeanor, and her appearance might as well have been sketched in charcoal—from her severely parted black hair, down her black buttoned frock, all the way to her polished black shoes.

"She looks like the typical housekeeper if you ask me."

"There is nothing typical about that woman," Hammond said. "You'll see. I swear, she moves through walls. Materializes out of thin air. You'll be walking down a perfectly empty corridor. Suddenly, there she is right in front of you."

Gabe had to admit, she'd certainly appeared out of nowhere last night.

"I'm an architect. If there were secret corridors in this house, I'd know—and there aren't. I'm telling you, she's some kind of spirit. I'm hoping you'll sack her, but I'm not certain it would work. You'll need an exorcism, I think."

"Finding and training a suitable replacement would be a monumental task on its own." Gabe knew the value of a competent employee—and after last night, he wasn't giving the woman any reason to go spreading vindictive rumors about. "So long as she's loyal, she stays."

"She's much *too* loyal. She doesn't want anything changed. Projects that were done one day will be mysteriously undone the next morning."

"So she's meddling?"

"That, or working incantations."

"I'm not going to sack her. When people are competent in their posts, I keep them on." He gave Hammond a look. "Even if they are annoying."

"I worried you'd say as much." Hammond sighed. "Whatever else can be said for the creature, she does know this house. Better than you know the face of a shilling."

I doubt that.

"But when she has you scared out of your wits," Hammond said, "don't come knocking at my door in the middle of the night. I won't let you in."

"How disappointing."

They made their way down the remainder of the stairs and into the breakfast room. A bowl of fruit sat on the table, waiting. Gabe's mouth watered, and yet—as always—his instinct was to hesitate.

Don't touch it, boy. That's not for the likes of you.

No matter how much wealth he amassed, it seemed he would never banish that voice. And no matter how much he devoured, satisfaction eluded him. The hunger never went away.

He reached for an apple, shined it on his waistcoat, and took a defiant bite.

"And then there's your third problem." Hammond nodded at the window. "Just out there, on the green. Lady Penelope Campion."

Gabe strolled to the window. She looked different this morning. Different, but no less pretty. The spring sunshine lent her fair hair a golden sheen, and a simple frock skimmed the contours of her tempting, graceful curves. Even from here, he could see her smile.

Lovely as she might be, she wasn't Gabe's usual sort. He wanted nothing to do with delicate, pampered misses possessing no knowledge of the world beyond Mayfair. They were painted china on a high shelf, and he was the bull charging through the shop.

All the more worrisome, then, that Lady Penelope was working her way under his skin.

He took another bite of his apple, snapping the crisp sweetness down to the core.

Gabe watched her move to the center of the green. In one gloved hand, she clutched a leash. The other end of the leash was attached to . . . something furry and brown that *rolled*.

"What is that?"

"That would be a mongrel with two lamed hind legs. Apparently, Her Ladyship's friend devised a little chariot for his rear half, and the dog careens around the neighborhood like a yapping billiard ball. If you think that's strange, wait until you see the goat."

"Hold a moment. There's a *goat*?"

"Oh, yes. She grazes it on the square every afternoon. Doesn't precisely elevate the atmosphere of Bloom Square, now does it?"

"I see the problem."

"I'm only getting started. Her Ladyship has single-handedly set us back a month on the improvements." Hammond pulled a collection of letters from a folio. He held one aloft and read from it. "'Dear Mr. Hammond, I must request that you delay completion of the parquet flooring. The fumes from the lacquer are dizzying the hens. Sincerely yours, Lady Penelope Campion.'"

He withdrew another. "'Dear Mr. Hammond, I'm afraid your improvements to the mews must be temporarily halted. I've located a litter of newborn kittens in the hayloft. Their mother is looking after them, but as their eyes are not yet open, they should not be displaced for another week. Thank you for your cooperation. Gratefully yours, Lady Penelope Campion.'"

Gabe sensed a theme.

"Oh, and here's my favorite." Hammond shook open a letter and cleared his throat for dramatic effect. "'Dear Mr. Hammond, if it is not too great an imposition, might I ask that your workers refrain from performing heavy labor between nine o'clock in the morning and half-three in the afternoon? Hedgehogs are nocturnal animals, and sensitive to loud noises. My dear Freya is losing quills. I feel certain this will concern you as much as it does me. Neighborly yours, Lady Penelope Campion.'" He tossed the folio of letters onto the table, where they landed with a smack. "Her *hedgehog*. Really."

Outside, Her Ladyship coaxed her dog back toward the house, lifting both dog and cart up the few steps to her door. Gabe turned away from the window, rubbing his temples.

"The situation is untenable, and that makes the house unsellable. No one wants to live next to a barnyard. I've tried reasoning with her, but when it comes to those animals, she's surprisingly tenacious."

Tenacious, indeed. And sufficiently reckless to trespass in a house after midnight and recover a parrot from a near-naked stranger's shoulder.

However, even that degree of tenacity had poor odds against sheer ruthlessness. Lady Penelope Campion had a softness for animals. Gabe had no softness at all.

"You make certain the work is done and bring in potential buyers." Gabe tossed the apple core into the fireplace grate. "I'll handle Lady Penelope Campion."

Chapter Three

$\mathcal{B}$y society's standards, Penny was rather lacking in accomplishments. As the daughter of an earl, she'd been given the best possible education. Governesses fluent in three languages, a full two years at finishing school, then private tutors in art, music, dancing.

None of it seemed to take. She'd never found an instrument willing to give up a tune for her, no matter how she strummed, plucked, or begged it. She'd attained only marginal competence in sketching.

And dancing? Impossible.

Penny did, however, emerge from adolescence with unparalleled accomplishment in one pursuit.

Caring.

Nothing pleased her more than looking after those around her. Feeding them, warming them, protecting them, giving them a home. She doled out affection from an endless supply.

The only problem was, she was running out of people to claim it.

She had her family, of course. But first her parents had gone to India as diplomats. Her eldest brother, Bradford, lived in Cumberland with his wife and managed the family estate. Timothy, the middle child of their threesome, had joined the Royal Navy.

Still, she had the most wonderful friends. Never mind that

the finishing school girls had scorned her. Penny welcomed the misfits of Bloom Square. Emma, Alexandra, Nicola. Together, they made the rounds of the bookshops, walked in the park, and gathered at her house for tea every Thursday.

Or at least they *had* done so, until her friends began to start families of their own. First, Emma's marriage to the Duke of Ashbury had transformed from a convenient arrangement into passionate devotion. Next, Alex had bewitched London's most infamous rake and became Mrs. Chase Reynaud. As for brilliant, inventive Nicola . . . ?

Penny scanned the note she'd just received, peering hard to make out the breathless scrawl of ink.

Can't today. Biscuits burned. Breakthrough near. Next Thursday?
Love, N

Penny laid aside the charred scrap of paper and regarded the tray of sandwiches on the tea table, all trimmed of their crusts and ready for a gathering that wouldn't take place.

Fortunately, in this house, food seldom went to waste.

Taking a sandwich, she crouched near to the floor and whistled. Bixby scampered down the corridor, his two front paws clicking over the floorboards and his lamed hind legs following right behind, rolling along in an ingenious chariot of Nicola's design.

After several excited sniffs, the dog gave the crustless triangle a cautious lick.

"Go on," she urged. "It's a new recipe. You'll like it."

Just as Bixby sank his dart-point teeth into the sandwich, the doorbell rang. Penny rushed to answer it. At the last moment, she hesitated with her hand on the door latch.

Could it be him?

It wouldn't be him, she told herself.

But what if it was?

Sensing her unease, Bixby whined and nosed at her ankles.

Taking a deep breath to calm her nerves, Penny opened the door.

"Oh," she said, trying not to sound dejected. "Aunt Caroline."

Her aunt entered the house in her usual manner—like a snobbish traveler disembarking on a foreign shore, visiting a land where the native people spoke a different language, exchanged different currency, worshipped different gods. Her eyes took in the place with a cool, smug sort of interest. As though, while she had no desire to truly understand this alien culture, she'd been reading up.

Most of all, she was careful where she stepped.

When she'd completed her quiet survey of the drawing room, she gave a weary sigh. "Oh, Penelope."

"It's lovely to see you, too, Aunt."

Her aunt's eyes fell on the quilt-lined basket near the hearth. "Is that still the same hedgehog?"

Penny decided to change the subject. "Do sit down, and I'll ring for a new pot of tea."

"Thank you, no." Her aunt plucked a tuft of cat hair from the armchair, pinching it between her thumb and forefinger and holding it away from her body. Frowning at the bit of fluff, she released it and watched it waft to the floor. "What I have to say won't take long, anyhow. I've had a letter from Bradford. He insists you return to Cumberland."

Penny was stunned. "For the summer?"

"For the remainder of your life, I believe."

No.

No, no, no.

Her aunt lifted a hand, barricading herself against dissent. "Your brother has asked me to tell you he'll be traveling to London in a month's time. He asked me to be certain you're prepared to join him for the return journey."

Penny's heart sank. She was a grown woman, and therefore could not be ordered to pick up and move to the farthest reaches of England. However, the snag was this—even if she was a grown woman, she was still a woman. This house belonged to her father, and while her father was out of the country, Bradford had control. Penny lived in Bloom Square at his pleasure. If he demanded she remove to Cumberland, she would have little choice in the matter.

"Aunt Caroline, please. Can't you write back and convince him to change his mind?"

"I'll do no such thing. I happen to agree with your brother. In fact, I ought to have suggested it myself. I did promise your parents I would look after you, but now that the war is over I intend to travel the Continent. You shouldn't be living alone."

"I'm six-and-twenty years old, and I'm not living alone. I have Mrs. Robbins."

Wordlessly, her aunt picked up the bell from the tea table and gave it a light ring.

Several moments passed. No Mrs. Robbins.

Aunt Caroline craned her neck toward the main corridor and lifted her voice. "Mrs. Robbins!"

Penny crossed her arms and sighed, fully aware of the point her aunt meant to make. "She's always looked after me."

"She isn't looking after you any longer. You are looking after her."

"Just because the old dear is a touch hard of hearing—"

Aunt Caroline stomped on the floor three times—*boom, boom, boom*—and shouted, "MRS. ROBBINS!"

At last, the sound of aged, shuffling footsteps made its way from the back of the house to the drawing room.

"My word!" Mrs. Robbins said. "If it isn't Lady Caroline. I didn't know you'd dropped by. Shall I bring tea?"

"No, thank you, Robbins. You've served your purpose already."

"Have I?" The older woman looked confused. "Yes, of course."

Once Mrs. Robbins had quit the room, Penny addressed her aunt. "I don't wish to leave. I'm happy living in Town. My life is here. All my friends are here."

"Your life and your friends are . . . where?" Aunt Caroline looked meaningfully at each one of the unoccupied chairs, at the trays of cold tea and uneaten sandwiches, and, finally, at the three kittens shredding the draperies with their tiny claws.

"I have human friends, as well," Penny said defensively.

Her aunt looked doubtful.

"I do. Several of them."

Her aunt glanced at the silver tray in the entrance hall. The one where calling cards and invitations were heaped—or would be, if Penny ever received them, which she didn't. The tray was empty.

"Some of my friends are out of Town." Aware of how absurd she sounded, she added, "And others are mad scientists."

Another pitying sigh from her aunt. "We must face the truth, Penelope. It's time."

It's time.

Penny didn't need to ask what her aunt meant by that. The implication was clear.

Aunt Caroline meant it was time to give up.

Time for Penny to return to the family home in Cumberland and resign herself to her destiny: spinsterhood. She must take on the role of maiden aunt and stop embarrassing both the family and herself.

After nine years in Town, she hadn't married. She hadn't even entertained any serious suitors. She rarely mingled in society. If she were being honest, she would strike "rarely" and replace it with "never." She didn't have any intellectual pursuits like art or science or poetry. No bluestocking salons, no social reform protests. She stayed home with her pets and invited her misfit friends to tea, and . . .

And outside her tiny sphere, people laughed at her.

Penny knew they did. She'd been an object of pity and ridicule ever since her disastrous debut. It didn't bother her, except—well, except for the times that it did.

As a person who wanted to like everyone, it hurt to know that not everyone liked her in return.

Society had long given up on her. Now her family, as well.

But Penny was not giving up on herself. When her aunt moved to leave, she grasped her by the arm.

"Wait. Is there nothing I can do to change your mind? If you advocated on my behalf, I know Bradford would reconsider."

Her aunt was silent.

"Aunt Caroline, please. I beg you."

Penny could not return to Cumberland, back to the house where she'd passed the darkest hours of her life. The house where she'd learned to bottle shame and store it in a dark place, out of view.

You know how to keep a secret, don't you?

Her aunt pursed her lips. "Very well. To begin, you might order a new wardrobe. Fur and feathers are all well and good—but only when they are worn on purpose, and in a fashionable way."

"I can order a new wardrobe." It wouldn't include fur and feather adornments, but Penny could promise it would be new.

"And once you have a new wardrobe, you must use it. The opera. A dinner party. A ball would be preferable, but we both know that's too much to ask."

Ouch. Penny would never live down that humiliating scene.

"Make an appearance *somewhere*," her aunt said. "Anywhere. I want to see you in the society column for once."

"I can do that, too." *I think.*

Considering how long she'd been out of circulation, invitations to dinner and the theater would be harder to come by than a few up-to-current-fashion gowns. Nevertheless, it could be accomplished.

"Lastly, and most importantly"—Aunt Caroline paused for effect—"you must do something about all these animals."

"What do you mean, 'do something' about them?"

"Be rid of them. All of them."

"All of them?" Penny reeled. Impossible. She could find homes for the kittens. That had always been her plan. But Delilah? Bixby? Angus, Marigold, Hubert, and the rest? "I can't. I simply can't."

"Then you can't." Her aunt tugged on her gloves. "I must be going. I have letters to write."

"Wait."

Surely there was a way to convince her aunt that didn't involve abandoning her pets. Perhaps she could trick her by hiding them in the attic?

"I hope you're not thinking you can hide them in the attic," her aunt said dryly. "I'll know."

Drat.

"Aunt Caroline, I'll . . . I'll try my best. I just need a little time."

"According to your brother, you have a month. Perhaps less. You know as well as I, it takes the mail the better part of a week to arrive from Cumberland."

"That leaves only three weeks. But that's nothing."

"It's what you have."

Penny immediately began to pray, very hard, for rain. Come to think of it, considering the amount of rain England typically saw in springtime, she probably ought to pray for something more. Torrential, bridge-flooding, road-rutting downpours. A biblical deluge. A plague of frogs.

"If, by your brother's arrival, I am convinced there's something keeping you in London other than an abundance of animal hair . . . ? Then, and only then, I might be persuaded to intervene."

"Very well," Penny said. "You have a bargain."

"A bargain? This isn't a bargain, my girl. I've made you no guarantees, and I'm not convinced you're up to the challenge at all. If anything, we have a wager—and you're facing very long odds."

Long odds, indeed. After her aunt had gone, Penny closed the door and slumped against it.

Three weeks.

Three weeks to save the creatures depending on her.

Three weeks to save herself.

Penny had no idea how she would accomplish it, but this was a wager she *had* to win.

Chapter Four

*A*fter that miserable encounter with her aunt, Penny could not have dreamed her day could grow any worse. But here worse came, in the form of Mr. Gabriel Duke, walking across the green directly toward her, right in the middle of Marigold's daily constitutional.

The Duke of Ruin, they said. Penny didn't know if the man lived up to his scandal-sheet moniker, but he was certainly the Duke of Ruining Her Afternoon.

"Lady Penelope." He inclined his head in the grudging suggestion of a bow.

Penny needed a few moments before she could look him in the eye. She took in his appearance from the ground up. His fine attire said "gentleman." The remainder of his appearance subtracted "gentle" and simply said "man." Though he must have shaved between last night and this afternoon, stubbly whiskers ranged up his throat and over his sharply cut jaw.

"Well?"

Drat. He must have asked her a question, and she'd been wandering so deep in the dark forest of his whiskers, she hadn't heard it.

She resolved to ignore his effect on her. Her resolution lasted approximately nine seconds.

When he spoke again, his voice was deliciously deep and intimate. "We need to have a chat."

She cringed. She'd been afraid he would say that. "Can't we agree to forget last night ever happened?"

"I'm afraid it was rather unforgettable."

With that, she could not argue. "I'm sorry about the parrot. And the trespassing. And the breaking and entering."

"I'm not here to talk about the parrot. Right now, my concern is the goat."

"Why would you care about Marigold?"

"Let me begin with this: I'm different from most men of your acquaintance."

She nearly laughed aloud. What an understatement.

Penny wasn't unused to men, but there was a difference between friendly acquaintance and a close-range confrontation with sheer masculine physicality. It felt like someone had taken a mallet to a gong of femininity hidden deep in her belly, and now the vibrations traveled through her bones, summoning an ancient, primal force.

Penny could think of only one name for it: lust.

It made no sense. She'd always been a romantic. She cheered on her friends' unlikely matches. She believed in destiny, soul mates, love at first sight.

Penny didn't want any of those things from Gabriel Duke. She wanted to tear off his clothes and look at him—all of him— the way she had last night. It had been too dark in the room, and she hadn't found the courage to stare. When would she see a man so very big, wearing so very little, again?

Never, that was when.

The thought made her irritable and sulky.

Good Lord, Penny. He's a person. Not merely a collection of muscles with an intriguing distribution of hair.

"Unlike most gentlemen, I did not inherit a fortune," he continued. "I built one. I did that by acquiring things that are undervalued, and then selling them for more than I paid. Hence, a profit. Do you follow me?"

"If you're asking whether I comprehend basic mathematics, then yes. I follow you."

"Good." He looked in the direction of the house that so inconveniently abutted hers. "When the Wendlebys could not pay their debts, I acquired their property. Now I mean to sell it at a profit."

"And therefore you've undertaken several months of improvements."

"The improvements to the house will add to its value, but the property's main selling point is right here."

"You mean the square?"

"I mean you."

His words took her by surprise. "Me?"

"Yes, you. Do you have any idea how much a social-climbing family would pay to take up residence next door to a lady?"

"No."

"Well, I do. And it's an outrageous figure. They envision themselves rubbing elbows with the elite, climbing the rungs of society, living in elegance and luxury. If they gaze out the drawing-room window and see their aristocratic neighbor playing goatherdess on the green like some absurd imitation of Marie Antoinette? It ruins the effect."

"People run their dogs on the green all the time."

"Dogs are pets."

"Marigold is a pet, too. And she needs to browse. She can't subsist on alfalfa alone. She's prone to bloating."

"Bloating?" he echoed, incredulous.

"She has sensitive digestion."

"That doesn't look like bloating to me." He tilted his head and regarded Marigold's swollen underbelly. "That looks like breeding."

Penny stepped back, offended. "She is not breeding. It's impossible. There are no bucks for miles."

"You're certain of that?"

"Yes, I'm certain. No one keeps goats in the middle of Mayf—" She bit her tongue before she made his argument for him. "I'm telling you, it's impossible. If she's not in the mews or the back garden, I keep her on a short lead."

His eyebrow quirked with derision. "Spoken like the guardian of many a ruined young female in this neighborhood, I'd wager."

"I beg your pardon. Marigold is not that kind of goat."

"Whatever you say. I don't care about the creature's virtue. I just want her removed from the square."

"I told you, she needs to browse. Her diet requires shrubs and fresh grasses. Hay and corn are well enough for Angus, but—"

"Hold a moment. Angus?"

"Angus is a Highland steer. I rescued him when he was a calf, but he's three years old now. Grown and healthy as anything."

He blinked at her. "You have a fully grown bull—"

"A steer."

"—living in your back garden."

"Don't be silly. Angus lives in the mews. The otter is in the back garden."

"An otter?" He grumbled something that sounded like *Holy immaculate mother of goats.* "This is ridiculous."

"Mr. Duke, the variety of pets I keep may be unusual, but an attachment to animals isn't. Have you never had a pet of your own?"

"No."

"Don't you like animals?"

"Certainly, I like animals. Roasted animals. Fried animals. Minced-and-baked-in-a-pie animals." He gestured expansively. "I like all kinds of animals."

Oh, this man was impossible.

No, Penny corrected. The man was not impossible. Even the

most untamed, ill-mannered creatures could be won over with a bit of patience. She'd made pets of worse beasts than Gabriel Duke.

She simply wasn't up to the effort this afternoon, that's all.

"Listen," he said, "I don't have time to compromise. They have to go. All of them. The goat, the cow, the otter, the parrot, that hedgehog, and whatever else you have in your rafters. I need them all gone."

"What a coincidence you should say that."

Ever since her aunt had left, Penny had been turning it over and over in her mind. She would have to find the animals new homes. Either she did so quickly and succeeded in convincing her aunt, or else she would be forced to leave Bloom Square—in which case, there would be no taking her pets with her. Bradford would never take them to Cumberland. If she defied her brother's wishes, one of Penny's friends would surely welcome her to stay with them—but she couldn't ask them to take in a few dozen animals, too.

One way or another, she would have to bid them farewell. And if she wanted any hope of remaining in Bloom Square, she must not only find her pets new homes, but undo a decade of social seclusion. In three weeks.

It all seemed hopeless.

"As it happens, Mr. Duke, you are going to get your wish. The animals will be gone within the month, one way or another."

"Good."

"In fact, it's entirely possible that I'll be gone, too."

"Wait." His eyebrows converged in a frown. "What did you say?"

"My brother is demanding I go home to the ancestral estate in Cumberland. He's coming to collect me in three weeks. That means I'll be leaving Bloom Square, too. Unless I work a miracle."

He swore under his breath. "This is unacceptable."

"I'm not happy about it, either, but I'm afraid neither of us has much say in the matter. I must be going." She gathered Marigold's lead. "Come along, sweeting."

He cut off her path. "The miracle."

"What?"

"You said you'll be leaving unless you work a miracle. Tell me about the miracle."

"I don't know why you should care."

"Oh, I care," he said. "I care a great deal. What ever this 'miracle' is, I will work it."

"You couldn't possibly."

"I can, and I will."

Heavens. His dark, intense stare nailed her slippers to the gravel path. Her heart pounded in her chest. And then he spoke the gruff, possessive words Penny had started to doubt she'd ever hear.

"I need you, Lady Penelope Campion. I'm not letting you go."

Chapter Five

*W*hen he made this firm declaration, Gabe had not been expecting Lady Penelope's reaction. First she looked surprised, and then she looked—

She looked hopeful?

"You . . ." Her cheeks flushed pink. "You *need* me?"

He would need to tread carefully here. She was sheltered, naïve. And she did not want to be a spinster. So much was clear from simply staring into her china-blue eyes. She'd been saving that soft, blushing sweetness for years, waiting to lavish it on the right man.

Gabe was not, and never would be, the right man. Not for her, not for anyone. If Her Ladyship had formed any notions otherwise, she was a fool.

"I need you," he clarified, "to continue residing in Bloom Square if I'm to sell the house at a handsome profit. Which I fully intend to do."

She blinked several times in succession. "Yes, of course. I knew that. It's kind of you to offer your help, that's all."

Kind?

What an innocent she was. If she could glimpse the ugliness in his past, the ruthless hunger that consumed his mind, the blackness of his heart, she would learn the enormity of her mistake. But he'd never allow anyone near the yawning, empty pit of his soul. Posted warnings were the best he could offer. For her own sake, she had better heed them.

"Listen to me," he said sternly. "My motives are never kind. Neither are they generous or charitable or good. They're money-driven and entirely selfish. You'd do well to remember that."

So would he.

"So," he said, "what are the terms of this miracle you've mentioned?"

"My aunt has promised she'll try to change my brother's mind about taking me home to the country—but only if I meet her conditions."

"And those would be . . . ?"

"A new, fashionable wardrobe, to begin."

"Well, that's not even a challenge. Certainly nothing approaching a miracle."

"It's the easy part, yes. My dear friend Emma was a seamstress before she married. I know she'd help." She took a deep breath. "But there's more. I also have to begin moving in society again."

He shook his head. "Do we have different definitions of the word 'miracle'? Because that doesn't sound difficult, either."

"You don't understand. I haven't socialized within the *ton* in almost a decade. By now, they've forgotten I even exist. Yet somehow I'm meant to make my grand reentrance. She wants to see me in the society column."

Gabe was forced to admit that sounded a touch more complicated than the first condition, and it certainly wasn't something well-suited to his own talents. He wouldn't be caught dead at a ball, and despite his many mentions in the papers, none was in the society column.

Nevertheless, the task was well within the realm of possibility. There were several lords and gentlemen in his debt he could press for invitations, if it came to that.

"You mentioned a third thing your aunt's demanding."

"The same thing you're demanding. Be rid of the animals." She gave the goat a fond scratch behind the ear. "It will break my heart, but I have no choice. I must find them new homes."

"Done."

"*Done?*"

He shrugged. "As good as done, anyway. I'll find them homes. All of them."

"Just like that."

"Just like that. It'll take a week, at the most."

"I don't think you understand," she said. "My pets came to me wounded, abandoned, untamed. They're the animals no one else wanted. It won't be an easy task finding them safe, loving homes, with people who'll treat them as part of the family."

Part of the *family*? She lived in a fantasy land. Even if such "safe, loving" homes existed in the real world, Gabe wouldn't know how to recognize them. Fortunately, he wasn't above a falsehood or two.

"Not to worry. Leave it to me. I'll find them excellent homes."

She scanned him with narrowed, doubting eyes. "Forgive me, Mr. Duke, but I'm not at all convinced you're qualified to take on this sort of—"

Her all-too-perceptive statement was interrupted by a flurry of barking. This would not have been remarkable, had said barking not been emanating from the pavement in front of her house.

She turned toward the noise. "Oh, no. Not again."

Again? Barking pavement was a regular occurrence outside her house? Of course it was.

"Hold this." She pressed the goat's leash into Gabe's hand, and then left the two of them standing there while she ran toward the noise.

As he looked on, utterly baffled, Lady Penelope Campion—daughter of an earl—knelt on the ground and shouted into the small, round iron plate embedded in the pavement. The coal hole.

"Bixby? Bixby, is that you?"

From below, a dog whined in response.

She cupped her hands around her eyes and peered through the hole in the iron plate. "Don't worry, darling. Be brave and hold tightly. I'm coming for you straightaway."

Lady Penelope picked herself up from the pavement, hiked her skirts with both hands, and disappeared into her house.

After a moment's internal debate, Gabe followed. The scene had piqued his curiosity, to say the least. Not to mention, his alternative seemed to be milling about the square tending the goat.

The hell he would.

"Come along, you," he grumbled.

He pulled the goat up the stairs and through the door Lady Penelope had just bashed open.

As he entered, the infernal parrot squawked at him from an adjacent room. *"Yes! Yes! Yes!"*

Gabe closed the front door behind him and loosed the goat to make a meal of something unfortunate. Hopefully the bird.

"I'm coming, Bixby!" Lady Penelope called in the distance.

Gabe followed the sound down the corridor and then down a flight of stairs. He emerged into the kitchen. There were no servants to be seen, and a kettle looked to be boiling dry on the hob. A jumble of felines curled by the fireplace.

"I'm here, Bixby! Just hold on a little longer."

A heavy door at one end of the kitchen stood ajar. Gabe crossed to it and nudged it open further.

Nothing but darkness.

A darkness that scurried.

After blinking a few times, he could discern that this was the coal store, and it sat directly beneath the iron plate she'd been shouting through a few moments ago. A small mountain of coal rose at a steep angle, leading from the ground to the coal chute at the top.

And there—somewhere in the darkness at the top of the heap—was Bixby, presumably. The dog emitted a feeble whine.

"Nearly there." Lady Penelope attempted to scale the mountain, scrambling up the heap on hands and knees, pushing aside loose chunks of coal as she went.

Gabe shook his arms free of his coat and flung it aside. "What the devil has he done?"

"He's stuck. It's happened before. He finds a rat, and then he chases it into the store and up to the chute, and then his cart gets stuck on the coal hole hook, and—"

Yes, the cart. So this was the rolling dog.

"His back legs are lamed, and—" She scrambled higher, dislodging yet more coal. "There's no time to explain. I have to unhook him, or he could slip and hang himself."

Gabe yanked open his cuffs and pushed his sleeves to his elbows. "I'll do it."

"I'm almost—" She lost her footing and slid back to the ground, losing all her progress.

He reached for a shovel propped against the wall. "Stand aside."

At last, she relented, backing away from the mountain of coal. Gabe climbed as far as the ceiling would allow and dug into the coal, lifting a shovelful of sooty lumps from the top and heaving them to the cellar floor.

Once he found a rhythm, he made quick work of it, jabbing the spade into the coal heap again and again, employing not only the force of his arms, but his back and legs, as well. His muscles retained the memory of what he'd tried to forget. Shoveling coal was nothing he hadn't done before. Just something he'd sworn to never do again.

While Gabe worked, she called out encouragement from below. Not to him, of course. To the dog.

"Just a bit longer, Bixby!"

The dog's whines grew mournful.

Gabe could nearly reach him now. He tossed the shovel aside and cleared more coal from beneath the chute. When he'd created enough space, he flattened himself on his belly and wriggled over the coal, using his elbows to drag himself forward until he'd reached the spot beneath the chute.

There he was, the little mongrel. Scarcely bigger than a rat himself. He was caught on the iron hook of the coal hole plate, hung up by a bit of leather strap and struggling against the dead weight of his stumpy hind legs and cart.

"Easy, there. Easy." Gabe stretched his hand up the chute, twisting for the best angle. Couldn't quite reach. Even if he could, he had no idea what he was reaching for. How did this cart fit together? Was there a buckle or button he'd need to undo in order to free the dog? If so, it was hopeless. He didn't have enough light or space to complete any maneuver requiring dexterity.

"Very well, dog. You'll have to do your part." Gabe turned onto his side and reached up into the chute again, this time fumbling blind. When his fingertips brushed against fur, he lifted the dog's weight in his palm and pushed upward, straining his shoulder nearly out of its socket, hoping he'd give Bixby enough slack to wriggle free.

"Come on, you little bastard," he said through gritted teeth. "I've destroyed a full suit of clothing on your account, and I'm not handing your mistress a dead dog at the end of it."

Thank God. It worked.

Gabe knew the moment Bixby was free, because the dog slid down the chute and landed on his face. With a scrabble of sharp little claws, he fled to his mistress. By the time Gabe disengaged the abandoned cart from the hook and made his way down, he found her seated on the kitchen floor, cooing over the soot-covered dog in her arms.

"Bixby." The pup licked at her neck and face. "You are a naughty, naughty, *naughty* boy, and I love you so very much."

Gabe cleared his throat. "Cart's broken."

"My friend Nicola will mend it."

He set the mangled contraption to the side and shut the door to the coal store.

The moment he turned around, Lady Penelope flung herself at him and wrapped her arms around his shoulders. "Thank you."

Gabe winced, pulling free of her embrace.

"You've hurt your shoulder."

"It's nothing."

"It's not out of joint, I hope?" She prodded his shoulder, undeterred by his grimace. "When we were children, my brother Timothy dislocated his shoulder when he fell out of a tree. Even after it healed, he could pop it in and out of joint whenever he pleased. He used to do it just to make me scream."

"It's not out of joint. Let it alone."

Ignoring his protests, she pushed him toward a kitchen stool and made him sit. After unknotting his cravat with bossy motions, she circled to stand behind him and slid her hand inside the collar of his shirt.

Holy God.

"You've a cramp in your muscle." She stroked her fingertips along his shoulder until she found the source of his pain. He sucked a breath through his teeth. "Oh, dear. That does hurt, doesn't it?"

Yes. Yes, it bloody well hurt. He flinched from her touch.

She shushed him. "Be still. It won't release until you've calmed."

"Your Ladyship, you are anything but calming."

"You're not particularly cuddly yourself," she said. "Luckily, I have some experience soothing prickly beasts." She pressed her fingers against the knot of muscle, kneading gently. "That's it," she whispered. "Just breathe."

Her fingers weaved through his hair, stroking it back from his brow. He was painfully aware of his soot-smeared, perspiring state. It made him feel like a starving boy again, dressed in rags and covered in dirt, salivating over food on the hob and discarded crusts on the gin house tables. He'd worked so hard, come so far to leave that childhood behind.

Resentment rose in his chest, pumping his heart at a furious pace. Red anger clouded his vision and his pulse filled his ears.

Gabe shrugged off her hands and pushed to his feet. He needed to leave before he vented his emotions in her direction. She might be part of this elite, privileged world he despised, but she hadn't chosen it. No more than he'd chosen to be born in the gutter.

She circled back, standing before him. "There now. Better?"

He gave a reluctant nod.

"Can you move your arm in all directions?"

He rolled his shoulder to prove it. "Yes."

"What about your grip?"

"My grip is strong."

"Perhaps I should wrap the arm in a sling."

"I do not need a sling."

"Wait here. I'll dash upstairs to fetch some linen and—"

"For the love of God, woman. My shoulder is fine." He took her by the waist and lifted her straight off the floor, until they were eye to eye. "There. Believe me now?"

She nodded, wide-eyed.

"Good."

In his hands, she was delicate, breakable. Her hair was a golden treasure he should never, ever touch. And oh, how he hungered for those soft, pink lips.

The familiar voice echoed in his ears.

Don't touch, boy. She's not for the likes of you.

Put. Her. Down.

But before Gabe could lower those beribboned pink slippers to the floor, she captured his sooty, sweaty face in her hands—

And kissed him on the lips.

Chapter Six

*T*he kiss lasted a triumphant, beautiful instant.

Then he dropped her to the floor.

Penny, you fool.

It was only a distance of a few inches, but the impact shivered up her legs and made her knees weak. She had to cling to him for balance, which naturally made it all the more awkward.

"I'm sorry," she said, releasing him. "That was an accident."

His eyebrow quirked.

"I mean, it wasn't an accident. People accidentally bump heads, don't they. Or knees. No one bumps lips on accident. I did it purposely." She could hear herself blathering, but she couldn't seem to stop. "I was grateful for your help with Bixby, and more than a little overwhelmed by that display of brute strength. All that flexing."

He stared hard at her mouth, likely in disbelief at the nonsensical words streaming out of it.

She bit her lip. "Would you believe me if I said I was dizzy from the altitude?"

"No."

"Very well, I . . ." She squeezed her eyes shut. "I wanted to kiss you. I can't explain why. I have no excuses. At any rate, don't worry. It was clearly a mistake, and I promise it won't happen agai—"

Again.

He kissed her *again*.

Or rather, *he* kissed *her* for the first time—and he was so much better at it than she.

This kiss could not be mistaken for an accidental collision of mouths. Oh, no. He kissed with purpose. His lips had ideas. His tongue had *plans*.

She closed her eyes and melted against him, flattening her hands on his muscled arms. He brushed his lips to hers in a series of chaste, yet masterful kisses. He swept a hand up her spine and into her hair, where he twisted and gathered the tangled locks in his fist. Then he tugged sharply, tipping her face to his and sending electric sensation over her every nerve.

When her mouth fell open in a gasp, he reclaimed her lips, sweeping his tongue between them. Her first instinct was to shy away, but Penny fought against it. She reached higher, lacing her arms about his neck and holding tight.

His tongue stroked hers, slow and insistent. He tasted of soot and salt and . . . and of apples, strangely. Tart, smoky, just a hint of sweet.

A lush, decadent pleasure unwound within her, snaking through her veins—as though it had lain coiled in anticipation for years. Waiting on this moment.

Waiting on this man.

And then, in a voice rough with yearning, he whispered a single word against her lips. *"Inventory."*

Penny's eyes snapped open. "What?"

"Send me an inventory," he said, releasing her from his embrace. "A list of the animals. I'll start on finding them homes."

He gathered his discarded coat and folded it over his arm. After a look at his soot-smeared cravat, he tossed it into the fire.

Suddenly, he was all business. Penny was all confusion.

When he left the kitchen and mounted the stairs, she followed him, because what else could she do?

"While I'm working on the animals," he went on, "confer with your seamstress friend. You can't attend balls and such until you have a gown to wear. And if you want to make the society column, it had better be a stunning one."

"If anyone can create something stunning, it's Emma."

"Good." He opened the front door. "We're all sorted, then."

"Are we?"

"I'll await your list." With a nod, he exited the house and shut the door behind him.

How irritating. Penny was still reeling and breathless from their kiss, and he . . . wasn't, apparently. Surely a considerate man would at least *pretend* to be a bit unmoored.

Then the door reopened, and he entered again. "Your Ladyship, I—"

After a lengthy pause, she prompted him. "You . . . ?"

He frowned at the floor. "We."

We.

He said this as though it were a complete sentence, but even after several moments of contemplation, Penny could not make sense of it.

With an annoyed shake of his head, he wrenched open the door for the third time, stormed through it, and slammed it behind him with such decisive force that the portraits rattled on the wall.

Penny smiled to herself.

With that, she could be satisfied.

TAP. TAP. TAP.

The next day, Gabe found himself sitting in his office. In fact, he'd been sitting there for hours now. Not reviewing any of the many papers, contracts, or ledgers awaiting his attention, but merely staring into space and tapping a shilling against the desk.

Tap. Tap. Tap.

She'd meant to kiss him. She'd *wanted* to kiss him. She'd said as much, explicitly, and she'd seemed perfectly content to be kissed in return. More than content.

He hadn't taken advantage of her.

He'd just been colossally stupid.

With a creaking groan, he allowed his head to slowly fall forward until his brow met the desk blotter. And then he stayed there, trying not to recall the sweet freshness of her kiss or the hot joy that had blazed through him when her breasts met his chest.

Colossally. Stupid.

"Mr. Duke, you'll never guess what—"

Gabe lifted his head.

Hammond fidgeted in the doorway. "I'd something to show you, but perhaps this isn't a good time."

"No, no." Gabe launched to his feet. "It's a good time."

It was, in fact, the best possible time. He'd never been so happy to be interrupted.

Hammond led him to the upstairs bath, where he gestured expansively toward the tub. "Behold, the latest in modern conveniences. Hot running water."

"You're certain this time?"

"The tradesman repaired the boiler yesterday. I tested it just this morning. Piping hot."

As his architect turned the tap, Gabe crossed his arms and kept a safe distance. He'd let Hammond take the chances today.

Happily, the tap did *not* explode like a cannon packed with icy shrapnel.

Unhappily, what pooled in the bathtub was a trickle of rusty sludge.

"Deuce it." Hammond closed the tap and kicked at the tiled floor. "I swear on everything holy, this was working an hour ago. Burns probably hexed it."

"The housekeeper? Don't start in on that nonsense again."

"I tell you, she's unnatural. I don't know if she's a ghost, a witch, a demon, or something worse. But that woman is of the Devil."

"*Ahem.*"

Startled, both Gabe and Hammond wheeled around.

There stood Mrs. Burns. Even Gabe had to admit, these sudden appearances were growing unsettling.

Hammond raised his fingers in the shape of a cross. "I rebuke thee."

"Good afternoon, Mrs. Burns," Gabe said. "We didn't hear your footsteps."

"I was always taught, Mr. Duke, that servants should draw as little attention to themselves as possible."

She certainly had their attention now.

Wordlessly, Hammond lifted his arm, extended a single finger, and poked the housekeeper in the shoulder.

Mrs. Burns stared at him. "Yes, Mr. Hammond?"

"Solid corporeal form," he muttered. "Interesting."

Gabe gave him an elbow to the ribs, sending the architect's "corporeal form" stumbling against the sludge-filled tub. "Is there something we can do for you, Mrs. Burns?"

"I only came to inform you that you have a letter, sir. It's just arrived."

"The post came this morning."

"This letter didn't come through the post, Mr. Duke. It's from Lady Penelope Campion."

***

Dear Mr. Duke,

As requested, here is an inventory of the animals in my care:

- *Bixby, a two-legged terrier.*
- *Marigold, a nanny goat of unimpeachable character, who is definitely not breeding.*
- *Angus, a three-year-old Highland steer.*
- *Regan, Goneril, and Cordelia—laying hens.*
- *Delilah, a parrot.*

- *Hubert, an otter.*
- *Freya, a hedgehog.*
- *Thirteen kittens of varying colors and dispositions.*

GABE LEAFED THROUGH the report in disbelief. It went on for pages. She'd given not only the names, breeds, and ages of every misbegotten creature, but she'd appended a chart of temperaments, sleeping schedules, preferred bedding, and a list of dietary requirements that would beggar a moderately successful tradesman. Along with the expected hay, alfalfa, corn, and seed, the animals required several pounds of mince weekly, daily pints of fresh cream, and an ungodly number of sardines.

The steer and the goat, she insisted, must go to the same loving home. Apparently they were tightly bonded, whatever that meant, and refused to eat if parted.

The laying hens did not actually lay with any regularity. Their previous owners had grown frustrated with this paltry production, and thus they had come into Her Ladyship's care.

And the lucky bastard who accepted a ten-year-old hedgehog? Well, he must not only provide a steady supply of mealworms, but remain ever mindful of certain "traumatic experiences in her youth."

He had to read that bit three times to believe it.

Traumatic experiences in her youth.

Unbelievable.

The world teemed with children who received less food and attention than she gave the least of these creatures. Gabe knew it well. He'd been one of them. At the workhouse, he'd subsisted on broth, bread, and a few morsels of cheese every week—when his diet hadn't been restricted as a punishment for misbehavior, which it usually was.

He didn't have time for this, and he didn't trust himself to linger over the task, either. That would mean calling on Lady Penelope at least as many times as there were creatures on this list. Considering they had less than a month to resettle the animals, that would mean seeing her virtually every day. Too many opportunities for stupidity.

Loving homes, his eye. He was tempted to escort all the creatures on a loving journey to the nearest butcher. What Her Ladyship didn't know wouldn't hurt her.

Then again, if Her Ladyship happened to discover it later, it would likely come back to hurt *him*. And even Gabe wasn't quite so ruthless as to send an innocent hedgehog to slaughter.

Not the butcher's, then. But there had to be somewhere he could take them all in one go. He didn't suppose a menagerie would be interested in an ancient hedgehog or a trio of non-laying laying hens. Releasing a compromised goat and its best friend, Angus the Highland steer, into the middle of Hyde Park . . . ? That seemed unlikely to go unnoticed.

A city the size of London offered few, if any, possibilities.

What he needed was a farm.

Chapter Seven

"hen what happened?" Emma held the measuring tape stretched from Penny's neck to her wrist, waiting on her answer.

"And then I kissed him," Penny answered quietly. "And he kissed me back."

"*No.*" Emma took three paces backward and stared at her from the opposite side of the Ashbury House morning room. "Oh, Penny."

"I was caught up in the moment. He'd just rescued Bixby, and I was grateful. And when his shoulder flexed beneath my hand, his muscles felt so—"

"You were feeling his *shoulders*?"

"Only one of them," she protested, as if this fact made it any less improper.

Penny stepped down from the dressmaker's box, sank onto the divan, and buried her face in her hands. Emma spooled her measuring tape and came to sit beside her.

Penny laid her head on her friend's shoulder. "It's such a relief to see you. I haven't had anyone to confide in. Thank you for coming to Town."

"Naturally, we came. You said you needed us. Besides, I ought to thank *you.* For years now I've been dying to give you a new wardrobe. I'll draw up sketches, make patterns. Then we'll see that you have the best of fabrics and the most talented dressmakers in London."

As a seamstress-turned-duchess, Emma could have abandoned needlework in favor of a life of leisure. Most women in her place certainly would have done so.

However, Emma was not the usual sort of woman, and Penny was ever grateful for it. Their common status on the fringes of genteel society was the reason they'd become close friends.

"I don't know what's come over me," Penny moaned. "Whenever he's near, I feel like an animal in mating season. I think I've fallen in lust."

"If you have, it isn't the worst thing in the world. Many a woman has fallen victim to the same contagion. Including me. If you don't wish to see Mr. Duke, simply avoid him."

"I can't avoid him. He's offered to help me with my aunt's demands, and even if he hadn't, he lives next door."

"Good God, Penny." The Duke of Ashbury stormed into the room. "Do you know what kind of brigand you have living next door?"

"Gabriel Duke," she answered.

"Gabriel Duke, that's who." Ash glowered at the window. He always looked fearsome, due to the battle scars twisting one half of his face. If not for the giggling child attached to his boot, he might have looked truly intimidating.

"Richmond, darling." Penny extended her arms, and the boy toddled into her embrace. "Look how big you've grown."

"Your new neighbor is an infamous blackguard," Ash continued. "And now Emma tells me you're consorting with the man?"

"I'm not *consorting* with him. My aunt has given me an ultimatum. If I don't earn her approval before the month is out, my brother will take me back to Cumberland."

Penny's stomach churned. Ever since her aunt's visit, the prospect of returning to Cumberland had loomed over her like a thundercloud, oppressive and dark. The mere idea of living in that house, sleeping in that room . . .

She couldn't go back. She wouldn't.

"Mr. Duke offered to assist me with a few tasks. It's in his financial interests that I remain in Bloom Square."

"Oh, I'm certain it's in his interests. Haven't you heard what he did to Lord Fairdale?"

Penny bounced Richmond on her knee. "I hadn't heard, actually."

"I'll tell you. First, he bought up all the man's paper. And I mean all of it. Tracked down every last creditor, from an unsettled wager at White's to his outstanding balance at the glover's, rolling them all into one insurmountable debt. Then he drove down the value of stock in a shipping company, leaving Fairdale with nothing of worth to sell. He was left with nothing but a bit of barren land and the crumbling ancestral house."

"Goodness."

"There was nothing of goodness in it. Sheer villainy. He not only mowed that family to field stubble, he salted the earth beneath them. And Fairdale hasn't been his only victim. The man means to gather England's best families into a bundle of sticks and break them over his knee. You cannot have anything to do with him. The danger is too great."

"The danger of what?"

He spread his arms. "Isn't it obvious? He wants to ruin *you*."

"Ash, please." Emma covered her son's ears. "Not in front of Richmond."

"He's isn't even two years old. It's not as if he can understand." Nevertheless, Ash ceded to his wife's request. "The man means to R-U-I-N you."

Penny sat up straight. "Are you suggesting Mr. Duke intends to S-E-D-U-C-E me? How absurd."

It *was* absurd, she told herself. Their kiss the other day was not an act of seduction. It was an accident. A moment of madness.

More to the point, it was all her doing.

If anything, she'd taken advantage of him.

Penny shook her head. "He R-U-I-N-S lords' fortunes, not ladies' reputations."

"You never know if he'll start branching out. If the villain has designs on your dowry, you are too inexperienced to handle him."

"Oh, I think Penny can handle him," Emma said innocently. "She's handled the man quite capably thus far."

Penny cast a look at her friend. *Please don't.*

"I won't stand for it," Ash said with force. "Neither will Chase."

"Chase?"

"As usual, it appears I need no introduction." Chase Reynaud entered the room, linked arm-in-arm with his excessively pregnant wife, Alexandra, and followed by their two wards, Rosamund and Daisy.

"Alex." Penny handed Richmond to Emma and rushed to embrace her friend tightly—or as tightly as possible, given the obstacle between them. While Rosamund and Daisy mobbed her with kisses, Penny helped her friend waddle to the divan. "I thought you'd entered your confinement."

"I'm weary of being confined." Alexandra dropped onto the divan with a thud. "Besides, Ash said we were needed at once. I'm not certain why."

Ash said, "Tell her, Chase."

Chase stood tall and leveled a finger at Penny with unconvincing severity. "You cannot live next to that man. Don't you know what he did to Lord Fairdale? The villain—"

"Bought up his debts, destroyed his investments, and left him with scarcely anything to his name."

"Yes. What if the bast—"

"Chase," Alexandra said sharply.

He sighed. "What if the B-A-S-T-E-R-D sets his eyes on you?"

"A," Rosamund corrected. "B-A-S-T-A-R-D."

Penny made a suggestion. "Girls, would you kindly run across the square to my house and have a look at Angus? He sneezed yesterday. Perhaps he has a cold."

"Maybe it's the plague!" Daisy cheered.

"Probably not," Penny said. "But you had better go see."

"Is there any chance he's dying? I don't *want* him to die, of course. But it's ever so exciting when there's a chance."

"Daisy, he's not dying." Rosamund tugged her younger sister by the hand. "They're trying to be rid of us so they can discuss adult matters."

The younger girl pouted. "Pooh."

Once the children were out of earshot, Ash continued with his lecture. "Penny, you don't have to listen to us. Just look at the papers. They've taken to calling him the Duke of Ruin."

"Not so very long ago, the papers called *you* the Monster of Mayfair," she pointed out. "I know better than to heed the scandal sheets."

"It's not merely rumor." Chase pulled up a chair. "The man's deliberately set about driving well-heeled families to the brink of insolvency."

"Not just driving them to the brink," Ash said. "He tips them over the edge. Who's to say he doesn't have the same in mind for you?"

"He would find it impossible. My brother Bradford keeps the estate finances on a foundation of bedrock."

"Even if he can't touch your family's money," Chase said, "you do have a dowry."

"If you won't protect yourself," Ash warned, "we will have to take protective measures on your behalf."

"What sort of protective measures?"

Nicola rushed into the room. Wisps of ginger hair floated about her head in an unkempt halo. In her hand, she carried a brown-paper packet. "I brought the poisoned biscuits," she said, breathless. "I'm still perfecting the spring-loaded trap for her door."

Wonderful. Yet another addition to the "Protect Penny" brigade.

"That's very kind of you, Nicola." Penny took the packet of

biscuits from her friend, tucked them behind her back, and while completing her circuit of the room, discreetly tossed them into the fire.

"Perhaps the men do have a point," Alexandra said. "Maybe there is some cause for concern."

"Alex. Not you, too."

"I'm sorry, dear. But we all know how tender your heart is. It's a wonderful quality, and we adore you for it. But you can be too trusting at times."

"At all times," Chase added.

Penny couldn't believe this. "So you not only believe he'll attempt to seduce me, but that I'll fall for this supposed ruse."

"None of us wants to see you hurt," Nicola said. "That's all."

Penny turned and stared out the window. She was beginning to take offense at her friends' complete lack of faith in her judgment. She was a grown woman, not a child. Any moment now, they'd begin spelling out words in front of her.

She heard yet another knock at the door.

Lord, who else had they recruited to this effort? This time, Penny didn't bother to turn around and find out.

"Yes," she said, exasperated. "My new neighbor is Gabriel Duke. Yes, I have heard what he did to Lord Fairdale. Yes, I know the papers are calling him the Duke of Ruin. No, I do not need protection. All he wants is to sell his house. All I want is to remain in mine. We have a mutually beneficial, *temporary* agreement. He is not attempting to seduce me, and I will absolutely not fall in love with him."

The ensuing silence spoke volumes. And those volumes were titled *Worst Moments of Penny's Life, vols. I–XIII.*

His virile heat filled the room, blanketing her with gooseflesh. She didn't even need to look to know he was there. She didn't *need* to look, perhaps, but eventually, tragically, she would have to face him. It wasn't as though she could dive behind the draperies and hide until he went away.

Or could she? She gave it more than a moment's thought before dismissing the idea.

At length, she forced herself to turn around.

There he stood in the morning room entryway, dark and devastating. When he spoke, he announced himself in a low, commanding voice.

"I'm here about the goat."

No one had the faintest notion how to respond.

"And the steer, and the chickens," he continued, speaking to Penny. "Your housekeeper told me I'd find you here. I've found a solution."

"Goodness. That was fast."

Penny's heart pinched. She hadn't prepared to say good-bye to Marigold and Angus so soon.

"I told you, I don't waste time. I'll come around tomorrow afternoon. We can discuss the particulars then."

"Hold a moment." Ash shook himself to life. "She's not discussing anything with you."

"That's right." Chase stood. "Neither is her goat."

Gabriel alternated a glare between one man and the other. "Who are you?"

Ash puffed his chest. "I'm the Duke of Ashbury."

Penny intervened. "Come now, Ash. We don't use titles. Our guest is your neighbor, too. Everyone, this is Gabriel. Gabriel, meet Alexandra, Chase, Nicola, Emma, and Ash. They're my good friends."

"Friends, you say? They seem to have mistaken themselves for your guardians."

"Listen to me, you B-A-S-T—" Ash bit off the words, growled in annoyance, and began again. "Listen to me, you bastard."

"No," Gabriel said.

This simple response left Ash nonplussed. But fuming.

"I'm listening to exactly one person in this room," Gabriel said evenly. "It isn't you. The lady can speak for herself."

Oh. Penny's heart fluttered in her chest.

If by chance he *did* mean to seduce her, repeating that sentence fifty times over might do the trick.

He spoke directly to her. Only to her. "Tomorrow afternoon. We're agreed?"

She nodded. "We're agreed."

He quit the room without the usual courtesy of taking his leave. The bang of the front door announced his departure.

At length, Chase broke the disbelieving silence. "Good God. That man is intolerable."

"Yes," Penny said. "He is."

Alexandra sat up—no small feat, in her condition—and regarded her with concern. "Oh, Penny."

"What?"

"The way you said that. You sounded . . . dreamy."

"I am not dreamy," she fibbed. "Chase remarked that he was intolerable, and I agreed. If you like, I'll add that he's ill-mannered and beastly."

"Precisely," Nicola said. "That's what worries us. He's just the sort of man you'd be drawn to. We all know how you love a challenge."

"Believe me, I have sufficient challenges in my life at the moment. I'm not looking to take on one more."

"At least promise us one thing," Alexandra pleaded. "Promise you won't be caught with him alone."

Penny relented. "Very well. I promise."

Chapter Eight

$\mathcal{P}$enny would have no difficulty keeping her promise to her friends. She was never truly alone. Her collection of unusual pets had successfully kept men at bay for a decade. She didn't see any reason that would change now.

The following afternoon, she was just bringing in Marigold from her browse in the square when the rumble of approaching cart wheels pulled her out of the stables and into the alley.

The cart was drawn by a team of the most massive draft horses Penny had ever seen. A middle-aged couple in simple attire sat on the driver's box. And standing on the bed of the cart, like the marshal of his own parade, was Gabriel Duke.

The team drew to a halt. He vaulted over the side rail of the cart and landed before her.

"What's all of this?" she asked.

He gestured to the driver and his companion alighting from the box. "Allow me to introduce Mr. and Mrs. Brown."

"Pleased to make your acquaintance," Penny said, though she wasn't at all sure *why* she was making their acquaintance.

Mr. Brown doffed his hat and held it over his heart as he bowed. "'Tis a true honor, Your Ladyship."

His wife made a deep curtsy. "Never thought to meet with a genuine lady."

"The Browns own a charming farm in Hertfordshire," Mr.

Duke said. "And they'd be delighted to take the animals off your hands."

"All of them?"

He grinned. "All of them. Today."

Penny couldn't believe it. "How did this happen? How did you meet?"

"It was Hammond who met with them in the market. They'd come into town with a load of . . . What was it, Brown?"

"Parsnips, sir."

"Parsnips." Mr. Duke nodded. "Hammond does love a fresh parsnip. Tell Her Ladyship about your farm, Mrs. Brown."

"It's a lovely patch of country, milady. Just a smallholding, but it's ours. Pasture for the horses, and fields of oats, alfalfa, clover."

"And parsnips," Penny said.

"Yes, of course. And parsnips." Mrs. Brown smiled. "There's even a little pond."

"Tell me, Mrs. Brown, would you say this little pond of yours would make a good home for an otter?" Mr. Duke asked.

"I daresay it would make the ideal home for an otter, sir."

"Well, then. How convenient. Did you hear that, Your Ladyship? They can take the otter, too. Go on, then. Box him up."

Penny narrowed her eyes, suspicious. "I assume Mr. Duke has explained to you that many of these animals require special care?"

Mrs. Brown clasped her hands together. "God never blessed us with children of our own, milady. It would be a true joy to look after the animals. We need creatures to love."

"Indeed." Mr. Brown gave Angus a smack on the rump. "I'd wager this old girl is a fine milker."

"That's a Highland steer," Penny said.

"Oh!" The farmer—if indeed he was a farmer—peeked under Angus's tail. "So he is. Out in Herefordshire—"

Mrs. Brown elbowed her husband. "Hertfordshire."

"Out in Hertfordshire, we don't often see this breed."

Penny could have pointed out that the breeding organs of cattle remained largely the same, regardless. She didn't bother. Whoever these people were, they were not parsnip farmers from Hertfordshire. They weren't farmers of any sort.

"Well, then." Mr. Duke clapped his hands. "Shall we load them all up?"

Just how far did he intend to carry this ruse? Did he think Penny had taken a headfirst tumble off a parsnip wagon?

"By all means," she said. "And while you do that, I'll fetch my things."

"Your things?"

"Yes, of course. With no offense intended to Mr. and Mrs. Brown, I have to see and judge the place for myself."

"The journey will take two days." His tone was clipped. "Each way."

She smiled. "I'll pack accordingly."

"Fine. You do that. Mr. and Mrs. Brown will be waiting."

Before she could take his bluff to the next level, "Mr. Brown" intervened. "Hold a moment, sir. What is this mischief, I ask you? Two days' journey, in either direction? Inconceivable."

The man's amiable country accent had transformed into full-throated Shakespearean declamation, complete with trilled R's and flourishes of the hand.

The woman purporting to be Mrs. Brown confronted Mr. Duke in a faintly Irish lilt. "We agreed to a onetime engagement, sir. A single afternoon playing the humble farmer and his wife. What's this about travelin' to Hertfordshire? We've a Drury Lane performance in a few hours. I'm not giving my scheming little understudy a chance at Lady Macbeth."

"I'll have you know I make an appearance in the first act, sir!" the farmer bellowed. "I cannot miss the curtain."

"As if anyone would notice, Harold. You're naught but scenery."

Harold puffed his chest. "In the theater, there are no insignificant roles."

"Oh, to be sure there aren't. Size doesn't matter. Keep tellin' yourself as much."

Mr. Duke dug in his pocket for money. "Just go, the both of you."

Penny waited until the actors had gone. "You are unbelievable. And unimaginative, too. A parsnip farm?"

"Very well, there's no farm. But in my defense, I had every intention of purchasing the first available bit of pasture."

"The *first* available? You promised me they'd have the *best* available. With people who care."

"You handed me a mile-long list of animals. Where am I supposed to find a pension home for aging livestock?"

"This was a terrible idea. I should never have accepted your offer to help. If you're going to mock me, there's no point in this at all. You agree with my aunt. I'm silly and pathetic, and it's time for me to give up." She turned to retreat into the house. "Perhaps you're right."

"Oh, no, you don't." He caught her by the wrist. "The two of us . . . We're from different breeds. Different species, even. I can't pretend to fathom what you're doing with all these animals. However, I doubt you approve of the way I live my life, either."

That was fair to say, she supposed.

"There is, however, one thing we have in common. I'm stubborn as hell, and I'd formed the impression that you don't surrender easily, either. Or was I mistaken?"

"You weren't mistaken."

"It's settled, then." His gaze held her captive. "I'm not giving up, and neither are you."

PINK BLOOMED ON her cheeks. Her gaze dropped to his mouth and lingered there. Good God. She was thinking about kissing him. Not merely remembering kissing him the other night, but thinking about kissing him again.

She was a fool. A naïve, trusting, sheltered fool.

And Gabe wanted to corrupt her so damned badly, his bones ached.

He had to get this absurd task accomplished, and soon.

"I'll buy some property in the country. We have to find a place to put them all at once. How do you feel about Surrey?"

"Surrey? I'm ambivalent about Surrey."

"Everyone's ambivalent about Surrey. I'm not certain there's any other way to feel about Surrey."

"It doesn't matter. We aren't 'putting them' on a random parcel of land. We're meant to be finding them homes. Ones with real people."

"The problem is, real people need to eat. They don't have time to take on animals with dietary restrictions and missing legs."

"Do you think I don't know that? That's precisely why they're all here with me. No one else would take them. Angus, for example." She moved toward the Highland steer. "Some foolish merchant traveled to Scotland on holiday and decided on impulse to bring his wife a pet calf from the Highlands. Never stopped to think about the fact that he would grow."

"Surely people aren't that stupid."

"Oh, it happens all the time. But usually they make that mistake with pups or ponies. Not cattle." She shook her head. "They dehorned him in the worst, most painful way. When he came to me, the poor dear's wounds were infected. Infested, too. He could have perished from the fly-strike alone. That man was stupid, indeed. The only thing he got right was his choice of calf. Angus *is* exceedingly adorable."

Adorable?

Gabe eyed the beast. The animal stood as tall as Gabe's shoulder, and it smelled . . . the way cattle smell. Shaggy red fur covered its eyes like a blindfold, and its black, spongy nose glistened.

"He's the best Highland steer in the world," she said. "Come meet him."

"That's not necessary."

She didn't give him a choice about it, leading him by the arm until they stood before the giant, shaggy beast.

"He loves being scratched between the ears." She stroked Angus's forelock. "There aren't many creatures who don't enjoy a scratch about the ears. Go on. Have a turn."

"I don't want to pet the cow."

"He's a steer."

"I don't want to pet the st—"

She reached for his hand and placed it atop Angus's flat head, guiding his hand back and forth. As if he were a child who needed to be taught.

"See? He's softer than he looks."

Gabe was less interested in the texture of Angus's hide than he was in the texture of Lady Penelope's skin. Her hand was small and graceful atop his, but it was not the soft, delicate hand he would expect of a fine lady. Her skin was crossed here and there with lines and scars—some faded, some still pink. They were healed bites and scratches, accumulated over years. She had a lifelong habit of extending care to animals too wild or frightened to accept it—which made her the bravest kind of fool.

Gabe wanted to kiss each and every one of those healed wounds—which made him just an ordinary fool.

Angus snuffled and bobbed his head.

She smiled. "I think he likes you."

Gabe stepped away, brushing his hand on his trousers. "I didn't invent a farm and hire those actors out of *complete* heartlessness. It's a practical matter. Settling the animals one by one will mean we'd be spending a great deal of time together. That's a bad idea."

"If you're worried about my reputation, don't. It won't be noticed. No one pays much attention to me."

The injustice in that statement confounded him. How could

no one be paying attention to her? Over the past few days, he'd been unable to concentrate on anyone or anything *but* her.

"We're adults," she said. "Surely we can behave ourselves. I promise not to kiss you again."

"It's not a mere kiss that should worry you."

"What else are you worried could happen?"

Good Lord. What *wasn't* he worried could happen. He'd been up half the night inventing possibilities.

"Look at your goat," he said. "You weren't paying attention to her, and now she's breeding."

"Marigold is *not* pregnant."

"See? You're too trusting. That's why this is dangerous. If we're spending all that time together unchaperoned, there's too much chance of—"

"Too much chance of what?"

He moved closer, letting the tension build between their bodies. "Of this."

Her golden eyelashes kissed her flushed cheeks. "You're worried for nothing. My animals are incompatible with attraction, courtship, romance, or marriage. I've been reminded of that regularly for years. They're exceptionally talented in discouraging gentlemen."

"I'm not a gentleman. And if I could be discouraged, I'd never have amassed the fortune I have now. When I set my mind on something, a herd of elephants won't stand in my way."

A beam of sunlight caught the swirling dust motes and turned them into a glittering halo about her head. Those sparks invaded his body, coursing through his veins until every inch of him was sharply aware of her beauty.

He bent his head to kiss her.

She stretched to meet him halfway.

And Angus sneezed, spraying him with whatever wet, sticky substances comprised the contents of a bovine nose. Gabe wasn't willing to contemplate specifics. He merely stood there, sputtering with horror, and—

And *dripping.*

Wiping his face with his sleeve, he cursed cattle, the Highlands, and the world in general.

Lady Penelope laughed. Of course she did.

She unknotted the fichu from about her neck and dabbed at his shirt, oblivious to the amount of cleavage she'd exposed to his view. Her lips curved in a fetching smile. "I think Angus has made my case for me."

He shook his head. "From now on, we communicate in writing."

"We live next door to each other. That's absurd."

"It's necessary. This will be the last time we find ourselves alone. Animals don't count as chaperones. Not even phlegmy ones. Do you understand me?"

"You're vastly underestimating my pets' ability to prevent scandal."

Swearing under his breath, he caught her chin and tipped her face to his. "Your Ladyship, you are vastly underestimating yourself."

Chapter Nine

*T*wo days later, and Gabe's plans had already gone to hell.

The lady was impossible. When he'd written her about the otter, he'd given explicit instructions in his note. Be ready to leave at half-seven, sharp. Dress for the weather. Most importantly, bring a companion.

She brought the parrot.

The *parrot.*

They were miles beyond London's borders already, and Gabe still couldn't believe it. Look at him. Trapped in a barouche with a lady, a parrot, and an otter. He'd landed in the center of an absurd joke. One certain to end in uproarious laughter—at his expense.

He shifted unhappily on the carriage seat. "Did you really have to bring that bird?"

"Yes." She stroked the otter's sleek brown coat. "I think Alexandra and Chase will take her in. Their two girls love to play pirates. But as you pointed out, Delilah's vocabulary needs a bit of reformation, so I'm trying to instill some wholesome phrases in her repertoire. Considering that I've only a fortnight, I can't afford to waste a day." She leaned in close to the birdcage and brightly cooed—as she had no fewer than a hundred times since they'd departed Bloom Square—"I love you."

The bird whistled. *"Pretty girl."*

"I love you."

"*Fancy a fuck, love?*"

"I *love* you."

The bird ruffled its garish plumage. "*Yes! Yes! Yes!*"

She was undaunted. "I love y—"

"It's pointless," he interjected. "A waste of time. Even if you succeed in teaching the bird a new phrase or two, it's never going to forget the old ones. Years of filth won't simply wash off with one good rain. That's like saying you'd lose your finishing school airs with a single"—*soul-stirring, passionate kiss*—"act of mild rebellion."

She squared her posture, pulling her spine fence-post straight. "I don't have finishing school airs."

"To be sure, you don't," he grumbled. "Keep telling yourself that, Your Ladyship."

"Will you please stop addressing me that way. Everyone I'm close to calls me Penny."

"We're not close."

"We are the very definition of close."

Good God. Did she have to point it out? They were altogether too close in this carriage, in a way that made him ache to be closer. His body was painfully aware of hers.

Gabe despised the aristocracy. He'd told himself he could never lust after a fine lady.

Apparently, he'd told himself lies.

"We are neighbors," she said. "Our houses stand right beside each other. That makes us close."

"It doesn't make us friends."

She turned her attention back to the parrot, resuming her singsong torture. "I love you. I *loooove* you."

"Enough." Gabe wrestled out of his coat—no small accomplishment in a carriage—and draped it over the birdcage. "The bird needs a rest." *I need a rest.*

She pouted a bit, and he was unmoved.

Pretty girl, fancy a fuck, I love you, I love you, I love you . . .

The words were becoming a jumble in his mind—and his

mind was a place where "fuck," "love," and one particular "pretty girl" must remain separate things.

"You can stop staring at me," he said.

"Sorry. I was wondering if I could actually watch your whiskers grow. When we left London, you were clean-shaven. Now it's not even noon, and you're raspy already. It's like weeds after a rain. Fascinating." She shook herself. "Tell me where it is we're going."

"The country home of a gentleman I know. His son has been begging for a ferret."

"Hubert isn't a ferret! He's an otter."

"As far as this boy is concerned, he's a ferret. Just follow my lead."

"Surely you're joking."

"He's five years old. He won't know the difference."

"He won't stay five years old forever."

"Yes, but by then it won't matter. It's like that children's story with the swan's egg in the duck's nest. He'll be The Ugly Ferret."

"A five-year-old child can't take proper care of an otter. Or a ferret for that matter."

"So you'll leave specific instructions."

She shook her head. "You may as well turn the carriage around now. This is not in the terms of our agreement."

"You wanted a loving home. He'll be adored."

"Perhaps," she said. "But not for himself. Not for the otter he truly is, deep down."

Gabe pinched the bridge of his nose. "We've come this far. I'm not turning back now."

"Waste the time if you like. I won't leave him there."

"I think you will. You can tell me you intend to refuse. But once we're there, and you're standing before a bright-eyed, hopeful boy? You won't be able to say no. Your heart is too soft."

Her body was too soft, too.

She leaned forward, holding the otter in one arm and reaching for a basket with the other—a pose which just happened to give him a view straight down her bodice. Her sweet, tempting breasts pushed across the muslin shelf of her bodice.

Gabe clenched his hands into fists at his sides.

Just when he'd managed to stop ogling her breasts—although he hadn't yet managed to cease thinking of them—the carriage slammed to a halt.

Lady Penelope bounced off her seat, straight into his lap.

Breasts and all.

As LANDINGS WENT, Penny's wasn't a graceful one. When the carriage abruptly halted, she wished she could claim she'd made an elegant slide into his waiting, heroically muscled arms.

Sadly, the truth was quite different.

When the carriage lurched to a halt, she'd been leaning forward to retrieve a morsel for Hubert. The force launched her from her seat, propelling her toward Gabriel. She landed with her nose mashed against his chest and her breasts spilled across his lap.

Marvelous. Simply marvelous. What a lady she was.

He hooked his hands under her arms and lifted, peeling her face from his satin waistcoat. He settled her on his knee. "Good God. Tell me you're not hurt."

"I'm not hurt."

"Can you move all your fingers? Your toes?"

"I think so."

Apparently, he found these assurances unsatisfactory. He untied her bonnet and flung it aside. His eyes darkened with concern as he searched her face. Taking hold of her chin, he turned her head to either side, scanning her cheeks and temples for bruises. Then he skimmed his hands over her shoulders and down her arms. All the way to her fingertips, which he gave a firm squeeze.

Inspection complete, he laid a hand to her cheek. His thumb brushed her bottom lip. "You're certain you're not injured?"

She shook her head.

Injured? No.

Electrified? Possibly.

Most definitely breathless.

She was dizzied by his closeness, his touch, and above all, his unexpected tenderness. A shaft of sunlight pierced the carriage, dividing her between hot and cool. She felt the fierce pounding of a heartbeat. Hers, probably, but she couldn't be certain.

Penny was so disoriented, in fact, that she did the unthinkable.

She completely forgot about the animals. For several seconds, at least. Perhaps a minute, or even two.

A squawk jolted her back to her senses.

"Delilah." She scrambled to her feet and searched the carriage. "Hubert."

Happily, she found both parrot and otter at her feet. By the way Delilah bounced and flapped about her upended cage, she was rattled but uninjured. Penny scooped Hubert into her arms, rolling him over to look for any wounds or bleeding.

Finding none, she exhaled with relief.

By now, Gabriel had alighted from the carriage, presumably to investigate the reason for their sudden stop. Within moments, he returned—looking every bit restored to his typically unpleasant self.

"These damned country roads. The carriage went into a rut, and now one of the wheels needs repair."

He offered her his hand, and she accepted it, rearranging her disheveled frock as she alighted from the coach and her boots met the rutted dirt road.

"There's a village we passed, a mile or two back. The coachman will walk there to find a smith or wheelwright." He looked about them, taking in the sunny countryside. "I suppose this is as good a place as any to stop. The horses will be needing a

rest and water, at any rate. Looks as though there's a stream."
He nodded toward a line of trees and shrubs not far from the
road.

"We may as well make the most of the delay." Penny retrieved a hamper from inside the coach and looped it over one
wrist, tucking Hubert under her other arm. "Are you hungry?"

"I'm always hungry."

"I brought sandwiches. Assuming they weren't completely
smashed in the upheaval."

She walked toward the creek and selected a spot that was
sufficiently shaded by budding branches, but not too damp underneath. She withdrew a square of gaily printed linen from
the hamper, snapped it open, and spread it over the ground.
"We can have a picnic."

He frowned. "What, on the ground?"

"That's what a picnic is, usually," she teased. "Have you
never attended a picnic before?"

He didn't answer, which was an answer itself. He had never
attended a picnic before. Too busy ruining fortunes and seiz-
ing property, she supposed.

"Then you must come and join this one," she said.

Penny made herself comfortable, tucking her ankles beneath
her skirts as she sat on the ground. Hubert stretched out beside
her, angling for a belly rub. She couldn't possibly refuse.

As it happened, the sandwiches were only slightly smashed.
Penny unpacked them from their brown paper wrapping and
arranged them prettily on a wooden cheeseboard.

"I packed fizzy lemonade, as well." She withdrew a corked
jug. "Although considering our recent tumble, we might want
to hold off on opening it." She presented him with the platter
of sandwiches. "Here."

He took one from the tray and angled it for inspection. "What
sort of sandwiches are these?"

"Just try them."

Penny knew from experience that revealing her recipes in

advance wasn't a good idea. People tended to look askance at her unconventional ingredients. But once given a fair try, her sandwiches never failed to win over even the most choosy of palates.

"Go on," she said. "I made them myself. Have a taste."

OH, GOD. THE *taste.*

As his teeth sank through the sandwich, Gabe experienced a sensation that, for him, was exceedingly rare.

Regret.

The flavor hit him like a punch to the face. His jaw muscles ceased to function. They simply refused to chew. The mouthful of . . . whatever this was, as it clearly did not qualify as food . . . sat on his tongue, growing softer and slimier.

"What," he said, finally choking it down, "was that?"

"It's my latest recipe." She beamed. "Roast leaf."

"It's gone off. That's not like any roast beef sandwich I've ever tasted."

"No, no. Not roast beef. Roast leaf."

He stared at her.

"I'm a vegetarian," she explained. "I don't eat meat. So I create my own substitutions with vegetables. Roast leaf, for example. I start with whatever greens are in the market, boil and mash them with salt, then press them into a roast for the oven. According to the cookery book, it's every bit as satisfying as the real thing."

"Your cookery book is a book of lies."

To her credit, she took it gamely. "I'm still perfecting the roast leaf. Perhaps it needs more work. Try the others. The ones on brown bread are tuna-ish—brined turnip flakes in place of fish—and the white bread is sham. Sham is everyone's favorite. Doesn't the color look just like ham? The secret is beetroot."

Gabe tried them both. The tuna-ish was a dubious improvement over the roast leaf. As for the sham . . . it might very well be his favorite of the three. But considering the choices, that wasn't saying much. He stuffed the remainder of the sandwich into his mouth and chewed.

"Well?" she prompted.

"Are you asking my honest opinion?"

"But of course."

"They're revolting." He swallowed with reluctance. "All of them."

"I like them. My friends like them."

"No, they don't. Your friends find your sandwiches revolting, too. They just don't want to tell you so, because they're afraid of hurting your feelings." He shook his head as he reached for another triangle of white bread and sham.

"If the sandwiches are so revolting, why are you eating more of them?"

"Because I'm hungry, and I don't waste food. Unlike you and your friends, I never had the luxury of being choosy."

He tore off half the sandwich with a resentful bite. As a boy on the streets, he would have begged for the scraps she threw her dog. In the workhouse, on the two days a week they were given meat, he'd sucked the gristle and marrow from every last bone.

This woman—no, this *lady*—could fill her dinner table until it creaked beneath the weight of roasts, joints of mutton, game fowl, lobster.

Instead, she ate *this*. On *purpose*.

The thought made him viscerally, irrationally angry.

He pulled the shilling from his waistcoat pocket and tapped it against his thigh. "I don't know why I'm bothering to explain. You wouldn't understand. Can't understand. You've never known true deprivation."

"You're right," she agreed.

Gabe didn't want her to agree. He wanted to stay angry.

"I haven't known that kind of hunger. I choose not to eat animals, and I know it's a luxury to have that choice. It's a luxury to have any choice. And I also know people find me ridiculous."

"Not ridiculous." He flipped the shilling into the air and caught it one-handed, his fingers trapping the coin against his palm. "Sheltered. Trusting and naïve."

"I'm not so sheltered and naïve as you imagine."

He could only laugh.

"I'm being sincere." She picked at a blade of grass. "My youth wasn't idyllic, either."

"Let me guess. Beau Brummell snubbed you at a party once. I can only imagine how the nightmares haunt you to this day."

"You know nothing of my life."

"So there were more trials, were there?" He flipped the shilling into the air again, catching it easily. "The milliner's ran out of pink ribbon."

"Stop being cruel."

"The world is cruel. *This* world is, anyway. Tell me, Your Ladyship, what's it like in your fairy-tale land?"

She snatched the shilling from his hand. As he looked on in irritation, she stood, cocked her arm, and winged the coin with all her strength.

He pushed to his feet. "You just tossed away a perfectly good shilling. I can't imagine a better example of your pampered existence. That's a day's wages for a workingman."

"You have millions of shillings, as you're so fond of telling everyone."

"Yes, but I never forget that I came from far less. I couldn't forget that, even if I tried."

"I *have* tried to forget. To forget where I came from, to deny the past. You don't know how I've tried." Her voice crumbled at the edges. "I may not have known poverty, but that doesn't mean I haven't known pain."

Gabe pushed a hand through his hair. He recognized the ring of truth in her voice. She was being honest, and he was being an ass.

Her character was finally coming into focus. He didn't know who or what had hurt her, but the blade had sunk deep. The world didn't hold enough kittens to fill that wound—but that hadn't stopped her from trying.

Gabe gentled his voice. "Listen . . ."

"Oh, no." She wheeled around. "Hubert's missing."

"Who's missing?"

"Hubert! The otter. The only reason we're stranded here in Buckinghamshire, remember?"

Oh, yes. *That* Hubert.

"How could I have been so careless?" She shaded her eyes with one hand and searched the area. "Where could he have gone?"

"Considering that he's a river otter, I'm going to take a wild guess and say the river."

She'd apparently come to the same conclusion. Gabe followed her as she raced toward the stream's edge.

"Hubert!" She cupped her hands around her mouth like a trumpet. "Hyoooo-bert!" She plopped down in the damp grasses and began tugging at her bootlaces.

"What are you doing?"

"I'm going to look for him."

Once she had the boots kicked off, she hiked up her skirts, untied a beguiling pink garter, and began rolling the white stocking down the tempting contours of her leg.

Sweet glory.

Gabe shook himself. This would be the moment to avert his gaze, he supposed. Actually, the gentlemanly moment would have been several seconds ago—but he didn't play by gentlemen's rules, and peeling one's gaze from that sort of beauty wasn't so easily accomplished. He was drawn to the sight the way an otter was drawn to the river.

Once she'd divested herself of both stockings, she stood and gathered her skirts in one hand, holding them above her ankles as she picked her way down the riverbank.

Gabe sighed. He should go after her. Not because he cared

about catching Hubert, but because she was likely to stumble on the rocks and break her neck.

"Let him be." He caught up to her and offered his hand as a means of balance. "You wanted them to have good homes. He's saved us the trouble and found one for himself."

"He's been living with me since he was a pup. He can't survive in the wild."

"The wild? We're in the English Midlands. This is hardly the wild."

Her demeanor brightened. "I see him. Over there."

Over by the opposite riverbank, a slinky brown tail disappeared beneath the water's surface with a splash.

She tugged him by the hand. "We have to rescue him."

"He doesn't need rescuing."

Ignoring him, she lifted her skirts to the knee and dipped her toes into the river.

"No." Gabe planted his foot on the muddy bank and held her back. "Absolutely not. We are not going into the water."

She lunged forward.

They were going into the water.

Goddamn, it was cold. By his second step, the river had swallowed him to the knee, sending water rushing to fill his boots. His new, finest-quality-outrageous-sums-of-money-could-buy boots.

Undeterred, she waded farther. Soon she was submerged to her waist. When Gabe joined her, his ballocks retreated so swiftly, he could have sworn they'd taken up lodgings in his rib cage.

He held her firmly by the wrist. This time, he would brook no argument. "Not another step."

She pointed. "He's just on the other side. I can see him. You needn't go with me. If I cross the stream—"

"Are you mad?"

"It isn't that deep. My head will stay above water."

"That leaves more than enough of your body to contract pneumonia, consumption, and the grippe."

"Maybe I'm willing to take that risk."

"Well, I'm not." He slid one arm about her waist, tucked the other beneath her knees, and hauled her out of the water, into his arms. Like a damned mermaid. A sparkling, golden-haired, ruby-lipped mermaid. "I can't lose you."

I CAN'T LOSE you, he said.

I can't feel my elbows, Penny thought.

She couldn't help but give a long, swooning sigh.

This man was so dangerous. He had a habit of blurting out these growly, possessive statements, punctuated by intense gazes and capped by displays of sheer virility.

And then he had a habit of immediately ruining them.

"If something happens to you, my—"

"I know, I know." She wriggled out of his arms. "Your property value will decrease. Goodness. We can't have that."

"Don't complain. If I didn't have a financial interest in your life, you'd be packed off to Cumberland by now."

With that, Penny couldn't argue. "I won't cross the river. But I'm not giving up."

She tromped along in the knee-deep water, calling for Hubert.

Gabriel tromped along behind her. "For God's sake, let the beast have his freedom. He's a red-blooded . . . whatever a male otter's called."

"Boars. The males are boars."

"He'll build his own little house . . ."

"It's called a holt."

". . . find a Mrs. Hubert . . ."

"Otters are polygynous. The boars mate with multiple sows."

"So he'll find multiple Mrs. Huberts. Even better. I never thought I'd envy an otter, but here I am."

She heaved a long-suffering sigh.

"Before long, he'll have sired a whole crop of otterlings."

"Pups." She wheeled to face him. "They're pups. Stop pretending you know what an otter wants. You don't know the slightest thing about them."

"I know that he's doing what he was born to do. And that you are being selfish."

"Selfish?"

"That animal is not your possession. He doesn't exist for your amusement. He has needs, instincts. Urges."

The way he said that word, in that deep, earthy growl, had chills rippling over her skin.

She swallowed hard. "Urges?"

"Yes. *Urges.*" He sauntered toward her—as much as a man could saunter in knee-deep water. "But what could a lady like you know about those?"

"Oh, I understand urges. Right now, I have the powerful urge to do this."

She shoved him hard in the chest, hoping to send him flailing backward into the river.

He didn't budge. Not a teeter. Not a totter.

Not even a blink.

Penny would not surrender. She took a step in reverse and then tried again, adding the weight of her body to the effort.

This time, he was ready for her. He caught her wrists in his hands, stopping her before she could even make contact.

"Now, now, Your Ladyship. This is most unbecoming behavior."

"I know that." She clenched her hands into fists. "You are so maddening. You have a way of provoking me, unlike anyone I've ever known. It's as though I become a different person when I'm around you, and I'm not certain I like her."

He pulled her to him. "I like her."

Penny expected he would shortly ruin that statement.

I like her—smoldering pause—*potential to increase the return on my property investment.*

Not this time.

Instead, he lowered his head until his mouth brushed hers.

Teased her lips apart, until his tongue brushed hers.

And then they tumbled together against the riverbank, and his everything brushed hers.

GABE DIDN'T WANT to want her. But he did. God above, he did. Even though it made no sense. Even though everything in him was against it.

"I shouldn't be doing this."

She pushed against his chest, making just enough distance between them to meet his eyes. "We're both doing this."

He kissed her deeply, exploring her sweetness with his tongue and pressing her body against the riverbank. Springy green grasses crushed under her back, making a bed against the cool damp of the earth. Her skirts tangled around his boots and held him in a tight embrace. And her body . . . Her curves yielded beneath him, welcoming all his hard edges and giving them a place to rest.

Her fingers teased through his hair, sending a shiver of joy down his spine.

She threw her arms around his neck and clung tight. "Gabriel."

Sweet heaven.

No, no. More like bloody hell.

He knew what this little dalliance on the riverbank could cost him, not only in shillings, but in pride. He knew what it could cost her, too. Yet he couldn't bring himself to stop.

She tasted too good, felt too soft beneath him.

He shouldn't be here. Didn't belong in her arms. He was a street urchin trespassing in a fine house, forbidden to touch. But that was precisely why he ached to touch her—all over. To take what he'd always been denied.

But once again, she upended all his thinking. Even the lowest born of men couldn't steal what was freely given.

As they kissed, she arched her body against his in a silent, instinctive plea. He slid a hand up her rib cage until his thumb grazed the underside of her breast. She tensed beneath him, and her fingernails bit into his neck.

He broke their kiss, staring down at her and drawing ragged breaths, until her body relaxed and her blue eyes gave him permission to continue.

"Yes?"

She nodded. "Yes."

When he cupped her breast in his palm, he was the one to sigh with pleasure. He'd been wanting this, dreaming about it both asleep and awake. Her flesh was cool, and the frigid stream had drawn her nipple to a firm knot. For a moment, he simply held the chilled softness in his hand, making it his purpose to warm her, banish the cold.

But he couldn't be satisfied with simple contact for long. He massaged the soft weight of her, then found her nipple with his thumb and gently strummed. Her breath caught. The small sound was a spark, igniting desire that raged into a blaze, kindling his every nerve.

He began to murmur foolish words against her skin—words like "want," and "need," and "Penny," and "God," and he buried his face in the sweet curve of her neck to keep them secret. Even from himself.

With fumbling fingers, he peeled the damp muslin from her skin, working the sleeve over her shoulder until he had just enough slack to slide his fingers beneath and lift her breast, drawing it free from her chemise and stays.

Her bared skin was like silk, and her ruched nipple was the same tender pink as her lips. A touch of sunlight drifted through the leafy branches above, dappling her skin with a warm glow. Bending his head, he caught her nipple in his mouth, drawing on it with his tongue and—when that wasn't enough—gently scraping with his teeth. She tasted like flowing water in spring. Fresh, pure, sweet. He lapped at her, greedy for more.

More.

When he'd entered the water, his ballocks had gone so deep into hiding, Gabe hadn't expected them to emerge for days. He'd underestimated the power of this woman. His cock hardened against his trousers placket, straining the buttons and insistently pressing against her hip. Her pelvis tilted, bringing him in exquisite contact with her cleft. The keen spear of pleasure damned near ran him through.

He sent his hand on a downward journey, exploring the rolling landscape of her waist, hips, thighs. Her soaked skirt clung to her legs, revealing the contours of her body. When he reached the hem of her frock, he worried the edge between fingers and thumb. He thought of her stockings, lying discarded on the grass.

He shouldn't.

He did.

Parting the clinging fabric from her skin, he reached beneath to encircle her bare ankle with his hand.

As he swept his touch up her calf, she jerked in surprise. Her hand caught his, trapping it just below her knee. He paused at once.

"Ticklish?" He could scarcely scrape the word from his throat.

She shook her head.

"What is it?"

"I . . ." Her kiss-flushed lips curved in a coy little smile. "I think it's the urges."

He couldn't help but grin in response.

These teasing hints of her naughty side were driving him mad with curiosity. He wanted to pry her open at the delicate pink seams and explore the sensual woman within.

But at the center of this woman was a heart. A soft, vulnerable one, made to be broken. He damned well didn't trust himself with that organ, and if she possessed any caution, she wouldn't let him anywhere near it.

"Mr. Duke!" The call came from the direction of the road. "Mr. Duke, are you there?"

"Oh, no." Pushing against his chest, Lady Penelope scrambled out from beneath him. "He's returned."

"One moment," Gabe called out. He offered a hand and helped her to her feet. "Stay here. I'll go ahead and make some excuse for you."

"What excuse?"

"I don't know. I'll tell him you've gone to relieve yourself."

"Really?" She wrinkled her nose. "Can't you at least say I'm gathering flowers or something?" She picked at her wet, muddy frock. "And slipped into the stream in the process, I suppose, with a good roll in the mud on the way down."

He shrugged. "If you prefer."

"It's just so embarrassing. As if I don't generate heaps of humiliations on my own. Now I have to go borrowing them."

"You, er . . ." He hesitated. "Not that I mind, but you may want to fix your frock."

She glanced downward. Seeing her exposed breast, she quickly tucked it back in her stays. "See what I mean? Heaps of humiliations. Heaps."

Gabe wondered if the past quarter hour went into her heaps of humiliations, or whether she regarded it as something else.

He wondered, but he wasn't going to ask.

On his part, he wouldn't be filing this memory under the heading of "Humiliations." Oh, no. It was going straight into the stash of "Fantasies" that every man kept under his mattress, figuratively if not literally.

He was never going to forget the taste of her, pure and sweet. The way her skin moved like satin under his hands, warming to his touch.

And the way she'd responded to him? That was already etched on his brain.

I think it's the urges, she'd said.

The worrisome part of it was, their urges had gone unsatisfied.

They would remain so, he told himself. This afternoon had been a mistake. An enjoyable mistake, but a mistake nonetheless. Time to revive his judgment. Gabe could survive deprivation of all sorts, including this one.

He would not put his hands on Lady Penelope Campion again.

Absolutely not.

Definitely not.

Probably not.

Damn.

Chapter Ten

To make her story plausible, Penny decided she might as well pick some wildflowers while she waited for the men to repair the carriage wheel.

So that was how she passed the next quarter hour: Picking wildflowers, standing in sunny places in a futile attempt to dry her frock, keeping an eye out for Hubert, and thinking about Gabriel's tongue on her nipple.

Licking. Swirling. Sucking.

Sigh.

Other ladies—and no doubt a good many gentlemen—would view their tangled, passionate interlude as a mistake. Penny? Never. She had not an inkling of regret.

She felt awake. Alive.

And rather proud of herself, really.

She'd never dreamed she would feel such raw, carnal sensations. Her friends had marriages where love and desire were intertwined—two strands in a tightly braided cord. But Penny had always believed it couldn't be that way for her. The chance had been stolen from her long ago, when she was too young to even understand what she'd lost.

But today . . .

She thought of the way he'd paused when she touched his hand. When she hadn't known whether she wished to drag his touch higher, or push it away. But he hadn't made any judgments or pressed to satisfy his own desire—he'd merely waited for her to decide. It was a revelation.

After packing up the picnic things—the ants wanted her sandwiches, even if Gabriel didn't—she cast a final look at the riverbank, scanning the reeds for any sign of a sleek brown otter.

Nothing.

If Hubert had wanted to return to her, she supposed he would have done so. Perhaps Gabriel was right. He was pursuing the life he was born to have. A life that didn't include Penny.

Farewell, Hubert. I wish you many happy years.

As she turned back toward the carriage, her bare feet squelched in her boots. She'd retrieved her stockings, but there seemed no point in putting them on when her wet skirts would immediately soak them through.

Penny was no wheelwright, but as she returned to the coach, even she could see that the carriage wheel had not yet been repaired. Her first hint was that it was lying on the side of the road.

"It's the bit that connects it to the axle that's broken." Gabriel swiped at his brow with his forearm. "This could take hours to mend."

"That's unfortunate."

"The two of us will walk ahead to the village," he said. "We'll wait on the carriage at the inn."

"Why can't we wait here?"

"I can't take you home looking like that." He swept a glance down her muddied, grass-stained frock. "We both need to wash."

"I can bathe at home."

"And you could do with a lie-down."

"If you're so concerned about my fatigue, why do you want me to walk two miles to the inn?"

"Because. I'm. Famished."

Penny blinked at him.

"There. Are you happy? I couldn't choke down enough of

your miserable sandwiches. I need to eat something. Something that once had a face."

She wrinkled her nose. "That's a horrid way of putting it."

"You asked. I tried to spare your feelings this time. Give me credit for that much."

"Go on by yourself, then. I can wait here."

"I'm not leaving you stranded on the side of the road."

"I wouldn't be alone. I'd be with the coachman and smith."

"You're not as important to them as you are to me. I'm not leaving you here." He picked up the birdcage and walked backward, in the direction of the village. "Just like you're not letting me walk away with your deuced parrot."

Impossible man.

The afternoon had grown warmer. Delilah, being a tropical bird, seemed to thrive in the heat. Penny did not. She was weary and thirsty, and growing testier by the moment. "I thought the village was only a mile or two."

"It can't be much farther now. Probably just after that bend in the road."

"You said that two bends in the road ago. I thought the coach would have caught us by now. Perhaps they can't mend it."

"All the more reason to find the village. If worse comes to worst and the carriage can't be mended, we can find other transportation. I can hire a—" He stopped in the road. "Fuck."

His blasphemy sent Delilah into a titter. *"Fancy a fuck, love? Ooh! Ooh! Yes! Pretty girl."*

"My coat," he said. "I left it in the carriage."

Penny paused and squinted at the cloudless sky and the cheerfully scorching sun. "I can't imagine you'll need it."

"I don't need the coat. I need the money that's in it." He set the birdcage on the ground and rubbed his face with both hands, cursing into them.

"What do we do?"

"I don't know. But one way or another, I'll have you back in London by nightfall. You needn't worry you'll be ruined."

"I'm not worried I'll be ruined. I can't be ruined."

He lowered his voice, though there was no one but Delilah to hear. "If this is about earlier, by the river . . . There's quite a gulf between what we did and the act of copulation. You haven't lost your virtue."

"For heaven's sake, I understand how matters work between a man and a woman." She wiped sweat from her brow. "I can't be ruined because that would suggest I have prospects to ruin in the first place. I'm still unmarried, despite being an earl's daughter, despite having a considerable dowry. No suitors are beating down my door."

"There is no way in hell that your unmarried state is due to a lack of interest."

"Please, enlighten me as to the reason."

"That's simple. You've been hiding yourself, and you're good at it. A master of camouflage."

She laughed. "Camouflage?"

"That's the only possible explanation. You've made a frock from the same silk covering the drawing room walls, trimmed it with cat hair and feathers. Then when gentlemen visit, you stand still and blend in."

"You have a surprisingly vivid imagination."

"What I have is experience." He stopped in the road and turned to face her. "I've built a fortune by spotting things that are undervalued, dusting them off, and selling them at the proper price. I know a hidden treasure when I see one."

"Oh."

Looking away, he pushed his hand through his hair. "Not this again."

"Not what again?"

"Every time I speak three words, you look as though you're going to swoon into my arms."

"I do not," Penny objected, knowing very well that she probably did.

"You sigh like a fool, blush like a beet. Your eyes are the

worst of it. They turn into these . . . these pools. Glassy blue pools with man-eating sharks beneath the surface."

"I hope you're not planning a career in poetry."

"For the good of us both, you have to cease gazing at me."

"Then you have to cease wooing me."

"*Wooing* you." He grimaced, as if the words were a pickled lemon on his tongue. "I don't *woo*."

"You do too woo." She lowered her voice to match his gruff timbre. "'I need you,' 'I'm not letting you go.' A woman can't help but go soft inside. Those sorts of declarations are unbearably romantic."

"You know very well I don't *mean* them that way."

She couldn't help but roll her eyes. "I suppose if I didn't already, I would now."

"Exactly. So don't go swooning on me."

"I assure you, you needn't worry about that. If I did swoon, it would be from the heat."

Pounding hoofbeats behind them announced the prospect of salvation. Penny turned, hoping to see the carriage.

It wasn't Gabriel's carriage, but it was the next best thing. A stagecoach, passing their way. Penny darted to the center of the road, waving her arms until the driver pulled his team to a stop.

"You're a guardian angel," Penny said. "Can we ride to the village?"

The driver looked them over warily, taking in their bedraggled attire. "In that state? You'd have to ride up top with the trunks."

"We can do that." Penny extended her hand to the driver. "Will you help me up?"

The driver didn't take her hand. "Not so hasty. I need the fare in advance."

"How much?" Gabriel asked.

"Let's see." The driver squinted. "Fare for the two of you, plus tuppence for the baggage—"

"Oh, this isn't baggage." Penny lifted the cage for him to see. "She's a parrot."

"Then that's fare for two of you, plus *thruppence* for the parrot . . . A shilling, all told."

Penny reached for her reticule.

She didn't have her reticule.

Her reticule was back in the carriage. Along with Gabriel's coat.

"Deuce it," Gabriel said dramatically. "If only I had a shilling."

She sighed.

"I was certain I had one here somewhere." He made a show of patting all his pockets. "Oh, that's right. Someone tossed it away."

"Please," Penny begged the driver. "Take pity on us. We've had an accident. It's only to the next village."

"Sorry, miss." The driver flicked the reins, setting the horses in motion. "No fare, no ride."

In silence, Penny and Gabriel watched the stagecoach travel down the road, until it rounded a curve and disappeared.

On they walked. There was simply nothing else to do.

"I always keep a shilling in my pocket," Gabriel muttered after a few minutes of angry silence. "Always. Do you know *why* I always keep a shilling in my pocket? Because everything I am today, everything I've earned—it all started there. I was once worth a single shilling. Now I'm worth hundreds of thousands of pounds."

"No, you aren't."

"Shall I produce the bank ledgers to prove it?"

"Ledgers are meaningless. I have a sum placed on me, you know. A dowry of forty thousand. And yet if I were to lose my virtue, some would deem me worthless."

"You could never be worthless."

"I could certainly drive down the price of your house. You never miss a chance to remind me."

He shook his head. "That's not the point."

"Here is the point." She stepped into his path, forcing him to meet her eyes. Man-eating sharks and all. "No one can be reduced to numbers in a ledger, or a stack of banknotes, or a single silver coin. We are humans, with souls and hearts and passion and love. Every last one of us is priceless. Even you."

She set her frustration aside and took his face in her hands.

He needed to hear this. Everyone needed to hear it, including her. Perhaps that was why she spoke the words so often, to so many creatures. Simply to hear them echo back.

"Gabriel Duke. You are priceless."

Chapter Eleven

You are priceless.

Gabe's heart kicked him in the ribs.

There were responses he'd prepared in his life—saved up for the day he might need them, no matter how unlikely. He had an acceptance speech ready for the London Business League award. He had his murderous threats well-rehearsed in case he crossed paths with that cruel bastard of a workhouse guardian someday.

Gabe even knew what he'd say to his mother, if she came back from the grave to hear it.

He had no idea how to respond to this. He couldn't have possibly prepared. Nothing in his life had taught him to imagine those words.

You are priceless.

"Goodness, you needn't look so panicked." She smiled and gave his head a little shake. "It's no more than I tell Bixby daily."

Right. Of course it wasn't. She was only exacting a bit of revenge after he'd mocked her for blushing and so on, and he likely deserved it. Gabe hated that he felt disappointed. Even betrayed.

He brushed her hands aside. "You've made your point. I'll do my best not to swoon."

"Gabriel, wait."

He continued walking. "You needn't worry about any further declarations from my quarter. We needn't talk at all."

AT LAST, THEY reached the village and its lone inn.

"As you can see, we've had a traveling mishap," Gabe told the wide-eyed innkeeper. "We'll take your largest suite of rooms. My sister will need an attendant to help her undress and bathe."

He could feel the questioning look Her Ladyship gave him. *Sister?*

"While she rests, her attire must be laundered and pressed dry. And we want dinner, as soon as it can be managed."

"Have your choice, sir." The innkeeper pointed toward a slate listing the kitchen's daily offerings in muddled chalk.

Gabe skimmed the list. Kidney pie, stewed beef, leg of mutton, braised rabbit. Meat, meat, meat, and meat. Brilliant.

"One of each," he said. "No, two of each."

Lady Penelope nudged him in the side. "You needn't order any for me."

"I didn't."

"Beastly man." She sighed under her breath.

"You're not a child. You can read the board as well as I can, and you don't need me to make choices for you."

She sighed again. *"Not-quite-so-beastly man."*

"That's more like it."

"Toast and butter, please," she told the innkeeper. "A wedge of cheese and some preserves, if you have them."

"One more thing," Gabe said. "I require writing paper, pen, and ink. I need to send a letter. There's a five-year-old boy in Buckinghamshire who'll be heartbroken that he's not getting his ferret."

"For heaven's sake," she muttered. "He was never going to have a ferret."

The innkeeper scribbled on a greasy bit of paper. "All together with the lodging . . . That'll be six shillings, eight."

"I don't have the coin on me," Gabe said. "I'll pay you when my coach and driver arrive."

"To be sure, you will. And I'll feed you dinner when my Parisian chef arrives."

Gabe cursed and pushed his hand through his hair. "Take my boots as collateral."

The innkeeper peered down at the muddy, waterlogged boots. "Look as though they've been through a war."

"I paid twelve pounds for them. They're certainly worth six shillings, eight in any condition. Just hold them until I can pay you in coin."

"Very well. I'll hold the boots—*and* the lady's washing. She can have her laundered and pressed frock once you've paid."

Fair enough.

They took the largest suite of rooms the inn had on offer. A bedchamber for Her Ladyship to bathe and have a lie-down, a sitting room where he could eat and dash off a letter, and— most importantly—an antechamber between the two.

At the door to the suite, they parted ways. The serving girls brought hot water to her room; trays of food to his. All was as it should be. Completely separate.

Once alone, Gabe tugged his shirt over his head and draped it over a chair near the fireplace to dry. Once he'd finished a much-needed wash at the basin, he sat down to his dinner.

A *proper* dinner. Real, actual food, rather than falsehoods on a plate. No shmidney pie or braised crabbit or whatever fool name she would invent. He picked up a knife and speared a bit of stewed beef with a satisfying jab.

He was on his second plate of steaming-hot kidney pie by the time his chewing slowed. And that's when he heard it. The faintest sounds escaping her room, sweeping across the antechamber, and sliding under the door to him.

The sounds of bathing.

A splash.

A trickle.

A faint series of drips.

It all added up to torture. Pure, liquid torture.

He pushed his plate away, propped his elbows on the table, and buried his face in his hands with a groan. Even plugging his ears didn't help.

When he closed his eyes, he could picture her. Naked in a shallow tub. Her feet dangling over the lip at one end, and her head reclined against the other. And all that water embracing her with heat, lapping at her nakedness, pouring over her most secret curves and furrows.

He was immediately, startlingly hard.

Gabe drummed the table with his fingers. This would be the perfect time for a rainstorm. A riot, an explosion, a choir of tuneless schoolchildren. Something, anything loud.

Nothing.

Nothing but soft, devastating, erotic sounds.

Perhaps he could trick his mind. He might convince himself the sounds weren't from bathing. Instead, he'd imagine her to be . . . making soup. Unappetizing soup. Workhouse soup. Watery broth with a few scattered lumps of—

She sighed a long, languid sigh.

Curse it. Strategy ruined. No one sighed languid sighs while making soup.

Christ alive, women took ridiculously long baths. Was it possible to die of priapism? Perhaps she'd volunteered him as some doctor's investigatory case.

Make haste, he silently willed her. *Be done with it.*

In his mind's eye, he saw her dipping a sponge beneath a blanket of soap bubbles, and then pressing it against the back of her neck—just beneath the frizzled golden curls at her nape. She gave the sponge a long, firm squeeze, sending a warm cascade down her back. One mischievous rivulet strayed, trickling over her collarbone, burrowing between her breasts, and sliding down to her navel before it disappeared into a tuft of honey-colored curls.

Enough.

He pushed back in his chair and unbuttoned his trousers. He took his cock in hand, spreading the moisture welling at the tip all the way down his shaft.

Closing his eyes, he pictured her naked. She was still in the bath, but now he was the water. Warming her. Caressing her. Licking her all over. He needn't content himself with a single rosy-pink nipple. Not this time. He pushed her breasts together and feasted on both, nibbling and sucking. She moaned and bucked beneath him, gripping his hair and guiding him downward, where he ran his tongue along the seam of her sweet, wet—

He tightened his grip, stroking faster.

Now she was holding him in her arms. Wrapping her legs around him until her locked ankles dug into the small of his back, urging him forward. Inside. Deeper.

And as he thrust into her, again and again, she held him close to her. So close and so tight. She whispered his name.

Gabriel.

Gabriel.

"Gabriel?"

Gabe's eyes snapped open. He nearly fell over in his chair. Grabbing the writing paper the inn had provided him, he launched to his feet, holding the paper strategically in front of his groin and praying like hell his loosened trousers didn't slip to his ankles.

She'd opened the door just wide enough to angle her head around the edge and peek in.

"Nothing," he declared.

She frowned in confusion. "Nothing what?"

"Nothing nothing."

He was a fool, and his pounding heartbeat reminded him so, multiple times a second. *You fool, you fool, you fool, you fool.*

She looked at the paper. "Are you writing your letter?"

"Yes." He cleared his throat. "I am writing my letter." Writing it with the tip of his cock, apparently.

"It's growing dark," she said.

"I'd noticed that."

"The carriage . . . Even if the driver and smith were to arrive soon, the horses will need to rest."

"Yes, I know." Gabe inwardly cursed. He had no money to pay the innkeeper, let alone hire another coach. Thanks to his lack of foresight, they would be confined in this suite until first light. "So long as we're stuck here, you may as well sleep."

"I can't sleep."

"Surely you're fatigued."

"Yes, but—" She bit her lip. "I need an animal in my bed."

He could only stare at her.

"At home, I always have at least one in bed with me. Usually more. Bixby, of course, and a kitten or two. I can't sleep alone."

"What about the bird? Surely it can keep you company."

"Delilah? She's asleep in her cage. And even if she weren't, one can't exactly snuggle with a parrot." Her eyes swept the sitting room. "I was hoping there might be a newspaper or book here, so I could pass the time."

"Well, there isn't."

She pushed the door open further, revealing herself to be clad in nothing but a Grecian-inspired arrangement of draped bed linens. The graceful angles of her bared shoulders and arms stood bright against the darkness. Her knot of steam-dampened hair could be so easily undone. A flick of his wrist would send it spilling free, flowing like molten gold between his fingers.

And those bed linens . . . a single tug, and they'd be a puddle on the floor.

She was trying to kill him. He was sure of it.

"What on earth are you wearing?"

"You told them to take all my clothes for laundering."

"I didn't think you'd give them your shift, as well."

"It was all mud at the hem. I couldn't wear it in that state."

He rubbed the bridge of his nose. "Do you mean to tell me you've no garments at all?"

Don't tell me that.

Please tell me that.

She stepped forward, trailing a swoop of white bedsheet behind her like the train of a bridal gown. "Are you certain there's nothing to read? I thought I spied a quarterly of some sort on the mantel."

"No."

She shrank behind the door again, looking like a kicked puppy. "You needn't shout at me."

"Go back to your room. Cover yourself with something other than bedsheets."

"I have a corset and I have stockings. Shall I wear those?"

Jesus God.

Holding his trousers closed with one hand, he lunged to one side and snagged his shirt from where it hung drying by the fire. He tossed it at her, and it hit her in the face.

As she slowly drew it downward, she gave him an offended look. "Was that truly necessary?"

"Yes. Go on, then. I'll be in once I've finished my letter."

Once she'd finally retreated and closed the door behind her, Gabe exhaled in relief. He tucked his now-softened cock back into his trousers. There was no way he could take up where he'd started. God only knew when she might decide to pop in again, and what she might be wearing—or not wearing—if she did.

Instead, he sat down and wrote his letter—with pen and ink. He took his time choosing every last word. His penmanship had never been so legible. But a few paragraphs simply refused to stretch into hours. Eventually, he ran out of excuses and crossed the antechamber. As he opened the door halfway, he sent up a prayer.

Please let her be asleep in bed.

She wasn't asleep. She wasn't in bed.

She was *on* the bed. Clad in his shirt, which he'd been a bloody fool to loan her.

Draped in bedsheets, she'd been a Grecian goddess. An aloof deity meant to be worshipped, adored, even feared—but never embraced.

Seeing her swimming in the billowing waves of his shirt, however, with her fair hair hanging loose about her shoulders . . . ? The intimacy of it shook him to his core.

She looked not only desirable, but necessary. A part of him. The better part, of course. The part where his redeeming qualities might be hiding, if indeed he possessed any. Gabe doubted he did, but he found himself longing to search her thoroughly, inside and out, just to be sure.

This was a dangerous situation. No otters. No carriage. No coachman. Just a man, a woman, and a bed.

"Gabriel?" Her voice was husky, sweet. "Aren't you coming in?"

Don't do it, he told himself. *Let her be. She's safer without you. Close the door, turn the latch, slide the bolt, and nail it shut for good measure. Leave.*

Instead, he entered.

Chapter Twelve

When his silhouette appeared in the doorway, Penny gulped. Audibly.

This was an ancient coaching establishment, centuries old. The floorboards had worn to a dark, grooved polish, and the floors tipped at drunken angles where the walls had settled into the ground. The rooms had low ceilings and even lower door mantels.

When Gabriel entered the room, this all conspired to impressive effect. He filled the doorway, looming and large, and as he walked toward the bed, the floor groaned and creaked beneath his feet.

Out of an instinct of self-preservation, she wriggled to the far side of the mattress and drew the quilt up to her neck. Rationally, she knew she had nothing to fear. Not from him, that was. But as he slung his formidable, masculine body onto the other side of the bed, she was a tiny bit afraid of herself.

He was so warm, and so big. He smelled like soap and clear water, and when she stole a look at him, the hair lightly furring his bared chest was visible in the dim firelight. Her fingers ached to touch him.

"There." He folded his arms over his chest and crossed his legs at the ankles. "You have an animal in your bed. Sleep."

Sleep? Impossible.

How could she sleep with such a riot of noise? Her pulse

pounded. Her whole *body* pounded. Her heart, her eardrums, her wrists, the hollows behind her knees—and, throbbing hardest of all, the secret, intimate pulse between her legs.

Falling in lust at first sight was bad enough. This afternoon she'd tumbled into a whole river of desire, all the way up to her neck. Now Penny was drowning in a sea of sensuality. She was confused by it, even a bit panicked—but drawn to him nevertheless.

Because he knew how to swim.

And he could teach her to swim, too.

She covered her face with her hands and groaned into them.

"What?"

"The animals," she lied. "They'll have missed their dinner tonight. And unless Mrs. Robbins takes him out—which is unlikely—Bixby will have piddled on the carpet by the time we're home."

"There's nothing to be done about it tonight. Save your strength. The otter was only one animal. We've still a dozen or more to get rid of. Not to mention, you have your wardrobe and social obligations to occupy you."

She stared up at the blackened ceiling beams. "This will never work. Even if we manage to find homes for the animals—and you must admit, we're not off to an auspicious start—I'll never meet my aunt's expectations when it comes to circulating in society."

"Oh, yes, you will. I'll make it happen. I've money and influence at my disposal."

"I've no doubt you do. But all the money and influence in the world can't change my nature."

"There's nothing wrong with your nature. Your nature is fine."

For that sentence alone, she could have kissed him.

"I'm a wallflower," she said. "No, I'm not even a wallflower. At a party, a wallflower stands against the wainscoting. I don't even make it through the door."

"Why not?" The bed creaked as he rolled onto his side. "That doesn't make sense. Aside from the whole daughter-of-an-earl bit, you're an amiable person. Far too amiable, in my estimation. Is it the crowds? The noise?"

"No, it's . . ." Cringing, she turned to face him. "It's the hedgehog."

To that, he had no response other than a blank look. She supposed she shouldn't have expected one.

"I was sixteen the year of my debut. I'd been dreading it for years. At finishing school, I hadn't fit in with the other girls. I was always more comfortable with animals than people. While the rest of the pupils were painting flowers with their watercolors, I was returning fledglings to their nests. Making friends with hedgehogs. Like Freya."

She picked at a loose thread on the quilt. "As you can imagine, the other pupils poked fun at me. Laughed at my expense. You know how girls are at that age."

"Actually, I'm not certain I do."

"It doesn't matter. Eventually, I found truer friends. But when I first came to London, I felt rather alone and completely unprepared. My parents were in India, and my Aunt Caroline was— is—a formidable woman. She insisted I enter society. I didn't want a formal debut, so we compromised, settling on an introduction at Almack's."

"Almack's?" He pulled a face.

"I know, it's horrid. Do you know they only serve lemonade and biscuits now? I hear they're not even good. Anyhow, I was so nervous. I didn't think I could face the ordeal on my own. So I tucked Freya into my pocket."

"Your gown had pockets?"

"Every gown should have pockets. My Aunt Caroline always insisted, and it's the one thing on which we agree." She frowned in concentration. "Where was I?"

"At Almack's for your grand social debut, eating dry biscuits and hiding a hedgehog in your pocket."

"Yes. Well, there's not much else to tell. My first dance was with Bernard Wendleby. He asked me out of family obligation, of course. He didn't wish to be there any more than I did. Our steps crossed during the quadrille, and his hip collided with mine. I suppose you can see where this is going."

He nodded slowly. "My mind is painting a picture."

"Good," she said brightly. "No need to describe it for you, then."

"Oh, no, you don't. I want to hear every last detail."

She'd feared he would say that. "Freya startled, pricking Bernard with her quills. Bernard jumped in alarm, stepping on my foot. I stumbled forward, sprawling onto the floor. And . . ."

"And . . . ?"

"And Freya fell out of my pocket. She rolled across the floor like a ball in lawn bowls. People scattered like pins."

A low rumble started in his chest.

"Don't laugh." She buffeted him with a pillow. "It's not kind."

He wrenched the pillow from her grasp. "I never claimed to be kind."

"I was humiliated. It wasn't funny."

"Not at the time, perhaps. Here and now? It is exceedingly funny, and you know it."

Penny supposed it was. It had been years, hadn't it?

At the time, her friends had attempted to console her. They'd told her that in time the mortification would fade and the episode would be an amusing story for dinner parties.

Except that she didn't attend many parties after that.

Now, so removed from that world of Mayfair snobbery, Penny could look back on the scene and appreciate the absurd humor. Once she started giggling, she couldn't stop.

"The worst of it . . ." She wiped away tears of laughter. "The worst of it was, one of the patronesses—I can't recall which one—fainted into the lemonade. She was standing behind me when I fell, and when she saw the hedgehog rolling across the floor . . ." She buried a giggle in her palm. "She thought it was my head. That I'd somehow decapitated myself when I hit the floor, and my head had gone rolling."

He shook his head. "Astounding. I never dreamed I'd say this about Almack's—but I wish I'd been there."

"If you want to visit, you'll have to find someone else to take you. My voucher was revoked," she said proudly. "For life."

"A pity." He propped his head on his folded arm and regarded her intently. "So what's the true reason?"

"The true reason for what?"

"Your retreat from society. Your life as a wallflower."

"I just told you."

"You told me a story about one embarrassing moment, years in the past. I'm to believe an earl's daughter was exiled from the *ton* over a hedgehog?" He shook his head. "No. There must be more to it than that."

A knot of panic rose in her throat. She didn't have another story prepared. Everyone accepted the hedgehog incident as reason enough.

Everyone but him, it would seem.

"I believe it's your turn," she said, deflecting the question. "If you want to hear more about my tragic youth, you had better share a story from your own."

"I don't have any stories fit for a lady's ears."

"Come now, man of mystery. Tell me something. Anything. Your family, your schooling, where you were raised. Surely you have a scar somewhere with an interesting story behind it." Smiling coyly, she poked him in the ribs. "Here, perhaps?"

He winced in indignation. "What do you think you're—"

She ran a tickling stroke down the underside of his arm. "Or maybe it's here?"

"Minx."

He grabbed her wrist and ducked his head under her arm, lifting her over his shoulder. She shrieked with laughter as he dragged her out from under the quilts. For a moment, she managed to wrestle out of his grasp, but he yanked her back with a tug on her ankle, turning her over his knee. She tickled his belly, and when he cursed and flinched, she gained the advantage.

She straddled his thighs. When he reached for her, she caught his hands and tucked them firmly under her knees. She braced her hands on his torso.

There. She had him pinned to the bed at his hips, hands, and chest. He could easily overpower her once he caught his breath, but for the moment he was her captive.

Her hair hung loose about her neck, and her shirt—*his* shirt—tugged to the side, slipping down over her shoulder as she gloated in triumph. "Every creature has a soft underbelly. I'm going to find yours."

"Search me if you like, Your Ladyship. I warn you, it's not softness you'll find."

Search me if you like.

Penny couldn't resist that invitation.

She trailed a light touch along his collarbone. Keeping his hands pinned with her knees, she ran her fingers over his chest, furrowing through the whorls of dark hair and tracing the contours of his muscles. She pressed her thumbs to his firm, flat nipples.

Years ago, Penny's mother had brought her a clockwork music box from Austria. It had a scene of a shepherd and a maiden on a mountaintop, and there were levers and handles on all sides. Sliding one made the shepherd bow. Cranking another made the maiden twirl. Turning the key produced a tinkling, friendly tune.

As she explored his body, Gabriel did not bob or twirl. He certainly didn't hum any tunes. He growled, moaned, winced, and cursed. Yet despite all these sounds of seeming displeasure, he made no effort to discourage her. He made his body hers to explore, just as she'd been longing to do ever since he'd come upon her that first night, draped in a towel and dripping wet.

With one finger, she drew a teasing line down the center of his chest, all the way down to his navel.

He bucked his hips. His erection grazed her sex, and she gasped at the sudden contact. Their bodies were separated by the fine lawn of his shirt and the wool of his trousers, but she could feel him—his length, his heat, his hardness.

His desire.

She'd felt triumphant in tackling him to the bed, but that was nothing compared to the surge of power rushing through her now. The thick, hot column of arousal wedged between her thighs—it was for her. All for her. Excitement rocketed through her body and came to settle in her sex, melting into a soft, throbbing ache.

Desperate to soothe that ache, she rocked against him. The friction sent a pulse of bliss through her body. Judging by his tortured groan, he felt it, too.

His head fell back against the mattress. "God. Yes. Again."

"Ask nicely." She levered her weight onto her knees, pressing his hands deeper into the straw-tick mattress and lifting her pelvis to break contact. "Ask me by my name."

After a grumble of complaint, he gave in. "Lady Penel—"

"Penny," she corrected. "Call me Penny."

She was every bit as desperate as he was for more, but she couldn't let the opportunity slip from her grasp. She'd been asking him to use her name for days now, and this might be her one chance to make him comply.

He gritted his teeth. "For the love of God, woman."

"Penny."

"Fine. Penny. There. Are you happy, Penny? How many times do you wish to hear it, Penny? Damn it, Penny. I've been craving this the whole cursed day, Penny. I'm going mad with lust, Penny. Penny, Penny, Pen—" She lowered her hips to his. "*Christ.*"

"That will do for now."

"Thank God."

She shifted gently, easing to and fro until his hardness nestled snug against her cleft.

Instinct took over. Penny braced herself on locked arms, hands flat against his chest, as she rubbed her body over his in a slow, steady rhythm.

"That's it," he murmured, rocking beneath her. "Just like that. It's good?"

She nodded, too drunk on sensation to be missish or shy. "So good."

"Go on, then."

"Go on and what?"

"Ride me," he whispered. "Use me. Take your pleasure."

She hesitated.

"Have you never . . . ? Perhaps they don't teach that at finishing school." He moved as though he would free his arms. "I'll show you."

"No." She clasped his biceps, holding him down. "I don't need help."

She had a big, beautiful man at her mercy, and she wasn't going to relinquish control. Oh, she was under no illusions that she had him physically overpowered. He could have flipped their places at any instant.

She hadn't *taken* the reins. He'd *given* her the reins. And that made it all the better.

She decided how to begin, when to stop. Whether to tease them both with grazing friction or grind her hips. She set the pace. It was hers to grant or deny him mercy when he pleaded in a whisper: *"Faster."*

With every motion—slow or quick, firm or gentle—her pleasure spiraled higher. Her breathing grew uneven, and she flushed with heat.

She fell forward to kiss him, searching his mouth. Exploring. As their tongues tangled, his whiskers scraped her lips and chin. Her nipples puckered to knots, exquisitely sensitive. With every movement, they kissed the hard planes of his chest.

Bliss rushed at her from all sides, propelling her toward that distant promise of satisfaction. Her rhythm lost all elegance. Her hips jerked and bounced as her urgency grew.

"Yes." His voice was strained. "Hold nothing back. I want to feel you come against me. I want to hear the sounds you make."

His words of encouragement had the opposite effect. For the first time, she felt a moment's trepidation. She'd never climaxed with another person. It had taken her years to feel comfortable with herself, let alone a man. When the pleasure broke, she would be bared to him. More naked than naked.

She let her brow fall against his shoulder, hiding her face. She whimpered against his skin. "Hold me."

In an instant, he freed his hands and wrapped his arms around her, stroking her hair and caressing her back, giving her the safety she needed. "I have you, love. I have you."

As she began to move once more, his hands slid down her back. He cupped and squeezed her bottom, guiding her. Urging her. Dragging her over his hard length again and again and again. Holding her through that last, unnerving moment of nothingness, and pushing her into the brightness on the other side.

Joy shivered over her skin and pulsed through her veins. She buried her cries of pleasure in the curve of his neck.

As the climax ebbed, the tension left her body, melting into his heat. A beautiful sense of peace drifted through her. As if she were sitting in a toasty room on a cold day, watching snowflakes land on the windowsill.

He didn't share the same languor. His erection jutted against her belly, still fiercely hard and unsatisfied. He drove a hand between their bodies and tugged at his trouser buttons.

"Sorry," he said. "Can't wait any longer."

Penny rolled to the side. Should she offer to help? It only seemed fair to repay him the favor. But then, she had no idea *how* to help. Perhaps her fumbling would do more harm than good.

As he slid his hand into his trousers, she came to one unwavering decision. Whether he desired her assistance or not, she was definitely going to watch.

Unfortunately, there wasn't much to see. Before her eyes could adjust to the firelight, he had his hand tightly wrapped around the object of her curiosity, and then he pumped his fist so quickly, she saw nothing but a shadowy blur. In a matter of moments, his body jerked and he made a low, guttural sound. With his free hand, he groped for a corner of tangled bedsheet. He drew it over his groin while he shuddered and finished with a few slower strokes.

"That"—he fell back against the bed—"was a close thing. It was all I could do to not spend in my trousers. But then we wouldn't have had a single clean article of clothing between us."

They lay on their backs, staring up at the ceiling. As their breathing eased, an awkward silence fell over them both.

When two people were in love, or at least true lovers, Penny supposed they would spend this time cuddling and settling in for a good, deep sleep. But she and Gabriel weren't in love, and despite what had just happened, they weren't truly lovers. They were neighbors with little in common, save for a shared interest in not being neighbors anymore. What were the rules for this? What did she *want* them to be?

The questions hovered above them like a cloud.

He offered the worst possible suggestion. "I should probably apologize."

"If you dare, I will beat you mercilessly with a pillow."

A loud knock came at the door of the suite. The voice on the other side of the door belonged to a sleepy innkeeper. "Sir, you asked to be roused at once if your coachman arrived."

"The hell I did," Gabriel muttered. "He just wants to be certain he's paid." He pushed to his feet and buttoned his trousers, then cleared his throat. "I, er . . . I'll need my shirt."

"Oh. Of course." Penny slid her arms from the sleeves, pulled it over her head, and buried herself beneath the quilt before passing it in his direction. Despite all her bravery a few minutes ago, she'd grown vulnerable and shy.

He pushed his hands through his hair in a vain attempt to tame it, and then he left her alone with that looming, unanswered question.

What now?

Chapter Thirteen

They returned to Bloom Square very late. Or very early, depending on how one looked at it.

For most of the journey, Gabe drifted in and out of sleep. He felt like a coward avoiding conversation, but he hadn't the faintest idea what to say, and drowsing gave him a chance to gather his memories and fix them in his mind before they could escape.

He recalled the way she'd touched him with such adorable, unashamed curiosity. The plump curves of her bottom filling his hands, and the hug of her cleft astride his cock. The lilting song of her cries as she'd climaxed.

If all that wasn't torture enough, her pleasure had been embossed on his shirt. Her scent lingered about him even now, warm and intoxicating.

The coachman slowed the horses to a walk as they entered Mayfair, keeping the noise to a minimum. As morning dawned, a drifting fog obscured the streets and wrapped the city in a blanket of hush.

Gabe looked down the alley in both directions before he handed her down from the carriage. As expected, even after a thorough laundering and pressing, her lacy, once blushing-pink frock was a shambles.

"I'll see you in."

They entered through the horse stalls—or, in Penny's case,

goat and steer stalls—and naturally, she had to stop to soothe them with loving pats and generous forkfuls of hay and alfalfa. As they moved through the back garden, she paused to scatter corn for the chickens and cast a sorrowful look toward Hubert's empty washtub.

"Come along." He drew her arm through his and pulled her toward the house. "Stay any longer out here and someone's bound to see you."

"And if they do? We are merely two neighbors having a morning chat in the back garden. How could that be scandalous?"

He exhaled. "Perhaps you're right."

"No one pays much attention to me, anyway."

Normally, Gabe would have paused to lecture her on the unlikelihood of this statement, or the injustice even if it were true. However, today her obscurity might work in their favor.

Maybe, just maybe, they'd gotten away with this.

When he followed Penny up the kitchen stairs to the entrance hall, however, he knew at once he'd been mistaken. They were instantly mobbed.

Her friends had been waiting. All of them. The duchess one, the freckled one, the pregnant one, the scarred duke one, and the aggravatingly charming one.

Five individuals who would defy even the closest observer to find a trait they all held in common. Except, of course, for one important quality: They all cared about Penny.

"Penny, is that you?"

"Thank heaven you're safe."

"We've been out of our minds with worry."

"Where the devil have you been?"

"Bixby piddled on the dining room carpet."

When they'd finished fussing over Penny, they turned to Gabe. Wouldn't you know, these five disparate people shared a second quality.

They were, every last one of them, furious with him.

The three ladies tugged Penny to one side, subjecting her to a stern, yet loving interrogation.

The two men slammed Gabe against a wall.

"What the hell did you do to her?" Ashbury snarled. His scarred face twisted with anger. "I demand answers."

"I demand answers, too," the other one said. Chase, Penny had called him.

"We were taking the otter out to the country. The carriage axle splintered, and we were delayed."

"Oh, please," Chase said. "A carriage accident? I've devised a great many excuses in my life, and that's the most hackneyed tale in the book."

"In the book?" Gabe asked. "There's no book."

"Yes, there is," Chase snapped, defensive. "And if there's not, I'm writing one."

"Forget the book." Ashbury shook him by the lapels, rattling the paintings and sketches mounted on the wall. "I want the truth."

"It *is* the truth. The carriage axle broke. We stopped and waited for the smith to come repair it."

"Then why is her frock a shambles?"

Gabe sighed. "The otter escaped into the river. She insisted on chasing after it. She rushed into the water, tumbled onto the muddy bank, and got tangled in the reeds."

Chase looked peevish. "Well, that sounds . . . entirely too plausible, where Penny is concerned."

"Then I assume we're done here." Gabe moved to leave.

"Not so fast." Ashbury slammed him back against the wall, rattling the artwork again. "What happened to her frock is inconsequential. I want to know where you were all night."

ACROSS THE HALL, Penny was relating the same story to her friends.

"We walked to the village, and after that, we—Oh! There

you are, darling." Bixby nosed at her ankles, and she crouched to smother him with love in return.

"After that, what?" Nicola prodded.

"After that, we stopped over at an inn."

At this, Emma and Alex exchanged concerned looks.

Nicola was not so delicate. "An *inn*?"

Penny hushed her, not wanting Ash or Chase to hear. "It was that or wait in the carriage. You're making it sound so terrible."

"Because it *is* terrible!"

"It wasn't. Truly, it was . . ." *Erotic. Wonderful. Confusing.* ". . . perfectly safe."

"You should have fed him the poisoned biscuits."

"Nicola," Alexandra said in a pointed murmur, "Penny says she found the arrangements acceptable."

"Well, I don't find them acceptable." Nicola raised her voice. "How can you be so calm about this? She spent the night with a *man*, Alex. *That* man. At an *inn*."

"An inn?" Ashbury growled. "You spent the night at an inn?"

"Her Ladyship needed to eat, rest, and stay warm. It was the best option, unless you would prefer me to have returned her home with pneumonia."

"I suppose there was only one room available. With one bed." Chase crossed his arms. "That one's in the book, too."

"The suite had three rooms."

"You shared the same suite?" Ashbury gave him another violent shake.

Chase intervened. "Ash, that's enough. Let the man go."

With reluctance, the duke released Gabe and fell back a few steps.

"It's my turn now." Chase took his place, grasping Gabe by the lapels and slamming him back against the wall.

Jesus Christ. The man was stronger than he looked. This time, one of the framed sketches tumbled to the floor.

"You know," Gabe said, "Lady Penelope might actually like some of this artwork. Take a bit more care."

Ash retrieved the small, oval frame from the floor. It held a phenomenally ugly sketch of a cross-eyed, squished-face pug. "This is hideous."

"Yes," Chase agreed. "It's probably her favorite."

Gabe grabbed the framed sketch from the duke's hands and rehung it on the nail. "I wasn't about to leave her unguarded in a strange inn. She needed protection."

"And we're to believe she was safe with you?" Ashbury asked, incredulous. "You're the one she needs protection from."

Gabe found it difficult to argue with that.

"I don't understand this," Chase said. "Penny promised us she'd take a companion."

Gabe chuckled wryly. "Oh, she did."

"Penny," Emma scolded in motherly fashion. "A parrot is not an acceptable companion."

Penny cast a glance toward the bird in her cage. "Delilah is more effective than you'd suppose. Certainly a better chaperone than Mrs. Robbins would be."

"Sadly accurate," Alex said.

"Tell us the truth," Nicola said. "Did he take advantage of you?"

"No," Penny said in all honesty. "He didn't take any liberties."

To the contrary, he'd *given* her liberties. The freedom to explore his body. The freedom to express herself. Part of her wished to tell them everything in detail—but she didn't want to confess it here and now.

"Something happened," Alex said. "I can see it on your face."

"What do you mean?" Penny might be a poor liar, but her talent for keeping secrets had been honed over the years. There were things she'd never told a soul.

Nicola's face fell. "You're smiling. This is horrible."

"It's horrible that I'm smiling?"

Emma took Penny's hand. "We love you. If there's anything you wish to say—anything at all—you can trust us."

"I know."

Then again, *could* she trust them entirely? Something Gabriel had said niggled in the back of her mind.

"Be honest," she said. "Do you find my sandwiches revolting?"

"You CALLED HER sandwiches revolting?" Chase went red with anger. "How dare you."

"I told her the truth. They *are* revolting."

"Of course they are." He jabbed a finger in Gabe's face. "And that's expressly why we never tell her so."

Gabe batted his finger away. "So you lie to her."

"Better than breaking her heart."

"Breaking her *heart*? Good God, man. They're sandwiches."

"Those are not mere sandwiches," Chase said through gritted teeth. "They're a test. You failed it."

Ashbury paced the narrow entrance hall, muttering angrily. "If anything happened between the two of you last night, so help me God . . ."

Gabe pulled his lapels straight. "If anything happened between us last night, it wouldn't be any of your concern."

"Unmannerly scut!" Ashbury shouted. "Thou reeky, burly-boned gudgeon."

Gabe had no idea how to respond to that.

"He curses in Shakespeare," Chase explained. "It's annoying, I know. You get used to it."

Gabe rubbed his face with one hand, weary. He would never get used to this aristocratic brand of madness, and he didn't intend to. A headache was brewing in his skull, and he'd reached the end of his patience with this cockish, swaggering display.

"Give us your word you didn't touch her," Ashbury demanded.

"I don't answer to you. Neither does she."

"Penny is our friend."

"Lady Penelope is a grown woman," Gabe said forcefully. "If you want to know what she did last night, here's an idea: Ask her yourself."

"Ooh! Ooh! Yes! Yes!"

Everyone in the hall went silent. In unison, they swiveled their heads toward the source of the cries: the birdcage. Inside, the parrot gaily bobbed on her perch.

Damn it. Gabe knew where this was going, and it wasn't anywhere good. At first opportunity, he was going to pluck that feathered menace and roast it for his dinner.

"Pretty girl," Delilah sang. *"Yes! Yes!"*

Don't say it, Gabe willed. *Don't say it.*

Delilah trilled for attention, coyly drawing out the suspense. *"Fancy a fuck, love?"*

Chapter Fourteen

$\mathcal{P}$enny closed her eyes in defeat. What a perfect encapsulation of her life. Betrayed by a parrot.

"What . . ." Emma tipped her head to the side. "What did that bird say?"

Alex wrinkled her nose in thought. "Fancy a cuppa?"

"No." Chase shook his head. "That's not it."

"Fancier fawn glove," Nicola suggested.

"Wrong again," Chase said.

"Well what else could it be?" Emma asked.

"'Fuck,'" Ash declared, exasperated. "It said 'fuck.' F-U-C-K, fuck. 'Fancy a fuck, love.' That's what it said."

Chase tutted. "Really, Ash. Which Shakespearean play would that word be in?"

"That would be in *Shut the Hell Up, Reynaud: A Tragedy in One Act.*"

Delilah ruffled her wings. *"Fancy a fuck, love? Fancy a fuck, love? Ooh! Yes! Ooh! Pretty girl."*

Ash and Chase turned murderous glares in Gabriel's direction.

"We're taking this outside," Chase said. "Now."

"Wait." Penny darted in front of Gabriel, shielding him. "It's not what you think. Delilah didn't learn any of that from us."

"You said she belonged to a little old lady," Emma said.

"A little old lady who lived in a brothel." Penny put a hand to her brow, realizing she might have coined the worst nursery rhyme ever. "Not that any of this matters."

"That's enough, all of you." Gabriel's touch grazed the small of her back as he moved to the center of the group. "We weren't off cavorting in the countryside. Even if we were, it would be none of your damned business."

The forceful way he advocated for her made Penny's heart swell.

"Her Ladyship wants to remain in London, in this house. Everyone here wants the same. Once her aunt and brother are convinced to let her stay, you'll have the added pleasure of being rid of me. We only have a fortnight. So instead of standing around reciting Shakespeare and interrogating a whorehouse parrot, I strongly suggest you offer to help."

"He's right," Nicola said. "We should make a plan."

"Finally." Gabriel threw up his hands. "At least one of you sees sense."

"I mainly wish to see you leave," she retorted. To the rest of the group, she said, "We should start with the animals."

"Hubert's on to happier waters," Penny said. "Bixby and Freya stay. Surely I'm allowed to keep a dog, and Freya doesn't trouble anyone."

Gabriel counted on his fingers. "That leaves Delilah, the kittens, Marigold and Angus, then Regan, Goneril, and Cordelia."

Penny was touched. He knew them all by name? Be still her heart.

"Chase, Alexandra . . . I was hoping you might take Delilah," Penny said. "Don't Daisy and Rosamund still enjoy playing pirates? You can't be a pirate without a parrot on your shoulder."

"If it were any other parrot, I'd happily agree," Chase said. "But *that* parrot? We'll have a baby in the house soon enough, and the girls are terrors as it is."

"I know, I know. Her vocabulary needs some reforming. I'm working on that. Will you consider it, assuming I succeed?"

"I'm certain the girls would be delighted," Alex said. "Even if Chase isn't."

"Our summer estate is only some ten miles from Town." Emma sent her husband a meaningful look. "It's lovely country. Plenty of pasture."

Ash grumbled. "Very well. I'll take the cow."

"He's a steer," Gabriel corrected. "And the goat goes with him."

"Fine. I'll take the goat, too."

"As long as you're doing that much, you may as well take the hens."

"For the love of—"

"We'd be happy to take the hens," Emma interjected.

"That leaves the kittens," Penny said, "and I can find homes for them. Kittens are something I understand. Society, on the other hand? That's the difficult part. I can't go anywhere without a gown, can I?"

"I've already made the patterns," Emma said. "But there's still a great deal to be done. Selecting silks, lace, ribbons. New slippers and gloves."

"Not to mention, I don't receive many invitations."

"Neither do we, I'm afraid," Emma said.

"I don't even bother to open the post," Nicola put in.

"I'd be glad to offer my services as a chaperone," said Chase. "But with Alexandra in her confinement . . ."

"You can't," Penny rushed to say. "You need to stay near home. I'd never ask it. We'll think of something. Or someone."

They turned to the only "someone" remaining in the room.

"Don't look at me," Gabriel said. "No one in Mayfair wants me at their parties, and Her Ladyship can't be seen in public with the Duke of Ruin."

"I might have an idea," Chase said. "One of the clubs is sponsoring a fete tomorrow. It's at a pleasure garden in Southwark. Dancing, supper, fireworks. It doesn't require an invitation or a new gown, and with a bit of planning, even the Duke of Ruin can escort you without causing a scandal."

"That sounds ideal," Penny said.

"It sounds impossible," Gabriel retorted. "There's no event safe enough for that. Not one that would make the society column."

"I assure you, there is." A slow grin spread across Chase's face. "But you're not going to like it."

GABE HATED TO admit it, but Chase was right.

He didn't like this one bit.

He stood with Penny at the edge of the garden, watching the throngs of masked lords and ladies float by, contemplating a subject that rarely occupied his mind: medieval history.

"How the devil did England win a single Crusade? I can't even walk in this. Or see, or eat, or drink." He fumbled with the visor of the helmet until it finally flipped up. "And this codpiece is much too small."

"Do stop complaining. It's not so bad."

"Easy for you to say. Your ballocks aren't dangling between two plates of metal." The armor creaked as he shifted from one foot to another—carefully.

A liveried manservant strolled in their direction, bearing a tray of crystal flutes. "Champagne?"

Gabe eagerly accepted. So eagerly, in fact, that he forgot the restrictions of his current attire. With one swipe of his plate-metal gauntlet, he cleared the tray, sending the crystal flutes to the ground and drenching the servant in champagne.

Brilliant.

As the servant walked away, Gabe filled his stifling helmet with profanity.

"You insisted you needed a true disguise—one that covered your face. This was the best we could do on such short notice. Be grateful that Ash loaned it to you. He did us a favor."

"Some favor," he muttered. "I don't suppose His Grace is going to do me the favor of holding my prick when I need to piss."

After that incident with the champagne glasses, Gabe wouldn't attempt it on his life. Perhaps a drink wasn't a good idea.

She gave him a teasing look. "If it helps at all, you do look rather gallant."

It helped a bit. A *tiny* bit.

"You may be uncomfortable now," she said. "But I'm the one bound for an eternity in perdition. Wearing my mourning attire to a masquerade? The last time I wore this gown, it was for my Uncle Jeremiah's funeral. He'll probably haunt me. Hairy ears and all."

With great effort, he swiveled his torso to look at her. She was dressed as a cat, naturally. A sinuous, alluring black cat. A pair of pointed ears perched atop her slicked-back golden hair. She'd tipped her eyes and the snub of her nose with charcoal, adding thin whiskers across her cheeks. And affixed to the back of her gown was a slinky black tail that waved and beckoned when she walked.

His codpiece was definitely too small.

He lowered the helmet's visor again.

A small orchestra gathered on a shell-shaped dais and began tuning their instruments.

"You should dance," he told her.

"I don't want to dance."

"I don't want to be wearing a metal codpiece, but here I am. This had better be worth it."

She was silent. "How can I dance when no one has asked me?"

"How can anyone ask you when you've installed yourself in the shrubbery? You're being a wallflower."

"No, I'm not. There aren't any walls."

"A shrubflower, then."

"You know, clanking at me isn't helping."

Gabe thought of asking what *would* help, but there seemed

little point. Whatever it was, he wouldn't be able to do it. He couldn't introduce her to anyone in this crowd of elites, couldn't make her feel confident when he had no idea what he was doing. And he damned well couldn't ask her to dance.

Even in a suit of shining armor, he wasn't fit to be her hero.

"I would do this for you if I could," he said. "But I can't."

"I know."

"You won't convince your aunt you're circulating in society if you spend the night hiding in the bushes."

"I'm frustrated with myself, believe me. A masquerade is supposed to be a chance to put on a different face, isn't it? An opportunity to be someone else for a few hours. Yet I can't seem to manage it. I'm still me, beneath the mask."

"I know what you mean." Gabe was still himself beneath the armor, too. An interloper among the aristocrats. Unwelcome. Inadequate. "We are who we are, I suppose."

"We are who we are," she agreed.

Gabe despised the defeated note in her voice. He *liked* who she was, beneath the mask. And when he was in her company, he almost liked who he was, too. The idea that anyone would overlook her made him vaguely furious.

"You don't have to dance." He gestured clumsily with a metal-plated arm. "Strike up a conversation with someone. Anyone."

"I do see someone I know." She lifted on tiptoe and craned her neck. "That man over there. He's a distant cousin."

"The one dressed as a Russian prince?"

"The one who actually is a Russian prince."

Of course he was. As if Gabe needed one more reminder of the vast gulf between their stations. "Go on, then."

She hesitated.

He creaked sideways, moving closer. "The hedgehog was ages ago. Everyone will have forgotten it."

She tensed. "I'm not so certain."

"Why, Lady Penelope Campion. Is that truly you?"

PENNY WINCED. OF all the people she could bump into at her first true social foray in years, it would be the Irving twins.

"My dear Lady Penelope." Thomasina took Penny's hands in hers and squeezed. "How long has it been?"

Not long enough.

Tansy and Thomasina Irving had been the bane of her life at finishing school. Unlike some of the other girls, they were never cruel outright—they would never risk making an enemy of an earl's daughter. However, they never missed an opportunity to needle her, and since there were two of them, they pricked from both sides.

Tonight, they were dressed as peacocks. They each wore a gown of shimmering teal-blue satin, with matching gloves and slippers. Fan-shaped arrays of peacock feathers sprouted from their posteriors.

"Why, we haven't seen you since your debut at—" Tansy conferred with her sister. "Almack's, wasn't it?"

"I can't say I recall," Thomasina answered blithely. Falsely. "It doesn't matter. What's wonderful is that you're here now."

Penny knew they were baiting her, and she felt helpless to challenge them. With Gabriel, she could be tart and witty, but with these girls she was straight back to her sixteenth summer. All the old feelings rose to the fore. Not because these girls were to blame for the humiliation at her debut, but she couldn't uncouple them from that time in her life. The years when she'd tried so hard to be good, to be quiet, to curl herself into a tight, impenetrable ball and go unnoticed.

Instead of going unnoticed, she'd made herself a spectacle, mowing down the crowd at Almack's.

"Won't you introduce us to your friend?" Thomasina swept an unsubtly flirtatious glance up Gabriel's armored figure. "What a fine figure you must strike at the Round Table."

"At any table." Tansy giggled.

Penny seethed. "It wouldn't be a masquerade if I gave him away, now would it?"

"I suppose we'll have to tease it out of him," Thomasina said. Was it Penny's imagination, or did her gaze linger on his codpiece?

Get your eyes off him, you vulture.

She chastened herself for entertaining a thought so mean. It was unkind to vultures.

"But you should be dancing, Lady Penelope," Tansy said. "Our brother is here. I'm certain he'd stand up with you."

"That's kind of you, but I don't wish to dance this evening."

"What a shame." Thomasina smiled. "How is that hedgehog of yours? Not still with us, I suppose."

"Actually, she is. Going on ten years now."

"By now, I'd wager she's in good company. You must have a houseful of dear little waifs."

Tansy latched on to her sister's arm. "Oh, Tommy. Remember the frog?"

As the sisters laughed, Penny wanted to inch backward until she disappeared into the shrubbery.

"What a sweet thing you were," said Thomasina. "Always so fond of God's lesser creatures. What's the latest beast in your collection, I wonder?"

"*Me.*" Metal clanged as Gabriel flipped the helmet's visor. "I'm her latest beast."

The Irving sisters choked on their laughter, then swallowed it hard.

He took a clanking step forward, towering over them. "Let me tell you, Lady Penelope has her hands full. I'm vicious. Untamed. I won't come to heel." He leaned forward, lowering his voice to a growl. "And I bite."

He turned, and—confronted with the wall of hedges—stormed through it like the Ottomans breaching the walls of Tyre. Once he'd cleared a path with his armored body, he extended a gauntlet, inviting Penny to follow.

She put her gloved hand in his shining one.

Rather than leading her through, he pulled her to him, slid

his hand to her backside, and lifted her off her feet, keeping her slippers free of the trampled shrubs.

Her beast in shining armor.

As he carried her through the hedge, she waved farewell to the bug-eyed Irving sisters. "It's been lovely seeing you."

Once he'd toted her a short distance from the pleasure garden, he set her down. After several moments of increasingly comic difficulty, he yanked the helmet off his head and chucked it aside with a curse.

Penny went to retrieve the helmet.

"Leave it," he said.

"It belongs to Ash."

"Exactly."

His face was the red-purple shade of beets, and his dark hair stood up at wild angles. In the darkness, he looked every bit as wild and dangerous as he'd just professed to be.

Penny took his face in her hands and gave him a firm kiss on the lips. "Thank you. That was magnificent."

"It was stupid. If rumors reach your aunt—or worse, the society column . . ."

She helped him remove his gauntlet. "We can't do anything about that tonight."

"I knew this was a mistake. I can't abide this society shite."

"The Irving twins have always been obnoxious."

"It's not only them. It's all of it." He stared at the scene of torches and merriment. "This is why I despise the aristocracy. The only way they survive is by holding themselves above the rest of the world. And it's not enough for them to sneer at the poor, or to abuse the working class. They have to turn on their own, as well. They'd mock you just because you don't like to waltz and you keep a pet hedgehog."

"You laughed at the hedgehog," she reminded him. "Understandably so. It's amusing."

"It's an amusing story. It's not who you are." He unbuckled a shin plate and shunted it to the ground with such force it bounced off the turf. "You're worth a thousand of any lady there."

"Let's leave, get you into some proper attire, and find ourselves some dinner." She stroked her fingertips over his brow. "I can tell from the pulsing vein in your forehead, you're hungry."

"I'm always hungry."

"My only regret is that we'll miss the fireworks."

"You want fireworks?" He cocked his eyebrow. "I can give you fireworks."

Well, then. Penny could scarcely wait.

Chapter Fifteen

*I*t wasn't the most lucrative of Gabe's investments, but there were times when owning one of the largest hotels in London came in useful. This was one of those times. For one thing, he kept spare clothing in his private suite, and thus was able to shed that ridiculous suit of armor.

For another, it offered a uniquely impressive location for a private dinner overlooking the fireworks display.

"Careful." He led her by the hand, helping her up the last few rungs of a ladder and guiding her onto the rooftop verandah. "We'll be able to view the fireworks from here."

"Yes. I should think we will." The awed hush in her voice thrilled him, as did the way she clutched his arm. "I feel like I'm floating in one of those hot-air balloons."

"I have the servants coming up with dinner soon."

"Thank you." She squeezed close to his side. "This is so much better than that silly masquerade."

She walked to the verandah's wrought-iron fencing and propped her forearms on the rail, gazing out over the London sprawl. The breeze plucked at her hair, teasing a few golden locks from their pins.

Gabe joined her. "I still can't believe the nerve of those sisters."

"Pity their parents," she said. "One Miss Irving would be bad enough. They had two in one go."

"I don't pity them at all. If you like, I could ruin the whole family for you."

She turned to him. *"What?"*

He shrugged. "It might take a few years, but I know how to be patient. It's only a matter of discreet inquiries here and there, paying attention to patterns. Somewhere there will be debts, unpaid taxes, poor investments—with luck, blackmail payments. No matter how impressive the family estate, there's always a loose brick somewhere. Every man has his weakness."

"I know they do." She lifted an eyebrow. "I'm still looking for yours."

Cheeky girl. She had to know she took his breath away.

God, she was lovely in moonlight. She was lovely in sunlight, for that matter, and in the pouring rain. Gabe suspected that even in total darkness, she would be radiant. Because though her features were exquisite, and her lips the pinkish hue of rose petals, her most beautiful feature by far was her heart.

Right now, soaring through the stars above the city, miles from everything that could keep them apart . . . he was dangerously close to telling her so.

He was saved by a timely interruption.

"My weakness is dinner," he said.

A parade of servants came through, bearing a table sized for two, chairs, a damask tablecloth, silver and china, candlesticks, crystal wineglasses, and trays loaded with divine-smelling food.

"My goodness." She laughed. "Now that was quite the trick."

"Impressed?" He held out her chair for her.

"Very."

Gabe settled into his seat and poured her some wine before filling his own glass. "I instructed the chef to prepare you dishes without any meat. I hope they're satisfactory."

She uncovered a small tureen and dipped a spoon into the steaming contents. As she stirred, the scent of exotic spices wafted through the air. "Vegetable curry? It smells divine. I'm ravenous."

Conversation was set aside by tacit agreement, as they both loaded their plates and tucked into their food.

Some minutes later, she sat back in her chair with a contented sigh, cradling her wineglass in one hand. "So tell me."

He paused, fork halfway to his mouth. "Tell you what?"

She shrugged. "Everything. How did you come to be the Duke of Ruin? Where did you learn so much about finances, and how to find those loose bricks in a fortune?"

Gabe carefully swallowed his bite and set his fork aside. "The truth?"

"But of course."

Very well, then. He'd known this would be coming eventually, and he'd been wondering how she would react. Tonight, they would both find out.

"When I was a young man, I worked for a pawnbroker. One with a reputation for discretion and a distinguished clientele. I learned how to judge the value of fine items—but more than that, I learned how to judge the fine people. Over time, you come to observe certain patterns. The lady who comes in monthly, like clockwork, letting go one more pearl from an ever-shrinking necklace? Blackmailed for a secret she can't afford her husband to know. The younger fellow who stumbles in of a morning, reeking of brandy and willing to accept shillings on the pound for his pocket watch? Gaming debts. The ones who weep as they hand over family heirlooms? They're poised on the brink of insolvency."

"And you use this knowledge to your advantage. You seize on their vulnerability to take what they have left."

"By perfectly legal means."

"You don't feel any sympathy for them?"

"None." He leaned forward, propping his elbows on the table. "Where do you think all that money comes from? Your own family's estate, for that matter. Parcels of land granted with the wave of a king's hand, centuries ago. That's the land here in Britain, of course. When that wasn't enough, they grabbed more from every corner of the world. The aristocracy built fortunes on the backs of serfs, peasants, tenant farmers. Slaves. I don't suffer a moment's shame when I take their wealth from them."

"You realize that when you say 'them,' you also mean me. My family, my friends."

"I'm aware of that."

She poked at a dish of sherry trifle with her spoon. "Before the pawnbroker, where were you?"

"On the streets. Thieving. How do you think I met the pawnbroker? I had to sell the pocket watches and baubles somewhere."

"And before that?"

"The workhouse, mostly."

"The workhouse? How dreadful."

"Could have been worse. I was out of the cold, at least. Meager meals are better than none. They taught us to read and write, and do sums." Gabe had also learned how to grind bones with a rock until his fingers bled, and how to survive savage beatings from a schoolmaster who took cruel joy in meting them out. But those were lessons better left unmentioned.

"What about your parents?"

"Never knew them." The one falsehood in his tale.

"I'm sorry," she said.

"I'm not."

"So you were raised in the workhouse—and here you are now, at the top of the world." She propped an elbow on the table and rested her chin in her hand. "It's remarkable, Gabriel. You must be proud."

Was he proud? He'd always thought so, but now he wasn't so sure. A sense of pride implied satisfaction. By now, everything he'd amassed ought to feel like enough—but it didn't. Satisfaction eluded him, again and again.

The hunger never went away.

He pushed back from the table. "The fireworks will be starting soon."

He guided her over to a heap of pillows and plush, sumptuous blankets. Velvet, satin, embroidered silk. They relaxed into the jumble of luxury and stared up at the clear night sky.

"Alexandra would know the name of each and every star up there," Penny said. "She found a comet, you know. It's named for her."

"That's impressive."

"I have remarkably accomplished friends. Alex is our astronomer. Emma's a magician with needle and thread, and Nicola . . . well, Nicola has a dozen brilliant ideas a day. Only half of them are new biscuit recipes."

"And what about you?"

"I'm the one who invites them over for tea and kittens. And horrid sandwiches." She nudged him in the ribs. "I don't have any remarkable talents. I just try to make my friends feel at home."

"That *is* a remarkable talent. A damned rare one, too."

She laughed in self-deprecating fashion.

"No, truly. Ask any hotelier. People with welcoming dispositions are in short supply."

"That's good to know. A spinster never knows when she might need respectable employment."

They lapsed into silence, staring into the vast, starry night. He'd stared into darkness many times in his life. Nothing ever made a man feel so alone.

He inched his hand to the side until his little finger brushed against hers. Just that feathery touch made his breath catch. They clasped hands, interlacing their fingers and holding tight. His heart was beating in his throat.

A rocket whistled into the air, exploding above them with a shock of sound and a burst of golden sparks.

"Make love to me," she said quietly.

His thudding heart stopped.

She rolled onto her side, facing him. Her fingers went to the buttons of his shirt, and she slipped them loose. One by one by one. Her hand stole under the fabric, caressing his chest.

Her lips brushed his. The sweetness of her kiss made his whole body ache.

"No, no, no." With heroic effort, he pulled away. "Your first time should be special."

"Gabriel. We're currently on a rooftop, lying atop a mountain of satin pillows, staring up at a sky bursting with fireworks. I should think this meets the 'special' requirement."

A burst of shimmering red bloomed amid the stars, conspiring with her against him.

"Your first time should be with some*one* special," he said.

"There's absolutely nothing ordinary about you. Once again, you can cross that requirement off the list."

"I meant your husband."

She flopped back on the pillows and groaned. "You're supposed to be dangerous and passionate. Not principled."

"I've made a career of ruining fortunes, but I've never ruined a woman. I damned well won't start with you."

"I despise that word. Ruined. As if passion is an unforgivable transgression, and virginity is the only measure of a woman's worth." She looked at him. "Is that what you believe? That making love tonight would make me worthless tomorrow?"

"Of course not."

"But it might make your property worthless tomorrow. Is that it?"

"No. I'm not thinking of that at all."

In fact, he'd forgotten it completely. His financial interests weren't the reason for their bargain anymore. At some point, he'd stopped caring about the damned house, and he'd—

He'd started caring about Penny instead.

"Nothing could make you less valuable tomorrow. But this might make you less marriageable tomorrow. If word got about."

"After the masquerade, word may already be about."

He cursed. "Don't remind me."

"What does it matter?" She propped herself on her elbow. "Perhaps I'll never marry. Perhaps my brother will cut off my funds. I have a bit of money stashed away. I have friends. Why should I care about my dwindling marriage prospects? I'd rather seize control of my life, be free to do anything I wish." She teased her fingertips through the hair on his chest. "And making love with you is the first item on my list."

"Don't tell me this nonsense about having no prospects. You could have all the prospects in the world, if you wished them. And something tells me you will wish them. Someday. In your heart, you must want to have a family. Children to love, to make feel at home. That talent shouldn't go unused." He touched her cheek. "Don't foreclose the possibility. You deserve good things. Promises. Tenderness. Love. Everything you've ever dreamed."

"Lately, all my dreams are of you." She kissed her way down his neck, nuzzling against his skin.

Desire and conscience warred within him, and there was no doubt which side was losing the battle. He slid his hand around her rib cage, feeling for the closures of her frock. "There could be consequences," he murmured against her ear. "I'd be a blackguard to ignore that."

"I'm fully aware of the risks to my reputation. As well as the risks to my body and my heart."

Good God, her heart?

Her *heart*.

"I want you, Gabriel."

Such a simple phrase, and yet it summed up the yearning of a lifetime. All these years of anger and striving, and he'd longed for nothing more than this: to be wanted.

Desire kindled in his chest with a ferocity that stunned him. Scared him.

As he wrestled to conquer it, he caught a flicker of doubt in her eyes. It was the final blow. Honor waved a white flag of surrender. He would never let her feel a moment's doubt. Not if he could help it.

"That is, of course . . ." She bit her lip. "If you want me."

Chapter Sixteen

*P*enny waited in quiet agony for his response.

"*If* I want you," he echoed. "*If.*"

"It's your choice as much as it is mine. If you need time to consider, I—"

"*If* I need time to consider?"

In the flash of a moment, he had her on her back. Penny lay beneath him, breathless.

His dark eyes held hers. "The only thing I'm considering is precisely how to remove the word 'if' from your vocabulary."

"Oh."

"First, I'm going to strip you naked. I'm going to stroke every part of you with my hands. Then I'm going to paint your body with my tongue. By the time I'm done with you, you will never—*ever*—ask *if* I want you again."

"Very well. *If* you insist."

He growled through a begrudging smile. "You little minx."

He kissed her more deeply than he ever had before, sucking her tongue and gently biting each of her lips in turn. His raw desire made it clear that in all their previous interactions, he'd been holding back. Now she would experience the full, primal force of his passion.

She couldn't wait.

He rolled her onto her side and started on the buttons of her frock. Her impatience was extreme. She couldn't remember exactly how many buttons there were, but judging by how long this was taking, she guessed the number to be seventy-eight, at minimum. His fingers plucked at the laces of her stays, pulling them through the grommets one by one until the corset fell away from her body.

"For heaven's sake. Hurry."

He took pity on her, grasping her chemise and splitting it down the middle. She saw his own shirt land in a heap at her side.

He rolled her over again and helped her work the stifling black shroud down her torso and over her hips, wadding it up and tossing it aside.

She lay naked to his view, save for her stockings.

Her black silk stockings.

He stared at them. "My God. Where did you . . ."

"Emma dyed them for the occasion. It wouldn't do to be a black cat with white stockings, would it?" She reached to untie her garter.

"Don't you dare." He ran his eyes over her body. "I have never seen anything so enticing in my life."

He ran his hand up her calf, over her knee, and up the sensitive slope of her thigh, until he cupped her mound in his palm. She gasped at the shock of pleasure. His fingers caressed her gently, stroking up and down the seam of her sex, teasing her with light passes until she was breathless.

She reached between their bodies, feeling for his trousers buttons and tugging at them with eager, inexpert fingers. At last, his placket fell open, and his erection sprang into her hand. Hot, hard, and heavy. She explored him the same way he touched her—skating her fingertips up and down his length, marveling at the silky softness of his skin and tracing the intriguing, yet entirely unfamiliar contours.

"Let me see you," she whispered.

He rose up on his knees, and his male organ jutted toward her.

The dark hair on his chest arrowed straight toward it, like a signpost indicating a point of natural interest: THIS WAY TO THE MANHOOD.

As if it could be missed.

Rude, large, framed by dark hair, and impressively male. No surprises, really. It simply looked like a part of him. An intimidatingly *large* part of him, considering what was about to occur and where she hoped he would put it. But it wasn't foreign or frightening. As was the case with all the other parts of his body, she found it bold, strong, unabashed in its nature, and arousing in the extreme. One more facet of a man she was coming to know and hold dear.

Perhaps even coming to love.

She curled her hand around his shaft, stroking up and down his length—the way she'd seen him do in the inn. He winced, but in what seemed to be a good way. He permitted her only a few easy strokes before pulling her hand away.

"Any more of that, and this will be over before it's even begun."

"We can't have that."

He shucked his trousers, tossed them aside, and returned to her, covering her nakedness with his body and settling his hips between her thighs. She arched against him, silently pleading. Once again, he made her wait.

He kissed her neck, suckled her breasts.

He reached between her thighs. "Let me kiss you here."

"Why?"

"Mainly because I suspect you'll enjoy it, and I want to give you pleasure. If you climax now, the pain will be less later. But also because I truly, deeply, very very much want to taste you."

She smiled. "Then by all means."

He ducked his head, and his whiskers scraped against her inner thighs as he settled between them. His broad shoulders pushed her knees apart, and he worked both hands beneath her hips and lifted, tilting her to the most favorable angle to receive his kiss.

For a moment, the intimacy was too much, too uncertain. But when she heard his deep moan of satisfaction, her hesitancy disappeared.

His tongue glided up the seam of her sex.

Oh. Oh, *God.*

She gripped the pillows on either side of her hips, sinking her fingers into the tasseled brocade.

The fireworks overhead were nothing to the sensations exploding through her with every pass of his tongue. He parted her with his thumbs, opening her to his explorations.

He centered his attention on the bundle of nerves at the apex of her cleft and worked it with his nimble, flickering tongue.

Penny's head rolled back, and she closed her eyes, surrendering to his erotic talent and the delicious, mounting pleasure. She twisted her hand in his hair and arched against him, seeking more contact, more joy. Climbing higher and higher, until she was dizzied and wary of looking down.

The pleasure rocketed through her, exploding into sparks of bliss. He rose up on his knees and took himself in hand, guiding his erection to where they both needed it to be. At the heart of her, where it belonged.

"Please," she begged.

When he pushed inside her, it hurt. He held her while she breathed, stretched. She sensed his struggle, the tension in his body.

"Are you—" A strangled noise. "Is it—"

In answer, she placed her hands on his back and pulled him deeper.

He moaned. "Penny."

He thrust deeper, working his length inside her in slight, inching thrusts. With his last push, he buried himself to the hilt, wrenching a cry of surprise from her chest.

"I'm well," she assured him. "It's fine."

"You're certain."

She nodded. "I'm fine."

As he set an easy, tender rhythm, the words rocked through her mind like a chant.

I'm well.

It's fine.

It's good.

So good.

I'm yours. Yours. Yours.

His pace quickened. He lifted her hips, angling her to take him deeper. His thrusts drove home again and again, each dig of his hips accompanied by a rasping, desperate sound. With a curse, he withdrew from her body and took himself in hand, stroking himself to completion.

Then he slumped against her chest, heavier than bricks. She wrapped her arms around his shoulders and held him tight, stroking her fingertips lightly down his back. Tears pressed to her eyes, but she forced them back. He'd mistake them for sadness, rather than joy.

There were no more fireworks overhead. No booming explosions or crackling lights. Only ragged breaths and pounding heartbeats.

The past, the future . . . none of it mattered. There was only this moment, this man. This one heartbeat, and then the next, stringing together to make this life.

A life that belonged to her. At last.

AFTER ROLLING ASIDE, Gabe observed her through the haze of fireworks lingering in the air. He believed she'd truly wanted this. He wouldn't have made love to her if he hadn't.

But that was before. It remained to be seen whether she'd feel the same way after.

"Gabriel." She rolled onto her back and stared up at the sky. "Ask me how it feels to be ruined."

"How does it feel to be ruined?"

He watched a grin spread across her face. "I have no idea."

Gabe exhaled, and the knot of dread in his chest unraveled. "So you're not regretful."

"Regretful?" She all but bounced to a sitting position. "Not in the least. I am delighted. I've wanted that since . . . since we met, I think. But I couldn't have imagined I'd ever work up the courage." She pressed her hand to her mouth and laughed. "I just lost my virginity on a rooftop. To"—she made a two-handed gesture at his nude body—"you."

Gabe folded one arm under his head. He supposed he would take that as a compliment.

"Emma, Nic, and Alex will never believe this."

"Hold a moment." It was his turn to bolt upright. "Surely you don't mean to tell them."

"I tell them everything. Almost."

"Yes, but . . ."

"Why shouldn't I tell them? Do you think I should be ashamed?"

"No," he answered. "But they will think *I* should be."

"Honestly, I'm not certain I could hide it. They'll guess the moment they see me."

Yes, he thought, it was likely they would. She was giddy, blushing. Radiant. Nothing could surpass his pleasure at knowing he'd helped put that look on her face. Not even the blood-stirring, soul-shattering climax he'd barely survived a few minutes past.

"Don't worry," she said. "They're my closest friends, and they wouldn't tell a soul. It's not as though I mean to put a notice in the *Times*."

This phrase gave him pause. Maybe she would expect a different notice in the *Times*. An engagement notice.

He cleared his throat. "So what are your expectations, moving forward?"

"Expectations?"

"Your hopes. If you have any."

"Oh, I do." She ducked her chin and looked at him through a golden fringe of eyelashes. "I hope we can do it again."

He stared at her, marveling.

"Not right now, necessarily," she hastened to say. "I know you must be fatigued. Another day would be fine."

He couldn't help but chuckle. With a flex of his arm, he drew her into a kiss—a kiss she returned with equal passion and a breathy, erotic moan. Despite her adorable concerns for his "fatigue," he could have risen to the challenge of another performance, easily.

"Good God," he said. "What have I unleashed?"

"Me." She lifted his hand and kissed it. "I'm in control of my life and my body, and you can't know what that means. I'm not sure *I* know what it means. But I'm all anticipation to find out."

So am I, he thought. *Bloody hell, so am I.*

He stroked the hair back from her face, admiring her beauty when bathed in starlight. She seemed an entirely new woman.

She startled. "Bixby. We have to go home. He'll be needing his walk."

Well, then. Perhaps not an entirely new woman after all.

Chapter Seventeen

$\mathcal{S}$everal days later, Penny sat at Nicola's kitchen table, staring at the fresh-off-the-presses copy of the weekly *Prattler*.

"I can't look," she said.

"Do you want me to read it?" Nicola reached for the newspaper.

"No." Penny slapped her hand over it. "I'll do it. When I'm ready." She looked at her empty plate. "Are there any more biscuits?"

"Between you and Bixby, the kitchen is bare."

"Oh. Did you have any plans of baking more?" Penny asked hopefully. "It might help."

Everything seemed a bit easier to face with a plate of fresh biscuits.

She tapped her fingers on the newspaper's front page. "I don't know why this is so difficult. It's not as though I can change the contents by waiting. What's printed is printed. I am either a scandal or a spinster already, depending on what's inside."

"Actually," Nicola mused, "while the paper remains closed, you're both."

"Both?"

"Right now, you're both a scandal and a spinster."

"I'm so sorry. I'm afraid I don't follow you." Penny frequently had difficulty following the twists and turns of Nicola's mind. Everyone did.

Nicola's eyes went unfocused, as though she were staring at the distant horizon. One that only she could see. "Imagine you took a cat," she said slowly, "and sealed it in a box."

"Seal a cat inside a box?" Penny was horrified. "I'd never do such a thing."

"Of course you wouldn't actually do it. I'm only trying to illustrate a philosophical conundrum."

"What sort of philosophical conundrum requires a person to imagine suffocating cats? Surely there's a better illustration."

"You're right. I'll think of something else." Nicola set aside her tinkering. "Penny, if there's anything you need to talk about, I'm always here for you. I know I'm not as sympathetic and comforting as Emma or Alexandra."

"Nic—"

"Don't worry. I'm not disparaging myself. I simply know my talents, and that's not one of them. However, I'm always here to listen. And when it comes to matters of the heart, I'm not completely inexperienced."

"You're . . . you're not?" Penny stared at her friend, amazed. In all their years of friendship, Nicola had never, not once, mentioned a sweetheart or a suitor. Much less being in love.

With a shake of her head, Nicola picked up a gear and turned it over in her hands. "Men can be terribly distracting."

A thousand questions crowded Penny's mind, but before she could ask any of them, the clocks began to strike the hour. From all around the house, they were bombarded by chimes, cuckoos, pendulum strikes, and clanging bells.

Nicola owned a great many clocks. Or rather, Nicola's father had owned a great many clocks, and Nicola couldn't bring herself to part with a single one of them. Although the hourly mayhem had a way of interrupting conversation, Penny never complained. How could she? A woman who took in kittens by the dozen had little room to criticize.

Today, it could have been worse. The clocks didn't go on too long this time, as the hour was merely three o'clock in the afternoon.

Goodness. Three o'clock in the afternoon? Penny had been sitting there for ages already.

No more dithering.

She reached for the copy of the *Prattler*, opened it to the society pages, and briefly squeezed her eyes shut. Strangely, she didn't know what to wish for. Perhaps Nicola had the right of it, and Penny had been delaying this because she enjoyed being a wallflower *and* a temptress—and she resented that society wouldn't let her be both.

The days since the masquerade had been the most thrilling days of her life. While she and Gabriel awaited the verdict, they'd made use of the time in a variety of passionate, and increasingly inventive, ways. It was as if all the clocks had stopped, and they'd carved out a secret haven free from prying eyes or consequence.

When she opened this newspaper, the clocks resumed ticking. Time had caught up with them, and one way or another, their stolen era of passion would come to an end.

Penny didn't want it to end.

Nevertheless, she couldn't avoid the reality any longer. If she didn't read this for herself, she would hear everything from Aunt Caroline. Better to be prepared.

"Read it aloud," Nicola said.

"'A Report from the Maximus Club's Spring Fete.'" She skimmed the contents, pulling out the most important words. "Southwark, pleasure garden, masquerade, orchestra, champagne . . . Ah. Here we are. Prominent guests in attendance."

Penny scanned through the list of names and titles. Her cousin the Russian prince received mention, naturally. Farther down, the Misses Irving were named. She'd nearly reached the end of the column, and no mention of Lady Penelope Campion yet.

Then she read the concluding paragraph.

"'In the usual fashion of masquerades, the identities of most guests were plain for all to see. However, one gentleman in attendance succeeded in generating a considerable amount of intrigue. As the evening drew to a close, only one question was on the guests' lips. Who was that knight in shining armor? The mystery remains. He was last seen in the company of . . .'"

Penny groaned.

"Well?" Nicola asked. "Which is it? Scandal or spinster?"

"Neither, apparently."

"Let me see." Nicola took the paper and found the point where Penny had left off. "'He was last seen in the company of an unidentified woman.'"

"Unidentified woman," Penny repeated, separating each syllable. She let her head drop to the table surface. "What could possibly be more depressing?"

"A suffocating cat?"

"True."

Nicola turned the page of the newspaper. "Hold a moment. Your neighbor is hosting a ball?"

"What?"

Penny rose from her chair and hurried to read over Nicola's shoulder. There it was, in black and white.

The *Prattler* has learned that one Mr. Gabriel Duke, better known to readers of this esteemed publication as the infamous Duke of Ruin, is planning to host a ball at the former Wendleby residence on Bloom Square. According to our sources, Mr. Duke has invited the better part of the London *ton*. Considering the host's financial influence, and the ruthless way in which he wields it, the question will not be who will accept his invitation—but rather, who would dare decline?

"Burns! *Burns!*"

Gabe winced. Just what he needed—another ridiculous conflict between his architect and his housekeeper. He rose from his desk and followed Hammond's bellowing into the dining room, hoping to head it off before it could begin.

He was too late, sadly. Mrs. Burns had already arrived.

"Yes, Mr. Hammond?" The housekeeper starched her spine. "Is there something I can do for you?"

Hammond gestured at the portrait on the wall. "You can explain to me why I'm looking at the inbred offspring of a suet pudding and a weak-chinned salamander."

"That's a portrait of Mrs. Bathsheba Wendleby."

"I expressly told the workmen to remove these paintings two days ago. Lo and behold, they have reappeared. As if by magic." His tone sharpened. "Dark magic."

Burns did not address Hammond's unspoken accusation of witchcraft. "These are family portraits, representing generations of Wendlebys."

"Those generations of Wendlebys don't live here any longer."

"Nevertheless, Mr. Hammond," she said with foreboding. "This house has a legacy, and it will not be forgotten."

"This house has a desirable address," Gabe interjected. "I'm going to sell it to some new-money upstart who wants to hobnob with aristocrats. Those buyers don't want moldering portraits of a crusty squire and his hunting dogs. They want modern water closets and gilded molding. If Sir Algernon Wendleby cared about his precious legacy, he shouldn't have frittered away the family fortune on cards and mistresses."

When he finished his tirade, Gabe felt rather shabby about it. He wasn't frustrated with the housekeeper. He was frustrated with himself.

After the last few days—and nights—with Penny, Gabe needed a reminder of just what the devil he was doing in Mayfair. He was here to sell this house for the highest possible price, and if the new occupants displeased the *ton,* so much the better. He wasn't here to stay.

He wasn't here to carry on a torrid *affaire* with the lady next door, either. With every tryst, he promised himself this time would be the last. It *must* be the last. The risks to Penny were too great.

Then she would whisper his name, or give him a coy smile, or breathe in his general vicinity, and all his resolutions turned to dust.

"As you like, Mr. Duke," the housekeeper said. "The paintings will be removed today."

"One more thing before you go." Hammond narrowed his eyes at her. "How did he die?"

"To whom are you referring, sir?"

"Mr. Burns. Your husband. You were widowed, I assume."

"It's customary for housekeepers to be addressed as Mrs., whether or not they are married. There was never a Mr. Burns." At the sound of the doorbell, she inclined her head. "If you will excuse me, I'll answer the door."

After the housekeeper left the room, Hammond approached Gabe and dropped his voice to a whisper. "No Mr. Burns? I don't believe that for a moment. She's hiding his corpse in a wardrobe somewhere."

Gabe sniffed the air hovering about his architect. "What is that smell?"

"Garlic." Hammond pulled a white, papery bulb from his pocket. "I've taken to carrying some at all times, and so should you. For protection. They don't like garlic."

"Housekeepers?"

"Vampiresses."

"For God's sake, this has to stop. Burns is *not* a vampiress."

"She's pale enough. But then, she does walk about during the day. Perhaps she's a wandering evil spirit who possessed the reanimated corpse of a virgin beauty." Hammond stalked away, scrubbing both hands through his silvered hair.

Gabe stared after the man. A virgin beauty? *Burns?*

If one looked past her gloomy attire and perpetually dour expression, Gabe supposed the woman might not be *un*attract-

ive. But a beauty? Maybe she truly did have Hammond bewitched.

Light footsteps approached from the corridor. "A *ball*? You're
hosting a *ball*? Were you planning to tell me about this?"

Penny. Speaking of enchanting beauties.

Gabe turned to greet her—but he found himself without
words.

God above, she was lovely.

Over the brief course of their acquaintance, they'd been
systematically destroying her frocks—first rescuing Bixby from
the coal store, then chasing after Hubert in the river . . . After
the masquerade, even her black mourning dress would never
be the same.

As a result, she'd been reaching further and further back into
her wardrobe, drawing out frocks she likely hadn't worn for
some time. Each one painted a portrait of a different, younger
Penny. In a strange way, he was growing acquainted with her
in reverse. There was a year she'd chosen brighter hues and
lower necklines, and a year she'd preferred demure lace, and a
year when a modiste must have talked her into an absurd number of flounces.

Today's frock must have been made several years ago, when
she was not merely younger, but slighter in form. Her figure
had matured since, and now the muslin clung to her body the
way limewash gripped stone. Praise heaven, he could make out
nipples.

His conscience niggled at him. There was something he'd
been reminding himself of a few minutes ago. Something about
selling this place, leaving Mayfair behind—and Lady Penelope
Campion with it. He was supposed to remember it.

He remembered nothing. Nothing, that was, except for her
silky thighs wrapped about his hips and the coarse saddle
blanket chafing his knees when he'd taken her in the hayloft
above the mews yesterday. He'd breathed in so much dust, the
sneezing had kept him awake half the night.

He had no regrets.

"I'm up here, Gabriel," she said tartly, yanking his gaze away from her breasts. Her brow wrinkled with concern as she held up a folded newspaper for his view. "And we need to talk about this."

Chapter Eighteen

"What's the meaning of this? You're hosting a ball?" Penny waited on Gabriel's explanation.

He offered none.

Instead, he strolled across the room to her, took the paper from her hand, and read through the notice of his impending ball.

"I see little to discuss. The *Prattler* has captured the details. In fact, it's shockingly accurate, considering the publication." He returned the paper.

"Yes, but—"

"While you're here . . ." He left the room, glancing back in a manner that invited her to follow. "I want your opinion on some wall coverings."

He mounted the stairs, and Penny followed. She hated trailing after him like a pup, but she wasn't going to let him get away. "According to the paper, you've sent invitations already. Perhaps mine was lost in the post?"

"Hammond likes the periwinkle blue," he went on. "But I don't trust his opinion on current fashions. Not for a lady's suite."

Penny growled behind clenched teeth. Wasn't he paying attention to her at all? Apparently not, or else she would have warned him that this ball scheme was a terrible idea.

He led her into a mostly empty bedchamber. The few pieces

of furniture had been pushed to the center of the room and draped with Holland cloths, and the walls were stretches of blank plaster. Three strips of silk damask had been tacked to one wall, each a different shade of blue.

"You've seen my house. I don't know anything about current fashions in wall coverings. Mr. Hammond's opinion is surely—"

He shut the door and pushed her up against it, crushing his mouth to hers in a possessive kiss. As his tongue found hers, a needy sigh rose in the back of her throat. The newspaper slipped from her grasp and fell to the floor. She couldn't recall why she'd been holding it in the first place. It didn't matter.

All she wanted to hold was Gabriel.

She took his face in her hands, sanding her palms on the delicious scruff of his whiskers before twining her fingers into his hair and holding tight. His hands roamed her body, claiming handfuls of her hips and skimming over her breasts.

"I need you," he murmured between kisses. "It's been ages."

"It's been"—she thought on it—"seventeen hours."

"Like I said. Ages." He bent to kiss her neck.

"We can't," she gasped. "Not here. There's no bed."

He grinned wickedly. "Love, we don't need a bed."

"Oh."

One of his hands caught the hem of her frock and hiked it above her knee, bunching her petticoats between their bodies. He swept his palm up her thigh, and pleasure rippled in the wake of his touch. While he nuzzled at her neck and licked at her breasts where they overflowed her bodice, his touch explored her intimate places. Her breathing quickened. Her nipples pulled to hard, aching peaks.

He slid a finger inside her. She melted against the door, her knees gone soft. She clutched his shoulders, clinging to him for strength as he stoked her desire with expert caresses.

"You don't understand what you've done to me," he whispered. "*I* don't understand what you've done to me."

"Whatever it is, you've done the same to me." She gasped as

he pushed a second finger inside her, and she caught him in a breathless, grappling kiss. They tugged at each other's clothing.

"I wanted you from the first," he said.

"I wanted you, too."

"Every time I closed my eyes, I saw you in my bed."

"I couldn't stop picturing you naked and wet."

"If you knew the things you've done in my imagination . . ."

"I touched myself while thinking of you."

He groaned against her lips. "Jesus Christ, that's one of them."

She whimpered in protest as his fingers withdrew from her body. He slid his hands to her bottom and lifted her off her feet, carrying her across the room, to where a floor-length mirror in a thick gilded frame stood propped against the wall. It must have been too heavy to move.

He spun her to face it, positioning himself behind her. Their gazes locked in the mirrored reflection. His eyes were dark, fierce, demanding.

"Show me." He yanked her skirts to her waist—frock, petticoat, chemise, and all—exposing her completely. "Show me how you touched yourself."

Penny's heartbeat stalled. The gruff command both scandalized and excited her.

With a rough flex of his arms, he hauled her to him. His erection throbbed against the small of her back.

"Show me."

Penny stared into the mirror. A bolder, naughtier version of herself gazed back. She placed a hand on her belly and eased it downward, until her fingertips disappeared into a thatch of amber curls. She hesitated, holding her breath.

"More," he demanded. "I want to see you."

His gruffness aroused her, but she wasn't intimidated. With him, she knew she was safe.

She raised her free arm above her head, clasping his neck for balance and resting her head against his chest. He wrapped his arm about her torso, holding her tight and pinning her lifted skirts at the waist. Her joints softened, and her thighs fell slightly apart.

"That's it. Spread yourself for me. Let me see."

The woman in the mirror did as she was told, sending her fingers downward to part the pink, swollen folds of her sex. A single fingertip settled over the sensitive bud at the crest, circling gently.

His ragged breath warmed her ear. "God, you're beautiful."

She stared at the reflection, transfixed by the eroticism of the image within. She felt like a woman in a boudoir painting, flushed with desire and unashamed of her body's curves and shadows. Aware of the power she held, even in her vulnerable, naked state.

As her excitement mounted, she strummed faster. She was panting, arching her back.

Suddenly, he worked his free hand between them, levering for space. His fingers made quick work of his buttons, and he pushed his trousers down over his hips. His freed erection pulsed between their bodies, so thick and hot and so very, very hard.

Yes. Take me.

He teased her instead, pushing against her cleft and gliding back and forth, spreading her slickness along his full length. Then he lifted and tilted her by the hips, thrusting inside. Deep, and then deeper, all the way to her core, giving her the fullness she craved.

He took her in long, steady strokes. His hardness was an anchor, balancing against the dizzying pleasure as she worked the hidden bud with her fingertips.

"Come." His voice was strained, but he held himself to a slow, devastating rhythm. "I need to see you come."

She held his gaze in the mirror for as long as she could, until the bliss overwhelmed her. She bit her lip, sealing in a cry as the climax broke. For a time, she was weightless in his arms, aware of nothing but the pleasure racking her body.

He ceased his thrusts as she quivered in the aftermath, supporting her boneless form. A courtesy on his part, surely. He was as hard as she'd ever felt him, and as her breathing slowed, the tension in his body increased.

She caught his gaze in the mirror and nodded.

Now.

"Lean over," he growled. "Hands on the frame."

The brusque command thrilled her. She did as he asked, bending forward at the waist and bracing her hands on either side of the mirror's gilt frame.

He lifted her by the hips and pushed deep, claiming her in one powerful motion. As he took her in pounding thrusts, his flanks met her backside with sharp, rhythmic smacks. They echoed through the room, obscene and arousing. Soon these sounds were joined by low, primal grunts of satisfaction.

She watched him, captivated by the display of raw, unfettered male desire. Sweat broke out on his brow. His jaw clenched so tightly, the tendons on his neck went rigid. He stared at the mirror, watching her breasts jiggle and sway with each thrust.

With a muttered curse, he redoubled his pace. Her observations were halted. It was all she could do to brace herself against the force of his thrusts. She would have bruises tomorrow from his viselike grip.

She felt him swell even larger within her, and his rhythm faltered. With a tortured groan, he pulled free of her sex and pressed her legs together, thrusting between her thighs until his seed spilled over her skin—hot and crude.

She felt marked, claimed.

But also wild and free.

Several panting, sweaty, sticky moments later, they crumpled together to the floor, sitting with their backs against the wall. Penny rested her head on his chest. He was lovely to snuggle. There was simply so much of him. She could be satisfied with just one of his arms to clutch, or a single shoulder to rest her head upon.

But Penny wanted him all.

She couldn't deny it any longer.

Closing her eyes, she pressed her ear to his pounding heartbeat. Like the rest of him, his heart was strong, defiant, loyal. Capable of lasting love. He might revel in denying it, but she knew the truth. If he ever permitted himself to love, he would love fiercely and without reserve. Only the most stubborn of women would be able to bear it.

And Penny loved nothing so much as a challenge.

Let me try, she silently willed. *Let me try.*

"So." He sat up and stretched, dislodging her from her resting place. "You were asking about the ball."

The ball.

She pulled herself from her musings. Yes, that was why she'd come over, wasn't it?

"When did you decide to host a ball?"

He stood, hiking his trousers. "Somewhere between delivering you home from the hotel that night and exerting a bit of influence over the Irving family the following morning."

Penny was agog. "You didn't."

"Would you rather those sisters spread vile gossip about you all over London?"

"I don't want you ruining families on my account."

"I didn't ruin the Irvings. I merely made it known that I *could* ruin them, if I so chose."

She moaned a little.

"Listen, it's not my fault their father backed the wrong company in the fur trade."

"The fur trade?" She accepted his hand, and he helped her to her feet. "Very well, I suppose I won't complain. This time."

So this was why she'd remained "unidentified woman" in the *Prattler.* She ought to have guessed.

She did her best to rearrange her attire. The seam under her arm had ripped. Yet one more frock for the mending heap. "This still doesn't explain why you're hosting a ball."

"I would say something about two birds and one stone, but

you'd complain about animal cruelty. Suffice it to say, by hiring an orchestra and inviting a crush of people to admire this place, we can solve both our problems in one evening. You can satisfy your aunt. I can sell the house." He clapped his hands in cheery fashion. "All sorted."

"How efficient."

"While you're here, you may as well give me your opinion on the wall coverings." He gestured at the strips of silk damask on the wall. "Tell me your preference."

"The blue."

"They're all blue. You're not even looking." He took her by the shoulders and swiveled her to face the samples. "Which is best for the lady of the house?"

"Why does it matter what I think?"

He tensed. "Why shouldn't it matter?"

"Because I'm *not* the lady of the house." She tried, and likely failed, to mask her discomposure. "It's not my bedchamber. It never will be. So it doesn't matter what I think, now does it?"

He rubbed the back of his neck with one hand. "Maybe not."

Penny smoothed her skirts and drew a breath to calm her emotions. He didn't deserve her frustration. Selling the house had always been his goal, and she was being churlish because she didn't want to be reminded of it.

It wasn't his fault that she was falling in love with him. For that, she had no one to blame but herself.

"Never mind me," she said gamely. "I have no eye for fashion. And to be truthful, I don't much like blue of any shade. That's all."

In a gesture she found irrationally dispiriting, he kissed her on the forehead. "Very well, then."

Penny decided to change the subject—to kittens. Kittens were always a welcome change of subject.

"Here is some good news. The last litter of kittens is fully weaned. They're ready for their new homes. We can take them tomorrow."

Chapter Nineteen

*M*ost people wouldn't consider kittens to be harbingers of doom. But then, most people weren't Gabe.

He had a bad feeling about this errand.

It began when she overruled him on their mode of transportation. He offered his carriage, but she insisted on taking a hackney cab. "I won't have any of your grumbling if one of the kittens claws the barouche's upholstery."

They piled into a hackney, three hampers of kittens between the two of them. Keeping them all contained proved to be an impossible task. They clung to his coat like burrs, and as soon as he plucked one from his shoulder and stuffed it back in a basket, another was scaling his trouser leg.

Meanwhile, Penny sat across from him—completely unmolested and laughing at his predicament.

"You could help."

"And ruin the amusement? Never."

Cursing, Gabe unhooked a miniature, translucent claw from his waistcoat embroidery.

"Perhaps they've mistaken you for a tree," she said.

"Perhaps you tucked a mackerel in my hatband." A set of tiny, predatory teeth nipped at his earlobe.

"We're nearly there."

Nearly there. Nearly where, exactly? Gabe craned his neck to look outside the cab. While he'd been fending off a feline siege, they'd traveled well into the East End.

He frowned. "What the devil are we doing in this neighborhood?"

"Taking the kittens to their new home."

The hackney came to a stop.

"This will be us, then," she announced.

"Here?"

"Yes, here."

She plucked one last intrepid kitten from his sleeve and tucked it into a hamper. The button on Gabe's cuff was left dangling by a thread.

They'd stopped before a building with a simple brick façade. It appeared to be well-tended, considering the environs—but Gabe didn't trust appearances.

"If you mean to release them into the streets, they'll find no shortage of rats hereabouts."

"I'd never dream of doing such a thing."

He knew she wouldn't, and that left him all the more disturbed. Loving homes in this warren of crime and drunkenness came scarce, and not only for kittens. A young, defenseless creature would find no comfort here. Only cold, hunger, and fear.

When Penny moved to exit the cab, he held her back. "Oh, no, you're not."

"Don't be silly. It's perfectly safe."

"What makes you think that?"

"Gabriel." Her eyes widened in disbelief. "You've truly *never* visited the place?"

Why would he have visited this place? He looked around, searching for street names or numbers, any signs posted overhead. He saw only a window with an astonishing number of faces smashed against the glass.

Children's faces.

The truth crept over him. *Penny, what have you done?*

She'd already alighted onto the pavement, carrying hampers in either hand and leaving him with the third. She beckoned him with a tilt of the head. "Come along, then."

"Wait."

He scrambled down from the cab to catch her. Stop her. But she'd already rung the bell. "Hammond told you, didn't he? It couldn't have been anyone else."

She gave him a gentle nudge with her elbow. "Don't be anxious."

"I'm not anxious," he lied.

"Don't be frightened, then."

"I'm not frightened. I'm livid. I'm going to sack that sorry excuse for an architect before he's—"

"Nonsense. You're not angry with Mr. Hammond. You're just put out that I finally found it."

"Found what?"

She gave him a smug little smile. "Your soft underbelly."

The door opened, and they were greeted by a woman of middle age, wearing a white smock over a dark green dress. Upon seeing Penny, she broke into a wide smile. "Lady Penny. What a delight to see you again. Do come in, come in." She waved them through the door.

"I've brought the surprise for the children, as we discussed." Penny lifted a hamper. "And I've brought a surprise for you, as well. Mrs. Baker, may I present Mr. Gabriel Duke. Your elusive benefactor."

"Mr. Duke?" The woman clapped a hand to her chest in shock. She turned to Gabe. "You are most welcome, sir. Most welcome."

Gabe mumbled a perfunctory greeting in reply. This Mrs. Baker wanted to make him welcome, and all he wanted was to make a half turn and walk out the way he'd come in. Next they'd be insisting he take some god-awful tour of the place.

"Perhaps you'd be so good as to give us a tour of the place," Penny suggested.

Gabe intervened. "That won't be necess—"

"Nothing would give me more pleasure," Mrs. Baker replied. "Please, this way. Mr. Duke, I hope you'll find everything to your standards."

It seemed there would be no escaping this.

As they proceeded down the corridor, Gabe spied a small, red-cheeked face peeking at him from behind a door. When he realized he'd been noticed, the child disappeared at once. The boy had been designated a scout, it would seem, judging by the flurry of whispers from behind the door as he went by.

"We have two-and-thirty children in residence at present."

Despite her evident pride in the place, apparently Mrs. Baker didn't believe in lingering—a quality Gabe appreciated. She led them through a bustling kitchen and scullery, then through a dining hall with long rows of tables and benches. They emerged into the corridor, and the matron immediately mounted a flight of stairs.

When Gabe hung back, Penny motioned impatiently for him to follow. He had no choice but to join them, unless he wanted to look like a mulish schoolboy dragging his feet.

"This floor is all bedchambers," Mrs. Baker said when they reached the landing. "Girls to one side, boys to the other. Four to a room."

At her urging, he looked in on one of the chambers. Simply furnished, but neat as a pin. Beds, a washstand, and a row of pegs on the wall on which coats were hung, in diminishing sizes. Beneath each coat sat a pair of sturdy boots, sized accordingly.

Gabe couldn't drag his gaze away from those boots.

Mrs. Baker noticed. "The children do have other shoes for every day, sir. Those are for church and outings."

"Yes, of course." He cleared his throat.

"Come back here, you little scoundrel." Penny hurried after a black kitten who'd escaped his hamper. She lifted the little explorer by the scruff.

Mrs. Baker laughed. "He's eager to meet the children, no doubt. We had best go upstairs straightaway." As Penny and Gabe followed, she forged ahead to the landing. "The younger children have a nursery to the left. The schoolroom is to the right. Naturally, many of the children come to us behind in their lessons, or unused to lessons at all. We're fortunate to have found patient tutors."

She clapped her hands for attention. The pupils bolted to their feet and stood straight. "All gather in the nursery, please. Our guests have brought us a treat."

The children left their slates behind, scrambling over one another to be first to the nursery.

Penny turned to Gabe. "Do you want to do the honors?"

"Why would I want that? They're your kittens."

"Yes, but the children are your charges."

"They are not," he said firmly. He gave this place money. He didn't take the children into his care.

"As you like."

Penny and Mrs. Baker went to the center of the circle and began lifting kittens from the hampers. Upon glimpsing the little balls of fluff, the children cried out with delight.

Boys bartered and argued over which kitten belonged to whom. Penny stepped into the fray, matching feline personalities to human ones.

Gabe disentangled the striped ginger kitten who'd found his trouser leg and looked about for somewhere to deposit it. Over to the side, a younger girl hung back, clutching her knees to her chest and watching the happy mayhem with longing in her eyes.

"Here. Have this one." Gabe placed the kitten in her lap.

When the girl remained hesitant, he crouched at her side and gave the cat a gentle stroke. "Behind the ears, like so. There aren't many creatures who don't like a scratch about the ears."

The girl snatched her hand away. "It's growling."

"Purring," he corrected. "Means he likes you." The tiny creature rubbed and curled in her arms. "You'd better give him a name."

As he stood, Gabe felt eyes on him. When he met Penny's gaze across the sea of furry mayhem, she was wearing that sweetly smug expression he'd come to expect.

The little smile that said, *I told you so.*

Damn it. He would never hear the end of this.

She didn't waste any time starting in on him, either. Upon leaving the charity home, they walked toward a busier street to find a hackney cab back to Bloom Square. They weren't halfway to the next corner when Penny stopped on the pavement and turned to him.

"Gabriel Duke. You are a complete hypocrite."

"A hypocrite? Me?"

"Yes, you. Mr. I-Know-a-Hidden-Treasure-When-I-See-It. You said you know how to spot undervalued things. Undervalued people. And yet you persist in selling yourself short. If I'm the crown jewels in camouflage, you're a . . ." She churned the air with one hand. ". . . a diamond tiara."

He grimaced.

"Fine, you can be something manlier. A thick, knobby scepter. Will that suffice?"

"I suppose it's an improvement."

"For weeks, you've been insisting you haven't the slightest idea what it means to give a creature a loving home. 'I'm too ruthless, Penny. I'm only motivated by self-interest, Penny. I'm a bad, bad man, Penny.' And all this time, you've been running an orphanage? I could kick you."

"I'm not running an orphanage. I give the orphanage money. That's all."

"You gave them kittens."

"No, *you* gave them kittens."

"You sent them gifts at Christmas. Playthings and sweets and geese to be roasted for their dinner."

"It was the only business I could attend to on Christmas,

and I don't like to waste the day. All the banks and offices are closed."

She skewered him with a look. "Really. You expect me to believe that?"

He pushed a hand through his hair. "What is your aim with this interrogation?"

"I want you to admit the truth. You are giving those children a home. A place of warmth and safety, and yes, even love. Meanwhile, you are stubbornly denying yourself all the same things."

"I can't be denying myself if it's something I don't want."

"Home isn't something a person *wants*. It's something every last one of us *needs*. And it's not too late for you, Gabriel." She gentled her voice. "You could have that for yourself."

"What, with you?"

She flinched at his mocking tone. "I didn't say that."

"But that's what you meant. Isn't it? You have this idea that you'll rescue me. Bring me in from the cold, put me on a leash, have me eating out of your hand. I'm not a lost puppy, and I don't need saving. You're being a fool."

Her chin jutted toward him. "Don't mock me. Don't you dare mock me just because you're afraid."

"You think *I'm* afraid. You don't know the meaning of fear. Or hunger, or cold, or loneliness."

"I know the meaning of love. I know that you deserve it. I know you are too good a man to be alone."

"Don't say such things," he warned her. "Don't make me prove you wrong."

She put her hand on his arm. "I'm not wrong."

He tipped his head back and cursed the sky. There was nothing for it. He couldn't convince her with words. She'd never understand unless he showed her the truth.

"Come along, then." He pulled her arm through his, roughly. "We're going to take a little stroll, you and I."

She pulled against his arm. "Where are you taking me?"

"On a tour of Hell."

PENNY STUMBLED AS he pulled her around a corner, off the bustling street of shops and onto a smaller, crowded lane. Passing women eyed her with a mix of curiosity and contempt. Men raked her with lascivious gazes.

"Stay close." His voice was dark and bitter. "This is where the ladies of the evening hawk their wares, and in a neighborhood like this one, it's evening 'round the clock."

Penny's face heated. As they stepped off the pavement, she lifted her hem to keep it out of the muck.

He clucked his tongue. "Mind you don't raise those skirts too high. Another inch, and you'll be mistaken for one of them."

The air was foul with the stench of filth and gin. People called and whistled to them from glassless windows and doorways on either side of the lane.

"Let's have a little tour of my childhood, shall we? I was likely conceived in one of the many rooms above this street. Fathered by a man who could be any of dozens, and born to a prostitute who was a slave to gin. Nonetheless, she made a better mother than many. She didn't abandon me to die of exposure. Not as an infant, at least."

Together, they weaved through a dense warren of twisting, fog-smothered passages. Derelict buildings crowded either side of the alleys. Streets so narrow, one couldn't see the sky.

Penny could have never retraced their steps. If he left her alone here, she would wander helpless in the fog forever.

But Gabriel never paused—and she didn't suppose it was because masculine pride made him reluctant to ask for directions. He knew precisely where he was going. Every twist and turn belonged to a map etched in his mind.

They passed a beggar woman with her palm outstretched for a farthing. Penny slowed on instinct, but he tugged her past.

"There's a cellar down that way that used to have a broken window." He tossed out the observation as if he were pointing out a church with unremarkable architecture. "I spent a winter sleeping in it. Along with a great many rats."

She tripped on a stone, and her boot sloshed into a shallow river of . . . well, of things probably best left unidentified. Gray gutter muck splashed her hem.

They ventured farther into the maze of tenements and doss-houses. Every minute or two, he paused to point out, in a tone of complete indifference, a doorway that could offer as many as six huddled urchins shelter from the wintry wind, or the baker's shop where it was easiest to steal bread. It wasn't difficult to imagine him here as a child. Everywhere they turned, she glimpsed the pale, grime-streaked face of a boy dressed in rags. A face that could have been Gabriel's, once.

By the time he brought them to an abrupt halt, Penny's feet were aching, her lungs were burning, and her heart was in tatters.

"Here's the best part." He took her by the shoulders and turned her to face the other side of the street. "That gin house, right there . . . ? That's where my mother sold me."

"Sold you? A mother can't sell her child."

"Happens in the rookery all the time. Husbands sell wives. Parents sell children. I was sold to the pub's owner."

"You said you were in the workhouse."

"I was, after the owner pushed me out the door. But not before I spent three years in that gin house. Hauling coal, carrying water, scrubbing vomit from the same floors I slept on at night."

"Gabriel . . ." She wanted to beg him to stop, but that didn't seem fair. She couldn't refuse to hear it, when he'd *lived* it.

"Do you want to know what those years of my life were worth? Can you guess the price a mother sets on her own child?"

Penny suspected she knew the answer. A sick feeling gathered in her stomach as he reached inside his coat.

"A shilling." He produced the coin from his pocket and held it up for her to see. "That's what I was worth. A single shilling."

"Don't say that. You were always worth more than a shilling."

"You're right," he said. "A shilling was an absurdly low price. If she weren't so desperate to buy gin, my mother could have haggled for as much as a half crown."

"I won't listen to you speak that way." Penny wrested the coin from his hand and tossed it on the ground.

"Oh, you will. You will listen, and you will hear."

He grabbed her by the wrist and led her down a dark pathway scarcely wide enough for the two of them to walk side by side. When they'd reached a place out of view, he turned to her.

"Do not speak to me of homes or comforts or love," he said through gritted teeth. "There is nothing the two of us could share. Nothing."

"Why not?"

He tugged at his hair. "Look around you. We're not in Bloom Square, Penny."

"I don't care whether you were born in a gutter or a palace, whether your mother was a beggar or a queen. It doesn't matter to me."

"Perhaps it matters to me. Have you thought of that? You're so enamored with the idea of deigning to be with a lowborn man, you haven't stopped to wonder if I want anything to do with a highborn lady."

"I thought you didn't believe in class distinctions."

"This isn't a matter of different classes. We come from different *worlds*. When you were eating buttered toast and jam for your tea, I was starving. While your nursemaid was dressing you in crisp white pinafores, I went without shoes. While you had candles burning in every room, fires laid every night, quilts heaped atop a warmed bed—I shivered in the street, in the dark. Waking at the slightest noise, ready to flee at any moment. I couldn't trust a soul in the world, and you've lived to the age of six-and-twenty believing every problem can be cured with a goddamned kitten."

"I do not believe every problem can be cured with a kitten. I do believe in love. And perhaps love can't cure every problem, but it makes the wounds heal a bit faster, with fewer scars. I understand why you don't believe that. How could you, if you've never known it yourself? But perhaps you should give it a try. Let someone care for you, Gabriel. It doesn't have to be me, but—" She broke off. "No. Forget that last. It does have to be me. I'm generous, but I'm not *that* generous. When it comes to this, I'm not willing to share."

"Penny, I haven't the faintest idea what you're on about."

"I love you." She exhaled in a huff. "There. Is that simple enough?"

Chapter Twenty

*S*imple?

Gabe stared at her. No, it wasn't simple. It was incomprehensible.

"I love you," she repeated.

"And what of it? You love everyone."

"Not this way." She reached for his hand and gave it a tender caress. "I love you."

"Penny, stop." Emotion held his throat in a vise. "You have to stop."

"I don't think I could if I tried. And I don't want to try." She brought his hand to her lips and kissed it.

Her gesture was wrong, so wrong. Gentlemen kissed ladies' hands, not the reverse. And they most certainly didn't do so in reeking, filthy slums.

His blood pounded at the door of his soul, and it would not be denied.

She kissed him first, bless her, moaning softly against his mouth, granting him permission to take control. He slid his hands to her backside and lifted, pushing her up against the brick wall.

"Here," he rasped. "Now."

"Yes."

They raced for the same goal, her tugging at the buttons of his trousers, him hiking her skirts. By the time her touch skimmed the shaft of his cock, he was already primed and aching. When he slid two fingers into her wet heat, triumph surged through him.

Yes, she wanted this. She wanted him.

He withdrew his touch and brought his fingers to his mouth, sucking them clean. God, she was sweet. And he was depraved, base.

She arched against him in a silent plea. He couldn't wait another moment. Reaching between them, he took his cock in hand and guided it home.

She gasped as his first thrust sank deep. Her fingernails bit into the nape of his neck, making him wince with joy.

She came quickly, her inner muscles clenching into a slick fist. He thrust through every sharp, keening wave of her pleasure, shredding her frock to tatters against the brick wall. Sheathing himself to the crude, thick hilt. Faster, harder. Her soft, rhythmic sobs of passion mingled with his harsh, guttural sounds.

He was surely hurting her, and yet he couldn't stop. He couldn't even bring himself to slow down. If he paused for a single instant, the truth would catch up with him. He'd be forced to reckon with the fact that he was taking her in an alleyway like a whoring brute. And he'd be reminded, once again, that he didn't deserve her—could never hope to deserve her.

So he galloped onward, desperate. Racing through that dark, lonely tunnel of yearning until he emerged into blinding light. The place where eternity was measured in heartbeats, and nothing mattered that wasn't joy.

In the aftermath, he slumped against her, shuddering with the pleasure of release.

And then, as the pleasure ebbed, the inevitable shame and disgust crept in. He looked around them, wrinkling his nose at the reeking alleyway and the puddled God-knew-what at his feet. Bile rose in his throat. He forced himself to meet her eyes—those lovely blue eyes. Eyes shining with an emotion he called foolishness and she called love. Perhaps they were one and the same.

Whatever name it went by, that emotion had found its way inside him, stretching his ribs and carving out space in his chest. Settling in.

How had she done it? Of all people, he knew how to lock up his heart, shutter the windows, bar the doors. She'd wormed through a keyhole somehow, made herself at home.

Damn it, Gabe couldn't let her stay. He knew how to force an eviction with a ruthless, cold-blooded strength. He'd allowed his willpower to slacken over recent weeks.

Now it was time to flex.

The danger was too great. Not to her reputation—her life was hers to do as she wished—but to her heart. Her lovely, shining soul. If he destroyed her trusting, generous nature, he wouldn't know how to live with himself.

Gabe lifted her in his arms and carried her out of the labyrinth of the rookery. He wasn't going to allow any further damage to her frocks. Not on his account.

When they reached the main thoroughfare, he waved for a hackney cab. "Mayfair," he told the driver. "Bloom Square."

He tucked Penny inside the cab, carefully settling her on the seat. She moved over to make room for him.

"I'm sorry," he said.

"For what?"

"For this." He slammed the door of the hackney shut and motioned to the driver.

"Gabriel, wai—"

The cab carried her and her objection into the London streets. When they'd gone, Gabe turned on his heel and walked the other way.

There. It was over. Forever.

IF GABRIEL THOUGHT this was over, he was fooling himself. Penny was not so easily deterred. However, she decided to allow him a day to recover his senses. When the hackney deposited her at home in Bloom Square, she wanted nothing more than to have a bath and perhaps a healthy cry.

However, when she entered the house, it became evident that both bath and tears would have to wait.

Aunt Caroline looked over her muddied, bedraggled frock. "Oh, Penelope."

"What a delight to see you, Aunt Caroline." With a dejected sigh, Penny dropped into a chair, unable to think of anything else to do. "Have you been waiting long?"

"Too long, I daresay. I've been having a disturbing conversation with your parrot."

"I don't suppose 'I love you' was part of the dialogue?"

Her aunt's eyes were steely. "No."

Drat. Penny couldn't convince anyone to believe those words, it seemed—man or bird.

"I've also been reading." Her aunt lifted a copy of the *Prattler*. "When I said I wanted to see you in the society column, this is *not* what I meant."

"I'm not in it."

"Don't lie to me." Her aunt held up the page and shook it at her. "It's right here in black and white. 'Unidentified woman'? That can only be you. Who else would attend a fete and leave before speaking to a soul in attendance?"

Penny covered her eyes with one hand and moaned. "I'm trying, Aunt Caroline. I truly am. The otter swam away, and the farm animals are headed to the country in a few days' time. Just this morning, we delivered the kittens to . . ." She couldn't bring herself to complete the sentence. "I'm trying."

And yet, somehow, all her effort wasn't enough. Not for her aunt; not for Gabriel. Not even for the parrot.

"Now about this ball your detestable neighbor is giving."

"You needn't worry. I don't plan to attend."

"Oh, yes, you will." Her aunt harrumphed. "You are running out of time. If you wish to remain in London, there is only one way certain to succeed. An engagement. Or at least the prospect of one. If you have a suitor or two waiting in the wings, Bradford won't drag you from Town."

"If it was so easy to line up a suitor or two in the wings, I wouldn't be in this situation."

"We both know very well that you haven't been trying. And this ball is your ideal opportunity. The Duke of Ruin has a great many lords and well-placed gentlemen dangling on the loose threads of his tailcoat. They won't fail to answer his invitation." She rose to her feet. "In short, you—and your handsome dowry—will be surrounded by financially desperate men. You'll never have a better chance at snaring one."

"As always, Aunt Caroline, you do wonders for my confidence." Penny accompanied her aunt to the door.

"It's given me no pleasure to watch you hide away all these years." Aunt Caroline patted her shoulder fondly. "Believe it or not, I'm pulling for you. You deserve to be an *identified* woman."

Penny was momentarily speechless. "Thank you."

Of all the places to find reassurance, she never would have expected it to come from her demanding Aunt Caroline. Her aunt's gesture wasn't precisely effusive, but Penny wasn't in a position to be choosy. She would take what she could get.

This rare display of affection concluded, her aunt opened the door to leave. "I'll see you at the ball, then. Do try to look . . ."

"Presentable," Penny finished. "I know."

Her aunt clucked her tongue. "Presentable won't do on this occasion, I'm afraid. If you want to win this little wager of ours, you had better look magnificent."

Magnificent.

Penny had no interest in accumulating desperate suitors of the *ton*. She had a singular interest in winning the heart of one man, which meant she'd be betting everything she had on love. If attending his ball and looking magnificent could help in the least . . . ?

Well, then. She had little time to waste.

Chapter Twenty-One

*H*urry along." Gabe kicked the blocks in place to keep the wagon wheels from moving, while Ash and Chase adjusted the wooden ramp to the wagon bed. "We need to have this done before the ladies return from the shops."

"What's the hurry?" Chase said.

Gabe hedged. "So they can arrive at Ashbury's country estate before nightfall. Safer for men and beasts that way."

In truth, he didn't want to risk meeting with Penny. Conversation was to be avoided at all costs. Nothing she could say would change his mind, and nothing he could say would make it any easier.

"Come on, then." He clapped his hands. "Angus is waiting. We need to have Marigold loaded before I can settle the hens."

"We have a problem," Ashbury called from the mews. "The goat won't move. She keeps stamping at the ground and bleating. Her belly doesn't look right. It keeps bunching and shifting."

Chase and Gabe followed him into the stalls.

"Penny always says the creature has sensitive digestion," Gabe said. "Perhaps the goat ate something that didn't agree with her."

"Or maybe it's something else," Chase said.

"Like what?"

"I've been reading up on things." Chase jammed his thumb in his waistband. "You know, since it will be Alexandra's time soon. Humans and goats are different animals, but some qualities among females must be universal. A contracting abdomen and a great deal of moaning being two of those qualities."

Ashbury wiped his brow with his sleeve. "Chase, what the hell are you saying?"

"I'm saying I think Marigold is preparing to give birth."

Gabe smacked his gloves against his thigh. "Damn it, I knew it. I knew this goat was breeding."

Ashbury braced his hands on his hips. "She's been too free with her favors, eh? The scarlet strumpet."

"Watch yourself," Gabe snapped. "Marigold's not that kind of goat."

"Yes, let's not shame the poor girl," Chase added. "Perhaps it was star-crossed love."

"Bringing this back to reality for a moment, if you don't mind," Gabe said. "What the hell are we supposed to do?"

"We definitely can't move her in this state," Ashbury said.

"Don't animals know what to do on their own?" Chase asked. "It's instinct. All we need to do is wait."

And so they waited.

And waited.

After what felt like hours, Gabe paced the stall back and forth. "Should she really be making that noise?"

Ashbury shrugged. "Have you ever heard a woman in her labors?"

"No," Gabe cautiously replied.

"I regret to inform you, it doesn't sound much different than this."

"Why are you telling me these things?" Chase complained.

"That's it," Gabe said. "I'm sending for a veterinarian. Two of them. Three. We'll wait on their advice."

And so they waited.

And waited.

After what felt like hours, no veterinarian had appeared.

Marigold braced her head against the side of her stall, pawing the ground and bleating. Her tail lifted.

"Hold a moment. I think something's happening." Gabe beckoned to the other two. "One of you should look."

"You do it, Ash," Chase said.

"Why me?"

"Because your wife's given birth. You said that you were there."

"I said I heard it. I didn't look."

Chase rose to his feet and went to the hind end of the goat. "I'll look. I'm not afraid. I intend to be there for every moment of the miracle of my own child's birth." He crouched and squinted. "And . . . I've changed my mind."

Chase retreated to the far corner of the stall and sat on a crate, his pallor having turned a pale, sickly green.

"Fine," Ashbury said. "I'll do it. If I could stomach my own injuries from that rocket blast, I can stomach this." He went to look, then reeled a step backward. "Oh, God. Something's coming out."

"Of course something's coming out," Gabe said. "A baby goat."

"No," Ash said grimly. "No."

"If it's not a goat, then what is it?"

"It's a punishment for all my earthly sins, is what it is."

"Describe it," Chase said. "I've done my research. What does it look like?"

"Picture a soap bubble," Ashbury said slowly. "Then picture a soap bubble blown in Hell, by a demon with a phlegmy cold."

Chase doubled over. "I think I just vomited in my mouth."

"Maybe it's the placenta," Ashbury suggested.

"Ash, you idiot." Chase had his head between his knees. "The placenta comes after. That's why they call it the afterbirth. Didn't you do any reading when Emma was pregnant?"

"Yes. I did all sorts of reading. I read every other type of book to take my mind off the entire affair."

"Rather cowardly, Ashbury."

"Yes, and you're an exemplar of courage over there, heaving your luncheon into a milk pail. Reading about it does nothing but tell you everything that can go wrong. I didn't need that. I could imagine too many things going wrong on my own."

"Thank God one of us prepared." Gathering himself, Chase wiped his brow with his sleeve. "That thing you're seeing is no doubt the bag of waters. Also known as the amniotic sac."

Ash stood up. "It went back in. Jesus. It went back in."

Gabe turned to Chase. "What does that mean?"

"I don't know what that means."

"You just said you've done your reading."

"That wasn't in the book."

"Wait, wait. She's pushing it out again. There's more of it this time, and it looks . . . phlegmier."

Chase retched. "Ash, please."

"You're right, I think it is the bag of waters."

"Well, what do you see inside? A nose? A leg?"

"How should I know? Why does it even matter what part it is?"

"A nose means it's headfirst. And that's good. A leg would be bad. I think."

"You think?"

"It depends on whether it's a foreleg or hind leg."

"How do we tell which it is?"

"I don't know!" Chase exclaimed. "I'm not a veterinarian!"

Ashbury threw up his arms and walked in a circle. "Now it's gone back in again."

Gabe lost his patience. He didn't know where the hell the veterinarian was, but it didn't matter. Sooner or later, Penny would return home, and Gabe would rather die than be the one to tell her Marigold was gone. "Listen, the two of you. This goat is not dying tonight. We need to stop bickering and do something."

The three of them gathered at the hind end of the goat. On her next contraction, they gathered their fortitude and crouched behind Marigold for a closer examination.

Chase sucked in his breath. "That's not a foreleg or a hind leg. That's a tail."

"Is that good or bad?"

"It's bad. Possibly very bad. That means the baby is in a breech position. She'll have a devil of a time delivering it that way. One or both of them could die."

"I told you, they're not going to die," Gabe said. "Not if there's anything we can do to prevent it. And there must be something we can do. What's it say in the book, Reynaud?"

"With a woman, the midwife will try to change the baby's position. So if both Marigold and the kid are going to survive, I think . . . I think we have to turn it."

Ashbury tilted his head. "How do you do that?"

"By fiddling a waltz," Chase quipped. "By reaching inside the womb, of course. With, you know, a hand."

The three men looked from one to the other, slowly pushing their hands into their pockets as they did.

Gabe looked at Chase. "It should be you."

"Why me?"

"You've read the book, and you're the smallest."

"I am not the smallest. I'm taller than both of you."

"Yes, but you're slender." Ashbury reached for his friend's arm and lifted it. "Look at that. I'd go so far as to say willowy."

Chase snatched his arm away. "I am not willowy, for Christ's sake. Why not you?" He took Ash's arm and flopped it up and down. "You're scarred and withered. You won't even feel the sliminess."

"We don't have time for this." With a curse, Gabe nudged the other two out of the way. He didn't need to read a book on childbirth to know that the longer this went on, the greater the danger to both Marigold and her kid. "I'll do it."

Gabe didn't know what the hell he was doing, but he was dead certain about one thing: He had to be in love with Lady Penelope Campion. Nothing less could have persuaded him to do this.

Penny, this is for you.

He rolled his sleeve to his biceps, drew a deep breath through his mouth, and shook out his hand. "I'm going in."

Chapter Twenty-Two

"Gabriel?" Penny dashed through the door, searching wildly through the rooms. "Gabriel!"

"Down here." The call came from the kitchen below.

She clattered down the stairs at once.

Ash's errand boy had found them at the draper's and told her there'd been some dire matter and she must return home at once. On the carriage ride back, a hundred terrible possibilities had sprinted through her mind, invoking terror but never pausing to be reasoned away.

When she emerged into the kitchen and saw him sitting by the fire, alive and unhurt, her breath returned for the first time in an hour.

She rushed to his side. "What happened?"

"This happened." He shifted his arms to reveal a bundle of tiny, knobby joints and fluffy patches of black and white.

A newborn goat.

"Oh, my goodness." She knelt behind him, peering over his shoulder. "Surely not Marigold?"

"I told you so," he said irritably.

As if she'd be intimidated by gruff words from a man cradling a newborn goat in his arms. She'd always known he had a capacity for gentleness.

I told you so, too.

She reached to stroke the little goat's fur.

Gabriel's shoulder muscle flinched in annoyance. "My shirt was ruined, I'll have you know. Completely unsalvageable. And then this runtish little thing wouldn't stop shivering."

"Would it help if I told you that I've never found you so wildly attractive as I do in this moment?"

"No."

She smiled and reached into her pocket to withdraw a parcel wrapped in brown paper and tied with twine. "Here. You need a biscuit."

He bristled. "I'm not the goddamned parrot."

"Of course not. Your vocabulary is much worse." She held the buttery round of shortbread to his lips. "Nicola made it fresh this morning. Go on, then. You know how you are on an empty stomach. Take this for now, and then I'll find you a proper supper."

He gave in, snapping the shortbread from her fingers with his teeth and devouring it in a single bite. "Where on earth have you been?"

She offered him another biscuit, and this time he accepted it without argument. "The shops. Emma helped me choose lace and stockings at the draper's. That's where Ash's errand boy caught up with us."

"Well, while you were dithering over lace, your goat nearly died. And so did her kid. For that matter, it was a close call for me, Ashbury, and Reynaud, too."

She paused in the act of brushing a crumb from the corner of his lips. "You delivered it yourselves? The three of you?"

"Mostly me. They were no help at all. At least Chase had this on him." He shifted the baby goat to one arm and handed her a silver object approximately the size of her hand.

Penny examined the makeshift feeding bottle fashioned from a silver flask. In place of a teat, he'd severed the fingertip of a leather glove, stretched it over the uncapped opening, and pricked a hole at the end.

"Marigold was too weak to let the baby nurse," he explained.

"We had to milk her, which was a miserable adventure on its own."

"This is ingenious. I doubt Nicola could have devised anything better. Though I do hope you emptied it of brandy first."

"Believe me, we'd already drained the brandy ourselves." He heaved a weary sigh. "It was a close thing, Penny. We nearly lost them both."

"But you did beautifully. Marigold survived, and he's perfect." She tilted her head. "Or is it a she?"

"Damned if I know. Never thought to investigate, and I don't care to. After today, I've seen enough of goat hindquarters to last me a lifetime."

She laughed a little. Hooking one of the baby goat's hind legs with a finger, she made her own examination. "It's a he. And he's darling."

"The veterinarian's already come and gone. He said Marigold would recover, but we mustn't be surprised if she refuses to nurse. Or she might reject the kid entirely. It happens, he said. Sometimes—" He stroked the kid's velvety ear with a single fingertip, as though he were afraid he might break it. "Sometimes, if she's ill or weakened, the mother knows she can't save both her offspring and herself. So she abandons her baby in order to survive."

Penny's heart squeezed. She rested her chin on his shoulder. "What a heartbreaking choice for a mother to make."

He stared into the fire. Amber warmth and cool shadows fought for dominion over his hard, unshaven jaw. "She's a goat. Goats have instincts. People have choices."

"You're right. People do have choices. Sometimes they make cruel, unforgivable ones. But we can choose to keep our little corner of the world warm and safe." She slid her arms around his chest and hugged him tight. "If Marigold isn't able to care for him, we will."

She reached to take the kid from his arms, but he pulled away.

"Oh, no, you don't. I'm not letting you coo over him. This one is mine, and I'll do with him as I please. Send him to Ashbury's estate. Banish him to a parsnip farm. Fatten him up for Christmas dinner. I told you she was breeding, and you didn't believe me. I delivered the thing, and you weren't here. You have no say in the matter."

"I suppose that's only fair."

Although, watching him tenderly hold the little dear, she didn't feel too worried about the kid's future. Nor Gabriel's. She would find it easier to part with him knowing he had some love in his life. Even if it came from a bottle-fed baby goat.

"Have you given him a name?"

"Considering what an insufferable pain he is, I'm leaning toward Ashbury."

Penny chuckled. "I'll tell you a secret about Ash. His Christian name is George. He hates it."

He nodded. "George it is."

George stirred and nosed at Gabriel's chest and gave a warbling, plaintive bleat.

"We should take him back to the mews, to be near Marigold," Penny suggested, "so they don't lose the scent of each other. Perhaps she'll feel strong enough to nurse him now. If not, I'll help with the milking."

GEORGE TOOK ANOTHER flask of milk a few hours later, and then again sometime after midnight, by the light of a lantern.

At some point, Penny must have fallen asleep, because she woke to the first glow of daylight. They'd leaned against each another in one corner of the stall, atop an uncomfortable heap of fresh straw.

Gabriel nudged her with his shoulder. "Look."

The newborn goat was standing on his own wobbly legs, taking drunken steps. When he toppled sideways, he bleated indignantly.

Gabriel started to reach for him, but Penny held him back. "Wait."

Marigold roused herself and ambled over to her kid, licking him about the head until George lurched and swayed himself to his hooves, and when he nosed at her swollen underside, she allowed him to nurse.

"Oh. That's lovely." Penny snuggled under Gabriel's arm.

"Thank God she finally took to him," he said.

"How could she not? Look how adorable he is. Best little goat in the world."

For a few minutes, they watched mother and kid in exhausted silence. Then Gabriel caught Penny's hand and brought it to his chest.

"They will all believe I ruined you," he said quietly. "Married you for your money."

They will. Penny tried not to betray how her heart leapt at those two simple words. Not "they would," or "they might," but "they will." "I don't care."

"Others will care. Your family. Your peers. In society's eyes, I'm unfit to stand on your carpet, much less share your bed."

She smiled. "I've shared my bed with far muddier, furrier creatures."

"You're the daughter of an earl. I'm a bastard from the rookery."

"You're a self-made marvel of business acumen. A brilliant financier. Besides, just look at Ash and Chase. They married a seamstress and a governess, respectively. It can be done."

"It's not the same. Emma and Alexandra were elevated by those matches. You'd be the lady who lowered herself to marry a commoner. Not merely a commoner, but a criminal from the streets. The rumors would be vicious."

She lifted her head. "And you believe I care what the gossips say? You can't think so meanly of me as that."

"I think that meanly of myself." His eyes were dark with an

emptiness that yearned to be filled. "You cannot understand. I can be wealthy as sin, live in the grandest houses, wear the finest clothes—and underneath, I'm still that starving, ragged boy from the streets. The hunger, the resentment . . . They never go away. I'll never belong in the *ton*. I can take their money. I can command their fear. But I will never have their acceptance, much less their respect."

"You'll have my love. And if I have yours, that will be more than enough."

"It's romantic to think so. But years from now, when the respectable ladies still snub you in church, or when our children come home bruised or crying because their schoolmates were cruel . . . ?"

She laid her head against his shoulder. "Then I will tell them an amusing story about a hedgehog in a ballroom and give them a hug and perhaps a kitten to hold, and you and I will remind ourselves that children are stronger than anyone suspects."

His chest rose and fell with a heavy breath. He released her hand and eased out of her embrace. "I need to go bathe and dress. I have a hundred things to do to prepare for the ball."

She cringed. "Do I truly need to attend?"

"Yes, you truly do." He brushed the hay from his trousers. "A lady must attend her own engagement ball."

Penny sat up straight. "Gabriel Duke. I know you did not just propose to me in the mews, without so much as going down on one knee, while my hair is a bird's nest and we both smell like goat."

"I didn't propose to you." He swung his arms into his coat. Before disappearing, he gave her a slight, mischievous grin and a single syllable that had her heart cartwheeling in her chest. "Yet."

Chapter Twenty-Three

$\mathcal{B}$etween the hasty campaign of plumbing repairs, the hanging of wall coverings and draperies, and other frantic last-minute work on the former Wendleby residence, Gabe had put up with a great deal of noise in recent days. However, on returning to the house the following afternoon, he heard the most unexpected sound yet.

Laughter. Feminine laughter. He followed the sound to the drawing room, and when he saw the source, he couldn't believe his eyes.

Mrs. Burns.

He cleared his throat. "What's going on in here?"

The housekeeper wheeled to face him. "Mr. Duke." She tried to school her expression, but not fast enough. Laughter had transformed the housekeeper's appearance. Her countenance was not dour and pale, but lively. Warm.

Human.

"I could have sworn I heard laughter."

"Did you, sir?"

"Yes. Perhaps it was a ghost? Or maybe a raving madwoman chained in the attic."

"It's my fault." Penny moved into view, carrying George in her arms. "I came to ask if there was anything I could do to help with the preparations."

"To begin, you could take the goat back to the mews. This

carpet was rescued from a French chateau. Its owner went to the guillotine. That kind of provenance comes dear."

"I know, but look." She set the kid on the floor, and George gamboled about the room, making high-pitched, chirping bleats. "He prances. Sideways. It's adorable."

The kid attempted a leap and stumbled drunkenly to the side, landing on the carpet before picking himself up and shaking his head.

Even Gabe had to admit it *was* rather adorable. Especially the way the newborn goat made its way to him from across the room, stopping at his boots to issue an entitled bleat. He was a demanding little thing already.

Gabe bent to give the kid a scratch between the ears.

"I'll take him back to his mother." Mrs. Burns gathered the baby goat in her arms.

As she was leaving, the housekeeper paused. She addressed Gabe directly. "Mr. Duke, you may trust that I—and all the house staff—are committed to making the ball a success. The heart of the matter is, this house *does* have a grand legacy. A legacy that I regard as my own. You are part of it now."

He arched an eyebrow. "I trust this means you take pride in your service. Not that you intend to trap my soul in a painting and hang it above the drawing room fireplace."

The housekeeper gave him a conspiratorial look. "Please don't tell Mr. Hammond. It's been too amusing, winding him up. I couldn't help it. But I'll put an end to it now."

"Oh, please. Feel free to continue. He deserves it."

"As you wish, sir." The housekeeper squared her shoulders, banished the smile from her face, and summoned her usual solemn tone of voice. "Far be it from me to disobey my employer's wishes."

The woman never failed to surprise.

Once the housekeeper had left them alone, Penny crossed the room to give him a sweet kiss. "I didn't expect to see you this afternoon. I was told you had urgent business matters."

"I had a great many calls to make. While you're here, I have something for you." He reached into his pocket and withdrew the stiffened bit of pasteboard scrawled with names in looping, elegant script.

She took the paper and turned it over to examine both sides. "What is it?"

"It's your dance card."

"My dance card?"

Gabe watched her closely as she scanned the card. He'd arranged dances—every set of the evening—to an assortment of highly placed, well-to-do, unmarried men. Peers, lords, gentlemen of note. All of them from families that stretched back generations, if not centuries.

"I don't understand. Why would you do this?"

"I'll be occupied with hosting, so I arranged suitable partners in advance."

She scanned the card. "Lord Brooking for the gavotte. A set of country dances promised to Sir Neville Chartwell. A midnight waltz with a royal duke?" Her eyebrows soared. "An ordinary duke wasn't good enough?"

"No man is good enough, where you're concerned. But these are the best ones available at the moment."

"Shouldn't I be the one to decide with whom I dance? Or if I wish to dance at all?"

"That's just it, Penny. Left to your own devices, you *won't* dance at all. You'll stand at the edge of the room. A wallflower."

She pushed the card back at him. "I don't want to dance with these men. I don't care about them. I care about you."

"Then do this *for* me," he said, unable to hide his mounting frustration. "I planned this entire occasion with you in mind, starting right after that asinine masquerade. The right guests, the best orchestra, the finest foods and wine. This ball was never about selling the house. It was meant to be your second chance at a proper debut."

"Why?"

"Because you deserve it. Because you've spent too many years hiding in the corners or among the shrubbery, when you ought to be the light of any party."

"That's lovely and thoughtful. But I'm going to marry you. It's not important anymore."

"It's more important than ever. Do you think *I* want to watch you dance with other men? Hell, no. I want the guests to see you dance. Before we announce our engagement, I want everyone to know you could have had your choice of any gentleman. Everyone, including your family. Your aunt, your brother."

"My brother? He won't be arriving until next week."

"I sent a rider to intercept him with an invitation to the ball. He's traveling in stages so he can arrive in time. I ought to speak with your father, of course. But I'm not patient enough to wait for correspondence from India."

She fell away from him, frowning. "You did all this without asking me first?"

Gabe was so taken aback, so unprepared for her displeasure, he needed time to search for words. "I planned it as a surprise. A happy one, I thought. If we marry—"

"*When* we marry."

He wreathed his arms about her waist and drew her close. "*When* we marry, I insist on doing it in the proper fashion, with your family's blessing. A lengthy engagement, a grand wedding."

"I don't need a grand wedding."

"I need you to have one. I'm the Duke of Ruin. If we rush to the altar in a slapdash manner, everyone will believe I compromised you in an effort to steal your dowry. Or even to purposely bring your family low and drag an aristocrat's title through the gutters where I was born. We'll never avoid rumor entirely, but speaking with your brother before announcing a betrothal is the least I can do."

She touched a hand to her temple. "I understand that you had good motives. I just wish you'd warned me."

"I didn't want you to worry. I've taken care of everything."

"I won't do this. I cannot do this." The dance card shook in her white-knuckled grip. "You don't understand."

"Then explain it to me. Because right now, it feels like you're making excuses. Hiding yourself again. Or perhaps hiding me." A sick feeling came over him. "That's it, isn't it? You're ashamed."

"No. Never. How could you think such a thing?"

"I'm good enough to fuck in an alleyway, but you don't want to be seen with me in public. Much less introduce me to your family. Is that it?" He took the dance card and held it before her face. "This is important. Unless people see that you have alternatives, they'll never believe you wanted me."

I won't believe you wanted me.

Gabe needed to be certain that she didn't see him as an escape—an easy way to avoid her rightful place in society. Or worse yet, as a last resort. She had options, and she deserved to know that before throwing them all away on him.

"Curse you, Gabriel. You are astonishingly self-absorbed." She dashed away a tear with an impatient swipe of her wrist. "I know it must be difficult to imagine, but sometimes I do have a thought or feeling that isn't about you."

"Then share it with me."

"I've never shared it with anyone. And even though I want to, I—" Her voice broke. She looked away, eyes red and welling with tears. "It's not that easy."

Gabe passed a hand over his face. She was right. He was being a self-absorbed jackass.

He drew a deep, slow breath, easing out from under the instinctive, defensive anger that had become as natural to him as breathing. In the past, that fire had kept him warm at night when the ground frosted beneath his bare feet. It had filled his belly when he hadn't eaten so much as a crust in days. It was the force that kept him pushing forward, struggling against the full weight of a world designed to hold him back.

That anger had been his companion when he didn't have a friend in the world.

But he wasn't alone anymore.

With Penny in his life, everything was different. *He* had to be different. If she was in danger, she was his to guard. If she was hurting, she was his to protect.

He drew her close, murmuring clumsy apologies in her ear. Taking her by the shoulders, he guided her to a divan, where they settled side by side.

"Tell me."

Chapter Twenty-Four

Tell me, he said.

Penny's heart clenched like a fist. Did she dare? Unburdening herself of those memories meant unpacking them from their strongbox, dragging their ugliness into the light. She'd avoided it for so long, hoping that someday the time would feel right to confide in someone.

Now she understood that the time would never feel right. There could be no feeling right about things that were so very wrong. No, there would never be a right time to share the memories. But there could be a right person to tell.

And the right person was here, holding her in his arms.

"When I was a girl, my father had a friend. Mr. Lambert." The name tasted foul on her lips, so she rushed on. "At the end of each summer, he came to visit. He and Father would go hunting, shooting. The usual autumn sport, you know."

He nodded, waiting for her to go on.

"And ever since I was a young girl, he'd . . . Well, he'd always made a favorite of me."

Penny could see it now, looking back, how early he'd started gaining her trust. Whenever he visited, he brought her lavish presents and demanded only a kiss in return. He'd given her attention at times when she felt overlooked, left out of Bradford and Timothy's games. The year she was learning her letters, he would pat his knee in invitation and she would go run to sit on his lap. *Come, poppet. Show me how well you read.*

And when he held her a bit tighter than she would have liked, or placed his hand beneath her skirt to stroke her leg, Penny didn't complain. She adored him.

"I looked forward to his visits more than I looked forward to my birthday, or Christmas. He always made me feel special."

Gabriel quietly took her hand in his.

"He passed me sweetmeats beneath the table, when Mother would have said no. He read to me from books of frightening tales that my nursemaid would never allow. But the treats had to be our secret, he said. I mustn't tell a soul, or my parents would be quite cross."

Penny became very good at keeping secrets.

It was the autumn she'd just turned ten when he began to touch her.

"The weather was miserable that year. The rain made sporting impossible most days. While everyone else was reading or doing needlework, Mr. Lambert proposed a new secret. Dancing lessons."

They met in the great hall on dark, rainy afternoons. Just the two of them. He showed her how a gentleman would bow to her, kiss her hand. Most important, she must carry herself as a lady. He showed her how to hold her body straight and corrected her posture with his hands. At first, he merely skimmed a touch down her body, from shoulders to hips. But then it grew worse. And worse. Gentlemen touched ladies in such a manner, he said.

Looking back, his ploy was so obvious. Like any girl of her age, Penny had been eager to grow up, chafing at her parents' restrictions. Lambert knew it, and he used it to manipulate her. She was wise beyond her years, he told her. Her parents wanted her to stay a little girl, but he understood she was growing up. Becoming a lady. He suspected as much from the maturity in her manner, but touching her beneath her clothing was the only way to be certain. He made it sound so reasonable, even if his cold hands made her insides squirm. Mr. Lambert was her father's oldest friend. Penny's friend, as well. He would never hurt her.

When he departed at the end of the visit, he reminded her sternly—the lessons had to remain their secret. If anyone knew—even the servants—they would tell her parents, and her parents would be angry. They would blame Penny. Not only for the grown-up dancing lessons, but for all their secrets. The forbidden sweets, the gifts, the stories she wasn't meant to hear and the pictures she wasn't meant to see . . . Everything.

It would disappoint them greatly to learn how she'd misbehaved over the years.

After that autumn, things were never quite the same.

She was never the same.

When he visited the following year, she feigned illness to avoid him—to the point of making herself vomit. She felt so queasy around him, it wasn't difficult to pretend. Headaches, colds, her courses . . . She invented every possible excuse.

However, she couldn't play sick forever. Mama had gently, but firmly, reprimanded her. Mr. Lambert had always made such a point of being kind to her. Penny didn't want to hurt his feelings, did she?

No, Penny had said dutifully, swallowing back the bile in her throat, she didn't.

That's my good girl, Mama replied with a smile.

Little did her mother know, Penny wasn't her good girl. Not any longer.

She was dirty. What would her parents think of her if they knew? Maybe they would feel the difference in her when she hugged them, she thought. And so she drew away. She dreaded Sundays. Even if she could hide the shame from her family, God must know. Perhaps the vicar could see it written on her face as she sat on the church bench, pretending to be the same good girl she'd always been.

Her entire upbringing had taught her that her innocence was her most important asset. If she surrendered that, she would be ruined. Worthless.

Only the animals were a comfort. She embraced family and friends less freely, but kittens never shied away. They curled in her lap and purred, and kneaded her with their velvet paws. She was especially drawn to the lost and defenseless creatures.

"They needed me," she told Gabriel. "And if I could save them, I still felt worthwhile."

As she talked, a series of objects drifted in and out of her hands. She didn't notice them being placed in her grasp, and she didn't recall setting them aside. They were merely there, in easy reach, exactly when she needed them.

A handkerchief.

A pillow.

A cup of tea to warm her trembling hands, and then later, when her throat was parched from talking, cool water to down in a single swallow.

At some point, the objects ceased moving into and out of her grasp, and she found herself clinging to one steady source of comfort: Gabriel's hand.

"I thought escaping to finishing school would be a relief," she went on, "but it was worse. So much worse."

Finishing schools ostensibly existed to instruct young ladies in playing the harpsichord and painting with watercolors. However, the lecture the matrons gave most frequently had nothing to do with art or music. The topic was virtue. The importance of staying pure, of never allowing gentlemen to take liberties before marriage. Not a kiss, not a touch. Without her innocence, a young lady was worthless.

By the time of her debut, Penny felt like a fraud. She wasn't the sort of young lady she'd been told a true gentleman would want, and she never could be again. The event was a lie. *She* was a lie. And of course, the mere idea of dancing made her ill.

So she tucked a hedgehog in her pocket. Freya was a protective talisman. Curled up in a tight ball, all her soft vulnerability hidden beneath rows of sharp quills.

And even now, when she'd grown old enough to understand it hadn't been her fault, and that her inner worth was intact, and the very idea of ruination was a falsehood . . .

She still couldn't bring herself to dance.

When she'd finally emptied herself of words and tears, it felt like hours had passed. Perhaps they had. She was wrung out, exhausted in both her body and her mind.

As she lifted her head, Penny gathered the frayed bits of her emotions and tried to prepare. Gabriel knew how it felt to be an unprotected, suffering child. He would want justice on her behalf.

She would have to make him assurances. He mustn't be angry or do anything rash, she prepared to tell him. She was better now, she'd say. So much better.

But the truth was, she didn't feel better. Not even though she'd unburdened herself of everything, purged that vast store of shame and pain and secrets. What remained when one unpacked an old wardrobe? An empty space. One that would take time—perhaps years—to fill.

So, no. She didn't feel better yet.

She didn't feel anything but numb, and she'd no strength in her body to pretend otherwise.

"Penny," he said. "If it's all right . . . may I hold you?"

She nodded, and he drew her into his arms, holding her close. He pressed a kiss to her crown. She couldn't have believed there were any more tears in her, but her eyes wrung out a few more.

"I don't have any kittens to offer," he said. "But if you're in need of some soothing, I may have just the thing."

Chapter Twenty-Five

*P*enny looked on with curiosity as Gabriel rolled his sleeves to the elbow, leaned over the immense copper tub, and gripped the water tap.

"Say a prayer to the gods of modern plumbing," he advised her. "And if you know any, a ward against witchcraft."

He turned the tap and water flowed into the tub—clear, plentiful, and steaming hot.

"That's more like it," he muttered.

"Hot running water?" She stretched her arm into the bath and swirled the water with her fingertips. "I hereby retract all my complaints about construction noise. This is a miracle."

"It certainly took an act of God to achieve."

He turned the other tap, adding cold water to balance the hot. Then he reached for a vial of attar roses and added a few drops to the bath. The room filled with fragrant steam.

"There are towels." He indicated a stack of immaculate white flannel towels, folded in perfect squares. "Soap is there, by the basin. I'll be seeing to a few things downstairs, but you've only to ring if you need anything and I'll come at once."

"Wait." She turned her back to him and lifted her hair. "Help me with the hooks, if you would?"

He undid the fastenings carefully and loosened the tapes of her corset, as well. His manner wasn't seductive, merely gentle.

"I'll hang a dressing gown on the hook outside the door," he said. "Take as long as you like."

Once he'd gone, Penny slid her arms free of her frock, untied her corset and petticoats, and unbuttoned her chemise. She pushed the layers of fabric down over her hips, shedding them all at once, like a skin. The tile was cold beneath her bare feet, but when she lowered herself into the deep tub, the heat enveloped her.

Heaven.

The bathwater wrapped around her like a hug. One that embraced every part of her equally. A hand, a knee, a breast, an earlobe—the water didn't distinguish between them. She submerged herself to the crown of her head and let the warmth flow over and around her.

The water had gone almost cold before she could bring herself to leave the bath. After drying herself with soft towels, she slipped into the comically enormous dressing gown he'd left her. She could have fit in one sleeve. The embroidered silk hem trailed behind her as she walked to the bed.

She must have fallen asleep the moment her head touched the pillow, because when Penny next opened her eyes, the windows revealed full darkness outside, and there was a toasty fire glowing in the fireplace. Across the room, Gabriel sat at an escritoire, poring over papers by the light of a single candle sconce.

When she rolled over and stretched, he lifted his head. "If it isn't Goldilocks. I hope this means the bed was just right."

"What?"

"Nothing. I'm glad you were able to sleep, that's all."

"So am I. Thank you." She came back to herself with a start. "Bixby. George. Marigold. Ang—"

"I've seen to them," he assured her. "All of them."

"Really? But how did you know what to do?"

He sifted through his stack of papers and withdrew a thick

envelope that looked familiar. "A few weeks past, someone was good enough to write out instructions in ridiculous detail."

She smiled and hugged her knees to her chest.

At her feet, a fold of the bed linens wriggled. A wet black nose appeared, followed by a whiskered snout.

"Bixby!" She reached for the dog and pulled him into her arms for cuddles and kisses. The pup was beside himself, turning in circles and licking her everywhere he could reach. "Oh, darling. Look at you. How did you end up here?"

Gabriel crossed the room to stand at the bedside. "I knew you needed an animal in your bed. And I didn't think it should be me tonight."

"There's room for another."

He joined her on the bed. Bixby nosed his hand, and he ruffled the dog's fur. They'd made friends, apparently.

Penny's heart swelled. "You," she said, "are the best man in the world."

He chuckled. "That is most definitely not the case."

"But it is." She smoothed the terrier's brown coat. "The night I found Bixby in the back alley, he was quivering and underfed, dragging his hind legs behind him. They'd been crushed by a cartwheel, or perhaps a horse's hoof. The veterinary surgeon came. He amputated the unsalvageable bits and set what remained with splints, but he gave him poor odds to survive the night. Don't name him, he warned me. It will only be harder when he dies."

She smiled and spoke to the pup in her arms. "But his warning was too late, wasn't it? You were already Bixby, and we both knew you had the heart and determination to survive. Two years later, and you're chasing squirrels across the green like the terror you were born to be."

She lifted her head to Gabriel. "This is the best dog in the world. And I don't need to meet any other dogs to feel sure of it."

His eyes narrowed. "Did you just compare me to a dog?"

"I know, I'm not certain you deserve the compliment, either."

She set Bixby down at her side. "I don't need to dance—or flirt, or walk, or go driving—with any other men to know you're the best of them all."

"I just hope that everything we shared was . . ." His fingers combed through her hair. "I mean, what happened in the alley was rather—"

"Extraordinary." She slid closer, taking one of his hands in both of hers. "What happened in the alley was nothing short of exhilarating. I mean, the part where you tried to leave me forever was quite poorly done, but up until that . . . ? Immensely satisfying."

He released a deep breath. "I'm glad of it."

"I'm glad of it, too. I know most girls spend their youths dreaming of the thrill of a first kiss, the passion in a first touch . . ." With the pad of her thumb, she drew small, lazy shapes in the palm of his hand. "I never expected to have those firsts myself. To be honest, I doubted I'd want them. And then I met you, and everything was different. I thought it was lust at first sight. I couldn't stop thinking about you. And not in a romantic, Prince Charming way. In a naked way."

He laughed a little.

"It was so unnerving."

"I can only imagine."

"But wonderful. Looking back, I don't think it was lust at first sight. It was trust at first sight. I felt safe with you. All those firsts that I believed had been stolen from me . . . With you, I got them all back. I *took* them back, on my own terms. I only wish I could go back and help recover all the firsts you missed, too."

"I've had some firsts of my own. First time being sneezed on by a Highland steer. First time playing midwife to a goat. First sham sandwich. That was a last, as well."

She poked him in the ribs. "You are terrible, and I love you."

He reached for her, cradling her cheek in his hand. "Hearing those words was a first."

"I know," she whispered. "But it won't be a last."

And because she knew he wouldn't take the lead tonight, she leaned forward to kiss him.

HER KISS WAS sweet and searching. Gabe wasn't certain how to respond. He didn't want to refuse her, but he'd be damned if he'd press her one touch further than she wished to proceed. So he let her take the lead, making himself open to everything she wanted to give—even when she kissed and caressed his body with a tenderness so foreign to him, he wasn't certain he could have borne it for anything less than love of her.

She hiked the hem of his shirt and shrugged out of the dressing gown he'd given her. They peeled away all the layers until they were both fully naked, and from there it was the simple, beautiful inevitability of joining. Clasping, holding, moving together in an unhurried rhythm that nonetheless quickly brought them to the brink. Her fingernails bit into his shoulders as she shivered and cried out with release. As he raced toward his own climax, she held him close, forbidding him to leave her embrace. He surrendered to the temptation, spending inside her with a primal, possessive joy.

Afterward, she snuggled in his arms. "You don't need to save my reputation, but I hope you know you're going to undermine your own. Long engagements and weddings in St. George Hanover Square? Not terribly ruthless or intimidating, Mr. The Duke of Ruin."

"I'm not going to undermine my reputation," he said. "I'm going to destroy it, thoroughly. For you."

"I know," she whispered. "I love you so dearly for it."

He was going to give her everything. Even if it meant living in her world, among the aristocrats he despised, choking back his pride and resentment.

The Duke of Ruin died here today, in her arms. And Gabe wasn't entirely certain who he'd be going forward, but he knew one thing. He would be her husband and protector. And he would never allow anyone to hurt her again.

Along that line of thought, he had best return her to her house before morning broke.

"I need to see you home," he said. "The last thing we need now is for a neighbor across the square to see you tiptoeing from my house to yours at dawn. Courting scandal at this stage would only give your family reason to object."

"I'm tempted to argue, but I won't."

"I'll check the corridor," Gabe said. "We don't want Mrs. Burns surprising us again."

"She wouldn't tell a soul."

"Perhaps not, but she might scare the soul out of me."

As Gabe ventured into the corridor, he paused and held his breath. From down the way, he heard the creak of floorboards. As he moved toward the sound, a ghostly figure appeared in the distance.

Gabe shook himself and rubbed his eyes. "Hammond?"

The architect's silvery hair stood at wild angles, and he was clad in only a white nightshirt. On one forearm, he balanced a tray of food. He had a bottle of wine tucked under his other arm, and a pair of wineglasses clutched in his free hand—the source of the clanking, Gabe presumed. The man was sweaty and breathless.

"What the devil is going on?" Gabe asked.

"Devil, indeed." Hammond leaned over his tray to whisper. "I finally learned the truth about Burns."

"Brilliant," Gabe muttered. "I thought you'd ruled out ghost, witch, and vampiress. What's left?"

"The woman's a succubus."

"What's a succubus?"

"A female demon." Hammond's eyebrows lifted. "One who feeds on sexual pleasure."

"Well, then. I am exceedingly sorry I asked."

"Gerard, is that you?" The sultry, smoky female voice came from within a nearby chamber. "I'm waiting."

"Good God. The enchantress calls." Hammond backed his way into the bedchamber, tray and wine in his hands. "If I'm dead in the morning, bury my corpse with a stake through the heart."

Numb with shock, Gabe returned to his own bedchamber. Penny lifted her shoulders in question. "Well?"

"I have good news and bad news."

"Let's have the bad first, please."

"The bad news is, I'll never, so long as I live, wipe the past two minutes from my memory." He scratched the back of his head. "The good news is, tonight we're in the clear."

Chapter Twenty-Six

$\mathcal{T}$he morning of the ball was so frantic with preparations that when Gabe met Penny at the door, he didn't even trouble with greetings.

"Come." He took her by the hand. "I have something for you in the study."

When he closed the door behind them, she blushed and dropped her voice to a whisper. "Er, Gabriel . . . I really would love to, but my hair's just been washed and pinned, and I'm down to my last few wearable frocks."

"I'm not after that," he assured her. "Not that I'd mind it, of course. But it's not my intent to bend you over the desk for a passionate tryst . . . today." After taking a moment to chase that tempting image from his brain, he patted the chair behind the desk. "Sit."

Gabe opened a strongbox hidden in a cabinet and withdrew a large, flat velvet box. He placed the box on the desk blotter, inordinately anxious. "Go on, then. Open it."

She lifted the top and peered inside. "Oh, Gabriel."

He moved behind the chair, looking over her shoulder at the sparkling array of rings. Diamond, ruby, sapphire, emerald . . . every precious gem he could think to request at the jeweler's, and a few he hadn't known existed.

"I thought you'd prefer to be surprised, but I didn't trust myself to choose one you liked. So I simply bought them all."

"They're exquisite."

He waved off her praise. "None of them are fine enough for you."

"I don't need even *one* ring so grand, let alone a tray of them."

"Too late. They're all yours. Wear them all at once, if you like. Or designate one for each day of the week."

She pried a ring from the velvet padding—a pale pink diamond set in gold and ringed with smaller sparkling stones. "I always did love pink."

"Try it on."

Penny slipped the ring on her third finger. She held her hand at a distance to admire the way the stone flashed in the light.

"It's beautiful." She rose from the chair and kissed him. "Thank you. I love it."

He exhaled, relieved. "Good. Now let's have it back. I'll lock it up for safekeeping."

She held her hand close to her chest. "Must I take it off?"

"Yes, you must. We're not engaged."

She arched one golden eyebrow and smiled. "Yet."

Good God. He didn't know where her faith in him originated—dropped off by pixies floating on the breeze with toadstool parasols, most likely—but at this point, he didn't bloody well care. If he pulled this off, he would be either the most cunning bastard in England, or the luckiest. Probably both.

Pouting a bit, she twisted the ring off her finger and dropped it into his hand. "We've agreed to marry each other. Bended knee or not, that seems to meet the definition of a betrothal."

"It doesn't meet my definition," he said firmly. "Not until I've spoken with your brother."

He replaced the rings in the safe, taking his time to be certain the strongbox was locked securely.

When he was finished, he turned to see Penny crouched on the floor, surrounded by scattered papers and correspondence. Papers she was never meant to see.

"Gabriel, what is all this?"

"It's not what you think."

"I can read." Clutching the papers in both hands, Penny shook her head. "You're planning to ruin my family."

PENNY HADN'T BEEN meaning to snoop, but as she'd risen from the desk chair, she'd knocked the papers to the floor. When she crouched to retrieve them, she saw her own name. It was a betrothal contract.

She scanned through the first few pages, feeling entirely justified in doing so. This would be her marriage, too. Apparently, he'd made several drafts. Just like the rings, he'd prepared for every possibility. Why hadn't he consulted her?

And then, at the bottom of the pile, she found an agreement that wasn't drafted in her name. It bore Bradford's name, and it wasn't a betrothal contract.

It was a betrayal.

"You were never meant to see those," he said.

"Oh, I can imagine I wasn't," she replied.

She certainly understood why Gabriel had kept these papers from her view. The reason was inscribed in black ink on crisp parchment, legible and stark, defying her to hope there could be any misunderstanding.

The truth was plain, and it was a dagger to her heart.

"This says you've purchased a loan from the bank. A loan taken against my family's property."

She lifted her head and found Gabriel staring back at her. His expression was inscrutable.

He didn't even attempt to deny it. "Yes, I did."

"That mortgage was drawn for the purpose of farmland improvements. It was meant to help tenants through the lean harvests, keep them from starving. Now you're threatening to call in the debt unless my brother agrees to our marriage?"

"No, no. You're misunderstanding."

She rattled the contract at him. "It's right here, in plain language."

"I'm not threatening to call in the debt. I'm offering to forgive the debt entirely. In exchange for your dowry."

Her jaw dropped. "That's supposed to sound better?"

He pushed a hand through his hair. "It was meant as a last resort, to be used only if he wouldn't give his consent. Call it insurance."

"I call it insulting. Because that's what it is. You planned to do this without my ever knowing? I'd blithely go about telling everyone how devoted we are to each other, and all the time my family would know the truth. That I was purchased." She let the paper slip to the floor as she stood. "When you said you insisted on doing this 'properly,' I had no idea this is what you intended."

"Don't make so much of it. We both know how aristocrat marriages work. No matter which man you married, your dowry would be a legal transaction."

"Yes, of course," she said bitterly. "Because what man would marry me without financial inducement."

"There's no financial inducement on my part." He gestured at the papers. "I'm not even coming out ahead. The amount of your brother's loan is far greater than your dowry. I'd be losing money on you."

The words hit her like pebbles winged by a cruel schoolboy.

He swore. "That came out worse than I intended."

"I certainly hope so. This is a nightmare." She retrieved the papers and ripped them down the center, shearing them in half. Then she took the halves of the sheets and slowly tore those into even smaller pieces. That still wasn't enough. She kept up her grim, methodical shredding until the pieces became bits, and the bits became snowflakes.

"My solicitor has copies of those," he said.

"I don't care. It was satisfying anyhow."

He came around the desk, closing the distance between them. "Your brother is never going to agree to our marriage unless some form of leverage is applied. Did you have a better idea?"

"Yes! Here is my wild idea. I will tell him that I love you with all my heart, and that I wish to spend the rest of my life with you. And if he says no, we'll marry without his blessing."

He took her by the shoulders. "Think about what you're suggesting. Your family would shun you. Everyone will say you've been ruined."

"I don't care what anyone says."

"Well, *I* care. I care what people say about you. What they say about us, our children. Penny, I'm telling you—"

"*Telling* me? I thought a proposal involved *asking* me. I fell in love with you partly because you respected my choices, on everything from my dinner to my engagement ring. Suddenly, you've become an autocrat."

He sighed wearily. "I'm trying to protect you. I'll do whatever is required to keep you from becoming a scandal, even if that means taking matters into my own hands."

"What does *that* mean?"

"If your brother knows how we've spent the past few weeks, I'm sure he'd agree we must wed."

Oh, Lord. Her stomach knotted. "You would tell him I'm ruined."

His expression was hard.

"Soiled in the eyes of society," she went on. "Worthless. That he has no choice but to bless the match, because how could anyone else ever want me."

"You know *I* don't see you that way."

"But you are willing to let my family see me that way, and then use that to your advantage. After everything you know of my past, I can't believe you would stand here and even suggest such a thing." She wrapped her arms about the hollowness in her chest and hugged tight. "Everyone warned me not to trust you. All my friends. I refused to listen."

"You knew my reputation from the first. I never claimed to be anything else."

"I suppose you didn't. I was naïve enough to fall in love with you anyway."

"Maybe you didn't fall in love with me," he snapped. "Maybe you fell in love with a man who doesn't exist."

"Maybe you don't truly love me at all."

She waited for him to contradict the statement. Assure her that yes, he loved her beyond anything. Instead, he released her and passed a hand over his face. "You're emotional. Fatigued. You should go home and rest."

"I'm going home, but not to rest. I'm going to pack my things. You're right, perhaps it's time I reached out to my family. I can leave with Bradford tonight."

"Penny, wait."

"No," she said. "I've waited long enough. I've lost ten years of my life to secrets and shame, and I refuse to surrender a single day more. Not even for you."

Chapter Twenty-Seven

"*M*RS. ROBBINS! MRS. ROBBINS!*"

Delilah—the bird who couldn't learn "I love you" after a thousand repetitions of the phrase—had learned to mimic this instead. The parrot had the poor housekeeper running all over the house.

Penny rose from the bed where she'd been moping all afternoon and dragged herself down the stairs before Mrs. Robbins could take the trouble to climb them.

When she arrived downstairs, however, she found the drawing room stacked with boxes. Small boxes, large boxes, hatboxes. In the middle of them all stood Emma.

"Surprise!" Emma spread her arms, gesturing toward the boxes with a tacit *voilà*. "Your wardrobe has arrived. I told you it would be finished in time. A full complement of frocks and underthings for daily wear, two evening gowns suitable for the opera or the theater, gloves and heeled slippers to match— and of course, your gown for the ball. I can't wait to show you everything."

"Don't bother." Penny removed a stack of boxes from a chair and numbly sat down.

"What?"

"Leave them boxed. It will save me the trouble of repacking them when I leave."

"Oh, no. Did your aunt refuse to help you?"

Penny shook your head.

"Your brother, then. He won't change his mind?"

"It's not my family. It's . . ." Tears pressed to her eyes. "Emma, I feel like such a fool."

Penny broke down and told her friend everything. Everything. From Cumberland and secret dancing lessons, all the way up through the contracts and heartbreak. She condensed a great many of the details by necessity, but she held nothing back.

By the end, the two of them were side by side on the divan, each of them dabbing their eyes with handkerchiefs. Even Delilah gave a mournful whistle. Mrs. Robbins brought a pot of comforting tea.

Emma embraced her. "Penny, dear. I am so sorry."

"I don't know what to do. You all attempted to warn me, and I thought I knew better. I believed he was good inside, at his core. I thought that he would set aside these ruthless vendettas once he came to believe that, too. My judgment failed me." She sniffed. "I ought to have known it when he insulted my sandwiches."

"You weren't a fool," Emma said. "You trusted your heart. And to be honest, I'm not convinced your heart was wrong."

"Were you listening to anything I said?"

"I know. What he did was horrible. I'm not excusing him for it. But men do nonsensical things when they're in love, and they become perfectly idiotic when they're afraid of losing it. Don't be too hard on yourself. The good qualities you saw in him do exist, even if he's allowed them to be vanquished by fear or anger. No one is entirely good or entirely bad." Emma took her by the hand. "You look for the best in people. It's one of the qualities I most admire in you. You're so brave."

"I'm not brave."

"You have more courage than anyone I know. Even having been hurt so deeply, you persist in opening your heart time and time again."

"To kittens, maybe."

"To people, too. Me, for one. I'll never forget how you invited me to tea the very week I married Ash. We'd never even met, and no other lady of the *ton* would have acknowledged my existence. A seamstress turned duchess? Somehow you understood how desperately I would need a friend."

Penny smiled at her friend. "Inviting you to tea was one of the wisest things I've ever done. Not the bravest."

"It was sheer courage. I could have been a murderer." Emma sipped her tea. "And it wasn't only me. Nicola, Alexandra, Ash, Chase . . . You're the paste that binds us all together. Reaching out takes courage, and holding on takes even more."

Penny cradled Freya in her hands, stroking her quills along the grain. The hedgehog rolled over and uncurled, exposing her white, fluffy belly for a scratch. "I felt safe with him. I told him *everything*. He told me I was a treasure, one impervious to tarnish. That I could never be ruined. And even if I knew that for myself in my mind, for the first time I felt safe to truly believe it in my heart."

"Penny."

"He betrayed my trust in him. But what's so much worse, he betrayed my trust in myself."

"Then borrow mine. Whatever it is you want to do next, I have absolute faith in you. We'll all be cheering you on, and we'll be there if you need us."

Penny gave Freya's tuft of fur a thoughtful stroke. What *did* she want to do next? Her heart and mind were too tattered to contemplate dreams of the future. She only knew what she *didn't* want to do. She didn't want to give up and hide.

Emma had taken the time and effort to produce this new wardrobe heaped in boxes around them. Penny had said goodbye to some of her animals, sending them out to be brave on their own. She owed it to Hubert to try, didn't she? To her friends, as well.

Mostly, she owed it to herself. Three weeks ago, she'd struck a wager with her aunt, and she'd already come this far. She wanted to win.

Penny gently set Freya in her basket, then surveyed the heaps of boxes surrounding them. "Which one of these has the ball gown?"

Emma jumped to her feet, clapping with excitement. "I was afraid you'd never ask." She navigated the room and found the largest of the boxes. "I didn't want to press you, but it would have killed me to leave it unused. Three seamstresses worked for days on the embroidery alone."

While Penny cleared the tea service, Emma lifted the box onto the tea table. She drummed her fingers on top, increasing the suspense. "Are you ready?"

She swallowed hard. "I think so."

Emma whisked the top off the box, revealing a cloud of tissue. "Prepare to be dazzled."

Chapter Twenty-Eight

$\mathcal{B}$eautiful."

"Remarkable."

"Stunning. Absolutely stunning."

Ever since arriving at the ball, Penny had heard many similar compliments. Sadly, none of them were directed *at* her. They were merely uttered *near* her.

"Never in my life have I seen so many craned necks." Nicola surveyed the crowded ballroom.

"You should attend a gathering of astronomers," Alexandra said.

"This is more like a gathering of ostriches."

The dancing hadn't yet begun, but the orchestra played light music while guests moved through the rooms, admiring the opulent decor. The mirrored walls, the paintings in gilt frames, the carved moldings, the waterfalls of blue velvet drapery framing the windows.

Here in the ballroom, the soaring ceilings drew the largest share of attention. Someone viewing the scene from afar might conclude that tipped heads and elongated necks were the latest fashion arrived from the Continent.

"They ought to be looking at your gown," Alexandra said. "That's the true work of art in the room."

Penny smoothed her gloved hands along the sheer silk netting that overlaid an underdress of ivory satin. The gauzy fabric was patterned with tiny pink roses connected by curling tendrils of green. The cap sleeves were fashioned from satin petals layered over creamy lace. A wide band of green velvet cinched her waist, and the daring neckline revealed the perfect amount of cleavage.

"Emma works miracles," she said.

"The beauty is all in the wearer," Emma said graciously.

"Let's hope that undeserving man shows up to appreciate it," Nicola grumbled.

Penny stood on her toes and scanned the growing crush of guests.

No sign of Gabriel. No sign of her brother yet, either.

Nicola shook her head. "I've been saying all along that he's not good enough for you. What sort of person fails to appear at his own ball?"

"He's here somewhere," Emma said. "Most likely occupied with hosting duties. He'll make an appearance before long."

A wandering servant offered flutes of champagne. Penny, Nicola, and Emma accepted eagerly. Alexandra declined, in favor of food.

"A toast to the three of you." Penny raised her glass. "You didn't have to come, but I'm grateful you did. Especially you, Alex. You should be at home with your feet propped on a cushion."

Alexandra balanced a plate of refreshments atop her immensely rounded belly. "We'd never abandon you to face this alone." She nibbled at a sandwich. "Besides, the food alone is worth the effort of attending. You've improved on this recipe remarkably, Penny."

"What do you mean? Which recipe?"

Alex held up a half-eaten finger sandwich. "The sham. It's not bad."

Nicola grimaced. "Surely that's the pregnancy speaking."

Alexandra offered a sample from her plate. "Taste for yourself."

"I'll try." Emma took a sandwich and sank her teeth into it, then chewed with caution. As she swallowed, her eyebrows rose in surprise. "That's almost tasty. What did you change, Penny?"

"I didn't change anything. Gabriel's chef must have made it. I had nothing to do with the refreshments."

"That's odd," Alex said. "I assumed you planned the entire menu. There's not a scrap of meat to be found anywhere."

"Truly? No meat whatsoever?"

"Not that I could find, and I did search." She looked down at her swollen belly. "This baby is quite the carnivore. It's all delicious, though. Onion tartlets, pastry puffs stuffed with cheese, a terrine of mushroom and hazelnuts. There's a pharaoh-sized pyramid of exotic fruits. The pineapples alone must have cost a small fortune. And, of course, there's the sham."

"Oh, Penny. He must truly love you," Emma said. "Ash and Chase ate the sham. Gabriel made more."

Penny couldn't believe it. He must have arranged the menu. Of course, he would have done so days ago, well before their argument today. Nevertheless, she was touched by the gesture. He truly had planned this evening for her, down to the last detail.

Just as Emma had worked tirelessly to create her gown, and Nicola and Alexandra were here to support her, despite the fact that they'd rather be anywhere else.

Yet here Penny was, tucked in a corner.

A wallflower, as always.

Tonight, she vowed, she would be different. She would leave the dancing to those who enjoyed it, but she would mingle, converse, make her rounds of the guests—if only to say that she had done it. Not for Gabriel, and not for Aunt Caroline. For herself.

Penny drew a deep breath and stepped away from the wall.

"Wait." Nicola grabbed her by the arm, yanking her back. Her voice was frantic. "Don't go."

Penny turned to her friend. "Heavens, Nic. You've gone white as paper."

"Are you ill?" Emma laid a hand to Nicola's brow, testing for fever in motherly fashion. "Do you need to sit down?"

"You look as though you've seen a ghost," Alex said.

"Worse than a ghost." Nicola shielded her face with one hand and lowered her head. "I've seen a fiancé."

"A fiancé?" Penny echoed. "Whose fiancé?"

She moaned faintly. "Mine, I think."

What?

Nicola, engaged to be married? Penny exchanged quizzical glances with Emma and Alex. They each shook their heads, as if to say this was news to them, as well.

Penny turned to look about them. "Where? Who?"

"For God's sake, don't look!" Nicola arranged the three of them shoulder to shoulder, making a human fence and then ducking behind it. "I can't let him see me. He'll recognize me from the hair alone."

The orchestra struck up the first strains of a quadrille. The dancing was about to begin.

"Come." Emma put her arm about their flame-haired friend's shoulders. "We'll find a place away from the crowd. And then you *must* tell us everything."

"Very well. But you have to conceal me until it's safe."

"There's a servants' door in the far corner of the ballroom," Penny said. "The corridor behind it leads to the rear of the house. We can make our escape through there."

The three of them shuffled sideways in an awkward, not-at-all-suspicious manner. Meanwhile Nicola crouched in their shadow, scurrying behind their human shield. Thank goodness everyone was more interested in pairing off for the quadrille than in watching a quartet of social misfits.

When they reached the corner, Penny prised open the hidden door, just a crack. "The three of you first. I'll stand guard."

She turned to face the ballroom and smiled innocently, fluffing her skirts to make a wider shield. Behind her, the others filed through the door, one by one.

And then she glimpsed Gabriel through the crowd, standing at the opposite end of the ballroom. He was magnificent in his full evening dress. Black tailcoat layered over a snow-white vest and cravat. His cheeks looked so smooth, she imagined that might be the reason for his tardiness. He'd probably been upstairs shaving at the last minute. By midnight, he'd have a forest of whiskers again. Their eyes met.

"Penny," Alexandra whispered. *"Aren't you coming?"*

"Not just now," she answered. "Go on without me."

As the quadrille came to an end, the dancers dispersed. He began to walk toward her.

She'd always dreamed of this scene. What girl hadn't? The dark, handsome man locking gazes with her across the crowded ballroom. Striding toward her, unwavering in his intent, drawn to her beauty, acting on an inexorable melding of desire and destiny.

It wouldn't happen that way. Not tonight. She refused to stand there meekly while Gabriel Duke made his manly strides across the ballroom to claim her.

Penny was going to meet him halfway.

WHEN SHE BEGAN to move toward him, Gabe cursed under his breath. This was a wrinkle in his plans. She was beautiful beyond words. Beyond his words, at any rate. And he'd counted on having a long, slow saunter across the floor to search his brain for a compliment that would be remotely sufficient.

Instead, she was going to intercept him before he had any chance.

When they met in the center of the ballroom, he was speechless.

She broke the silence. "I want to say something witty or cutting. One of those worldly remarks that brings a man to his knees. But I can't think of anything, so . . . The ball is lovely. You look quite handsome."

"And here I was just cursing myself for my complete inability to describe how beautiful you look. You deserve a sonnet. An ode? I don't even know the difference between the two. Next time, I'll hire a poet."

She smiled and shrugged. "We are who we are."

"We are who we are."

God, he loved who she was. But what was more, he loved who they were together. He couldn't lose that.

"I don't want to take you away from the party," he said. "I just had a brief question to ask you."

"I have a question for you, too."

"You go first," he said.

"No, you go first."

"I insist."

"I insist more."

"Fine," he said. "Will you marry me?"

She stared at him. "This was your brief question? *This.*"

"It's four words on my part. Your answer only requires one. That's the definition of brief."

"Is it?"

He reached for her hands. "I know it's not a romantic proposal, but I wanted to ask before your brother arrives. I need you to know that *your* answer is the only one that matters. The things I said to you were unforgivable. That contract was a horrid, thoughtless mistake. You were right to shred it to bits, and I've made certain my solicitor's copy was torn to pieces, too. The thing of it is, I was afraid. I'm afraid no one will believe you married me for love, because I find it so difficult to believe it myself. It seems impossible that you could love me. But then it once seemed impossible that I could love anyone, and now I love you with a ferocity I can't describe. Not because I need a poet, but because I don't want to frighten you away. You're the kindest soul I'll ever meet, and we're astounding together in bed. I don't think I could live without you. Well, I don't know. Perhaps I could. In the past, I learned to survive without a great many things. But I don't *want* to live without you. I realize you might not forgive me yet for being a shameless, presumptuous prick, but—"

"Yes," she interrupted. "The answer is yes. Adorable as it is to watch you nervously rattling on, if you want my answer before my brother arrives, we don't have all evening. So yes."

"Thank God." He closed his eyes and exhaled gruffly. "Damn it. I left the ring in the safe."

She laughed. "Best proposal in the world."

"So what was your question?" he asked.

"I'd almost forgotten. I was going to ask if you'd care to dance. With me."

"Penny." His heart clenched like a fist. "You don't have to do that."

"I know I don't have to. I *want* to, so long as it's with you. Everything is different with you." She licked her lips, anxious. "They're playing a waltz. The waltz wasn't in England yet when I . . . when I first learned to dance. It would be entirely new for me."

He brought both her hands to his lips and kissed them. "I'm so honored. And I wish like hell that I knew how. Neither of us would know what we're doing, I'm afraid."

"It couldn't possibly be a more alarming scene than my last attempt at dancing in public."

He supposed that was true.

"Even if it is a disaster, what's the worst that could happen? No one will invite us to another ball for a decade. What a shame that would be."

"In that case . . ." He waved his arm in the direction of the dancing. "After you."

To Gabe, the waltz seemed to be nothing but a great deal of mincing, turning, and mincing while turning. He felt like a clumsy ass, but he did his best for Penny's sake. For the remainder of his life, he'd do his best for Penny's sake.

She stopped in the middle of a mincing turn. The music continued, and the dancing went on, but Penny was frozen in place, staring at something over his shoulder.

"Penny?"

Her gaze held emotions he'd never seen in her before. Emotions he wouldn't have even believed to be in her character. Fear. Fury. Hatred.

And Gabe knew—he just *knew*, in his soul—there could be only one reason for it.

She pasted a false smile on her face and threaded her arm through his, turning him to face a pair of men. The younger of the two looked to be about the same age as Gabe, but he had Penny's light hair and blue eyes.

This one must be Bradford.

The other man was older, though not *old*. He had brown hair gone gray at the temples, and an insidiously average-looking face.

This one must be the Devil.

"There you are, Penelope," her brother said. "We've been looking for you." He settled cold, suspicious eyes on Gabe. "Introduce us to your friend?"

"Bradford, this is Mr. Gabriel Duke. Gabriel, this is my brother Bradford. And this is Mr. Lambert. He's Bradford's father-in-law."

Chapter Twenty-Nine

*H*im.

Penny clung to Gabriel's arm. She thought she might be sick. A cold sweat covered the back of her neck, trickling down between her shoulder blades.

This was the possibility she'd been dreading ever since she'd learned that Bradford was coming to Town. Perhaps, she'd told herself, he was traveling alone. Maybe Mr. Lambert wasn't coming to Town for the Season this year.

Yet here he was. Smiling at her as though none of it had ever happened. Because, as far as her family knew, none of it ever had. Lambert knew that Penny would never tell.

When she'd gone away to finishing school, she thought she'd finally be free of him. And then she'd learned the news in a letter from her mother. Bradford was betrothed to Alice Lambert.

Once Bradford's engagement was announced, she ought to have found the courage to speak. But she couldn't bring herself to tell the truth. She'd have been driving a wedge into Bradford's happiness with Alice. Ruining one of her father's oldest friendships. Perhaps her mother would gently accuse her of seeking attention again.

In short, telling the truth would be asking her family to choose between her and Mr. Lambert. They couldn't be loyal to both. And Penny knew which of the two stories they would prefer to believe.

So she said nothing.

On the day of her brother's wedding, Penny had vowed that if Bradford and Alice ever had a baby girl, she would break her silence. No matter how painful. But they'd had only sons, thank heavens, and by now speaking the truth seemed pointless.

What good could it do? Penny would be tied to him forever. Lambert would always be, much as it repulsed her to think it, family.

"Come, poppet. Is this any way to greet me?" Lambert kissed her on the cheek. She would be scrubbing it for days. "How lovely to see you dancing. I do hope you'll favor me with the next set?"

No. Everything in her screamed the word. Yet for some reason she couldn't speak.

"Actually," Gabriel said smoothly, "I have a request of my own. I had planned to ask for a private conversation with His Lordship. However, now that you're here, Mr. Lambert, perhaps you'd care to join us? Since you are family, this matter concerns you, as well." He looked to Penny. "You will excuse us, I hope?"

She managed to nod.

"Excellent." He turned to Bradford and Lambert, making a welcoming gesture in the direction of the corridor. "Shall we? I have brandy in my study."

She watched the men as they left the ballroom, paralyzed with indecision. The little girl inside her still trembled with fear. But she wasn't a little girl any longer. The woman she'd become refused to stand by, silent and ashamed.

She ran after them, pushing open the door of the study—

Just in time to see Gabriel's fist connect with Lambert's jaw.

Penny shrieked.

Bradford launched himself at Gabriel, dragging him backward before he could land another blow.

"You miserable blackguard." Gabriel struggled against Bradford's restraint. "I can't believe you would show your face in this house."

"What the devil is this about?" Bradford asked.

"Ask him," Gabriel spat. "Your father-in-law."

"I've not the slightest notion, Bradford," Lambert said. "No idea what he's on about."

"You know precisely what I'm on about." Gabriel pushed away from Bradford, grabbed Lambert by the lapels, and slammed him against the wall. "You've avoided the reckoning for years, but now it's arrived. You're going to pay for what you did to her."

"Stop, please," Penny cried. "Bradford, we need to talk."

"We'll have plenty of time to talk," her brother said. "A whole week's journey to Cumberland. You're leaving with me."

"Get away from her," Gabriel threatened. "Or I swear I'll take you down, too."

"Gabriel, he doesn't know."

"Then he deserves to pay for that." He let Lambert drop to the floor, then turned on Bradford. "How could you? How could you not know? Didn't you see her changing before your eyes? A bright, lively little girl turning shy and withdrawn. Hiding from you, from everyone. Surely you knew something was wrong. You never bothered to ask."

After a moment passed in silence, Bradford turned to her. His eyes were full of questions. "Penny?"

Lambert pressed a handkerchief to his lip. "She's confused, Bradford. Not difficult to see why, if she's fallen under the influence of this brigand." He glared at Gabriel. "See here, Duke. I demand an apology."

"Go to Hell," Gabriel snarled.

"Then I demand satisfaction."

"I'd be glad to give it."

Penny's lungs seized. A duel? She couldn't let this happen.

"Name your second, then. Bradford will serve as mine. They can set the time and place."

Gabriel shook his head. "I do my own negotiations, and I'm

not giving you any time to escape. Tomorrow. Pistols at dawn in St. James Park."

Lambert tugged on the lapels of his coat. "I look forward to it. I'm an excellent sportsman and a keen shot." He glanced at Penny. "Isn't that right, poppet?"

Gabriel cocked a fist. "Get out of my house before I grind you into pulp beneath my boots."

Before they could go, Penny ran to plead with her brother. "Bradford, you can't allow this to happen."

He regarded her with disappointment in his eyes. "It seems as though *you've* allowed this to happen. What were you thinking, associating with such a man?"

"He's a good person. You don't know him." *You don't truly know Lambert, either.*

"I know enough," he said. "I know he's gone unchecked for too long, destroying our peers and neighbors. For God's sake, we are standing in a house he shamelessly stole from the Wendlebys."

"He didn't steal it."

"I'll brook no more argument. I'm only too happy to help bring him to account."

Penny knew her brother well enough to recognize the expression on his face. His mind was made up. No amount of dissent would sway him now.

She stepped back and gave him the space to leave.

Once Bradford and Lambert had departed the room, Penny rushed to Gabriel. Perhaps he could be made to see sense. "A duel? Surely you don't mean to do this."

"I do mean to do this. I wish I could find a way to go back in time and hunt him down there, but I can't. This is the next best alternative."

"If going back in time were possible, we'd miss one another entirely—because I'd go back in time and rescue you from everything you endured. We've known pain, the both of us. No one came to our rescue. We are survivors, and we didn't come through all that only to lose our lives now." Her voice broke. "Gabriel, he stole years from me already. Don't let him take our future from us, too."

"He already has your future. Part of it, at least. I saw the way you reacted when he entered that ballroom. I *felt* it. As long as he's alive and connected to your family, you'll never be free of him."

"Can't there be some other way? Why must it be a duel?"

He gave her a wry smile. "I swore you'd marry nothing less than a gentleman. Dueling is the gentleman's way."

She rolled her eyes. "I don't want a dead gentleman. I'd prefer a living bastard, thank you. And what about George? You have a goat now, and he's depending on you. If nothing else, think of your kid."

"Penny." He touched her cheek. His eyes brimmed with tenderness. "I'm only thinking of you. If I don't defend you, I'm not worthy of you. Not in the world's eyes, nor in my own."

"WE HAVE TO do something," Penny said firmly. "Ideas?"

She looked around at her friends. After Gabriel left, she'd sent for Ash and Chase, and they'd all adjourned to her house for an urgent strategy session. In the most direct and matter-of-fact of summaries, she'd relayed the facts of the situation and the imminent danger. Considering the formidable amount of wits and determination represented in her drawing room, surely they could come up with a brilliant way to avert disaster.

Unfortunately, no one was quick with a suggestion.

She turned to Chase and Ash. "Can't you go after him? Punch him in the jaw, or tie him to a chair, or hold him at knifepoint until well after dawn?"

After conferring with Chase by eye contact, Ash rubbed the back of his neck. "As delightful as that all sounds, I don't think we can."

"Surely the two of you put together can overpower him."

"It's not that." Chase sat across from her and leaned forward, resting his elbows on his knees. "Perhaps we *could* restrain him. But I'm not convinced we *should*."

"Why not?"

"Because we agree with Gabe, that's why." Ash crossed his arms. "In his position, I'd do the same. In fact, I'd be tempted to call Lambert out myself if he hadn't already. The man deserves to die."

Chase reached forward and took her hand. "Penny, what he did to you . . . I can't imagine what you suffered. But I believe I can come uncomfortably *close* to imagining it, when I think of Rosamund and Daisy. I can certainly understand why Gabe feels the need to defend you."

"I don't need defending," she protested. "It's in the past. And while I'm sure you do have strong emotions, aren't *my* feelings and wishes more important right now? Perhaps Lambert deserves to die. But we all know it's far more likely that Gabriel will be the one wounded or worse."

Nicola joined her argument. "Dueling is an archaic, barbarous, stupid practice in which men pretend to defend a woman's honor by robbing her of any self-determination."

"Is that so?" Ash looked at his wife. "Emma didn't mind it when I snuck through her despicable father's window at night and made him piss the bed with fear."

"That was different!" Emma said. "There were no bullets involved."

Alexandra spoke up. "I was highly put out with Chase when he punched a man on my behalf."

"At the *time*," Chase argued. "Looking back, would you rather I hadn't?"

Alexandra went silent.

"See?" Chase said.

Penny jumped to her feet. "Listen, all of you. This isn't a matter of punching or climbing through windows. A duel means life and death, and considering that Lambert spent every autumn shooting partridges with my father, I have reason to believe he's the superior marksman of the two. I love Gabriel. I mean to marry him, have a family with him. In order for that to happen, he needs to not *die* tomorrow morning. And if you care about me at all, you'll do everything you can to prevent it."

After a moment of quiet, her friends mumbled and nodded in agreement.

Chase rose from the chair. "Ash and I will go after him. We may not be able to stop the duel, but there are ways of settling these things without bloodshed."

Penny exhaled with relief. "Thank you."

"Besides, he's going to need a second," Chase said.

Ash nodded. "I'll do my best to negotiate a resolution that doesn't involve black powder."

"Hold a moment," Chase objected, pulling on his coat. "Who said you were the second? I'm the second."

"You can be the third."

"The *third*? There's no such thing as a *third*."

Ash groaned. "We'll sort it out on the way."

After the men had left, Penny paced the floor. "There has to be something more we can do," she told Alex, Emma, and Nicola. "I can't simply sit here and sip tea all night."

"If I could move," Alexandra said, "I'd be a great deal more help. Perhaps you could set me rolling like a giant pumpkin, and I could mow them down?"

"Tempting." Penny was grateful for the smile that image brought.

"To be truthful, I'm not certain we can stop them," Emma added. "Nicola's right when she calls it archaic and stupid, but these are men we're talking about. Wounded male pride has caused the world more destruction than the Black Death and the Great Flood put together."

Nicola's eyebrows lifted. "Are we entirely certain men's bruised feelings weren't to blame for the plague and the deluge, too?"

"A fair point," Emma conceded.

"If men are bent on destroying the world, we women must

be the ones holding it together," a newcomer to their gathering said. "The earth hasn't crumbled yet."

Penny turned toward the familiar voice. "Aunt Caroline." Tears welled in her eyes, and she rushed to her aunt and clasped her in a hug.

"Oh, Penelope." Her aunt patted her on the shoulder. "That's enough."

Penny drew back.

"Now"—Aunt Caroline sat in the nearest chair without even inspecting it for cat hair first—"tell me everything."

Chapter Thirty

$\mathcal{I}$n St. James Park, fog swamped the new shoots of grass and wound through the budding tree branches. At the opposite end of the green, Lambert and Bradford were indecipherable figures in the mist.

"We'll have to reschedule," Chase said. "As your second, I'll go have a chat with the enemy."

Ashbury grabbed his friend by the collar, holding him back. "As the second, *I'll* do it."

"No one is postponing anything," Gabe said. "This bastard will not live to see another dawn. Not if I have something to say about it."

"Precisely how much shooting have you done?" Chase asked.

"A fair amount."

"Right." Ashbury looked grim. "So scarcely any."

"I'm not in the country shooting pheasants. The man's going to be standing right in front of me."

"To be sure he will be. Right in front of you, somewhere in this soup of fog," Ashbury complained. "You can scarcely see twenty paces, let alone hit a target with any accuracy."

Gabe shrugged. "His weather isn't any better than mine."

"But his facility with a pistol is," Ash replied. "Don't be a clod. In particular, don't be a dead clod."

Gabe extended his right arm, arranging his fingers into a mock pistol, and sized up the shot.

"Allow me." Chase nudged his friend aside. "Listen, Gabe. I feel bound to explain the potential consequences here. Dueling is illegal, to begin. It's also bloody dangerous. Men die."

"Yes," Gabe said impatiently. "That's the point."

"There's a solid chance you'll be grievously, if not mortally, wounded. And if by some miracle you do kill Lambert, your chance of dying only increases. Odds are, you'd be charged with murder and hang for it."

Gabe shrugged. "Not much I can do about it now, is there?"

"There is," Ashbury said. "*Delope*. Count off the paces, and when you turn, fire your pistol straight up into the air. Then pray Lambert does the same."

"Why the hell would I do that?"

"It's a sort of truce. Means honor is satisfied."

"I will not be satisfied until that villain is dead. He doesn't deserve honor. What he did to Penny was not merely despicable. It was unforgivable."

"We know. Her suffering is unfathomable. So if you love her, don't put her through even more pain. If you were to die, she'd be devastated. Hell, even Chase and I would be . . ." He looked to his friend for the word.

"Disappointed?" Chase suggested.

"Let's go with inconvenienced," Ashbury replied.

Chase nodded. "Someone has to eat the sandwiches."

"Thank you both for this touching moment." Gabe shoved past them. "If you'll excuse me, I have a rotting pile of human filth to murder."

"She loves you," Chase said.

"She loves anything with a face." Gabe gestured at Ashbury's scarred visage. "In your instance, half a face. If I die, she will find someone else."

"I've known Penny since we were children," Ashbury said. "Yes, she'll extend love to the most miserable of creatures. But much as I hate to admit it, this is different. I've never seen her like this before."

"*Delope*," Chase said. "Do it for her."

Gabe spoke through a clenched jaw. "Everything I will ever do for the remainder of my life—whether that life lasts ten minutes or fifty years—is for her. I don't require your approval, and I don't need you as my goddamned second and third." When neither of the two men moved, Gabe bellowed at them, "Begone."

Before walking away, Chase leaned close. "Just as a point of clarification, in case you *do* die . . . Which of us would you say was the second, and which the third?"

"For Christ's sake." Gabe was going to finish this. Now. He stalked across the green, took one of the prepared dueling pistols from the case, and approached Lambert until they stood toe-to-toe. "We don't have to do this."

"Are you offering to apologize for this grievous misunderstanding?"

"No." He jammed the barrel of the pistol into Lambert's gut. "I'm thinking I'll skip over the ten paces nonsense and shoot you right now in cold blood."

Lambert made a croaking noise. "You'd hang for that."

"Perhaps."

The fact might have dissuaded Gabe—if he wasn't a dead man already.

Ash and Chase were right. He would be at a disadvantage shooting from any distance, and he'd be committing a crime punishable by death. Maybe he'd survive the duel, but he'd be captured soon afterward—and if he didn't succeed in killing Lambert, it would have been for nothing. If he was going to swing from the end of a noose, he might as well go out knowing he'd meet this monster in Hell.

"You won't get away with it," Lambert said. "Everyone knows what you are. Word about the *ton* is that you're nothing but a lowborn guttersnipe."

"The word about the *ton* is right." Gabe cocked the pistol. "And this lowborn guttersnipe is sending you to Hell."

"*Wait!*"

The cry pierced the fog. It was a high-pitched, desperate cry. Female. Familiar.

Gabe closed his eyes and cursed.

Penny.

"WAIT!" PENNY CRIED, dashing over the damp grass with her hem hiked to her ankles. By the time she arrived at Gabriel's side, she was panting. "Wait. Don't shoot him."

"Penny, what are you doing here?"

"Isn't it obvious?" she hissed. "I'm preventing you from doing something that will get you killed."

"You need to leave. You don't belong here."

"You're wrong. I do belong here. If anyone's going to defend my honor this morning, it's going to be me." She put her hand over the barrel of the pistol. "I'm the only one who can do this."

Gabriel reluctantly fell back a step.

Penny took his place, standing directly in front of Lambert. She looked him in the eye. "I have things to say to you. You're going to listen. Silently. Not one word. Otherwise, Mr. Duke will have my permission to do with you what he will. Understood?"

"Now, poppet. We—"

"Not. One. Word," she growled.

Gabriel aimed the pistol.

Lambert displayed his open hands. Silently.

"I was a child. I trusted you. My family trusted you. What you did to me was an unconscionable betrayal of that trust."

Bradford turned to his father-in-law. "What does she mean?"

"I can't imagine," Lambert said.

"He touched me," Penny told her brother. Her voice was flat, drained of emotion. "In ways a grown man should never touch a girl. He did it for years."

"I would never hurt you, poppet. You must have misunderstood."

"I understood perfectly. You gained my trust with gifts and attention, and then you manipulated that trust to hurt me. You drove a wedge between me and my parents. You made me feel dirty and ashamed."

"Penny," her brother said. "If what you're saying is true, why did you never say anything before now?"

"Oh, Bradford. Because of this. Precisely this. I knew you would doubt me."

"I don't doubt you *believe* you're telling the truth. But I do wonder if you might be confused."

"Calling me 'confused' *is* doubting me." She kept her gaze on Lambert. "I'm not confused. I recall everything. Every hug that lasted too long. Every kiss in exchange for a sweetmeat. Every 'dancing lesson' in the ballroom that one rainy autumn. And I remember every caution to keep those things secret. I knew it was wrong, even as a child. You knew it was wrong, too."

"Wrong isn't the word," Gabriel interjected. "Sick. Monstrous. Evil. Death is too good for you, you—"

"Thank you," Penny cut in. "I appreciate your support, but I'll choose my own words today. And I'll take my own retribution."

Lambert chuckled. "Retribution?"

"I will never forgive you for ruining those years that should have been happy, or for ruining those relationships. But know this: You did not ruin me. You could never ruin me." She reached into her pocket and withdrew a tightly rolled sheaf of papers. "I'm the one who is going to ruin you."

"I can't imagine what you mean."

"Can't you? This might spark your memory." She unrolled the papers. "Perhaps you remember borrowing a large sum of money from my Aunt Caroline to pay off gambling debts? And perhaps you remember accumulating more gambling debts without repaying that loan. My aunt wasn't the only one you bilked, either. You've quite a trail of unpaid debts, Mr. Lambert. They amount to tens of thousands of pounds. And as of this morning, you have only one creditor. Me."

Gabriel took the papers from her hands and sifted through them. "Penny, how on earth did you accomplish this?"

"I learned from the best. And I had help." She nodded toward the edge of the park, where a dark coach and team were just visible through the fog. "My aunt and I spent all night tracking down people who'd loaned him money. She bought up all the debts, and she sold the entire bundle of paper to me. For a shilling."

"You are a wonder."

"Is it all in order?" she asked. "Will it hold in court?"

Gabriel nodded. "As far as I can see."

"Good." She said to Lambert, "This will be easier for us both if you'll surrender your assets willingly. If you won't, I'll go through Chancery and ruthlessly take from you whatever I can claim. I could burn your life to the ground. But if you agree to my terms, you'll keep your house and a modest income."

"Like hell he will," Gabriel interjected. "Leave him with nothing."

Penny never took her eyes from Lambert. "He needs his house and the income to keep it. Because he must agree to never leave that home again."

"What?"

"Allow me to tell you what's happened this morning, here in this park. You've been injured, most grievously, in this duel. As a result, you're going home to the country to recover. Except that you won't recover. Ever."

"Ever?"

"As far as the remainder of the world is concerned, you will remain a homebound invalid for the rest of your life. You may have the bare minimum of servants—old, unpleasant, male ones. No callers."

"No callers?"

"None."

"Not even my grandchildren?"

"*Especially* not your grandchildren. If you care anything for them, you will do precisely as I say. If I find you've broken this agreement, I will expose not only your perversion but your insolvency. Your children and grandchildren will be tainted by association. And Mr. Duke will have my full support to do what he will with you."

"Insupportable," Lambert snarled. "I won't be subordinate to a guttersnipe."

"Mr. Duke is worth hundreds of you. Thousands."

"Only because he stole that money from decent families."

"I'm not talking about his fortune. I'm speaking of his worth as a man. As for decency . . . ? You have no grounds to speak on that matter."

He fished about for another argument. "Bradford, surely you won't permit her to do this."

"My brother has no choice in the matter. Even if he offers you mercy, I will not."

Lambert's chin quavered. The reality of his situation seemed to finally be sinking in. "Surely we can come to some other agreement. Think of your parents, my friendship with your father. We can find a way to settle this misunderstanding, poppet."

"Don't you ever—*ever*—call me that again. Or I swear, I will shoot you dead myself." Penny stared directly into his repulsive, cowardly eyes. "I'm not your 'poppet' any longer. I *own* you. And in the future, if you address me at all, it will be as Lady Penelope Duke." A more fitting idea struck her, and a cold smile touched her lips. "Better yet, you may call me the Duchess of Ruin."

Aunt Caroline joined them. "Time for you to be on your way, Lambert. There's a carriage waiting. These gentlemen will see you to it."

Two giants emerged from the fog to take Lambert by either arm and drag him away.

The older woman smiled. "Now, *that* was satisfying. I never knew until this moment how much I wanted to have henchmen." With a pat to Penny's shoulder and a swish of skirts, she turned to follow.

Only Bradford lingered. "Penny . . ." He pushed a hand through his hair. "Deuced if I know what to make of all this."

"There are two alternatives. You believe me, or you don't." She drew a steadying breath. "You should know this. I've decided that I can't have anything to do with that man, ever again. If you choose to maintain a relationship with him—of any sort—I can't have a relationship with you."

He searched her eyes. "You're going to make me choose?"

"I have to. Otherwise, I'll never be at peace."

He looked into the distance and was silent for a long moment. "He's my wife's father."

"I know." Penny forced down the emotion choking her throat. His decision was nothing she hadn't expected. She'd always known which of them he would chose. "Safe travels, Bradford."

He went to join his father-in-law.

She turned and walked in the other direction, not wanting to watch them leave. Gabriel walked alongside her.

"Are they gone?" she asked, a few minutes later.

He looked over his shoulder. "Yes."

"Good."

She promptly crumpled to the ground. Her knees buckled beneath her and she leaned forward, bracing her palms on the turf for strength. She watched the damp earth seep under her fingernails. She felt cold droplets of dew wetting her stockings. Her heartbeat drummed in her ears. But none of it felt real. She floated above herself, an observer.

Then Gabriel's arms went around her, tethering her to the earth. Air flooded her lungs, then rushed out as a tearless sob. She turned and buried her face in his chest, clinging to his coat.

He rocked her gently, murmuring words of love in her ear and stroking her hair. "That was the bravest thing I've ever seen."

"I want to go home," she whispered. "I want to cry, and sleep for days, and possibly break things."

"That can be arranged. Mrs. Burns has Bathsheba Wendleby's old china stashed in the cellar. Service for eighteen."

"Perfect." She closed her eyes. "I'm also going to find a new litter of kittens, and I don't want to hear anything about it."

"You won't hear a word from me. Even if you have a hundred kittens." His hand stilled on her back, and he added, "That was hyperbole, you understand."

She lifted her head. "And in a few weeks, or maybe months, I want to start planning a wedding. The biggest, grandest wedding Mayfair has ever seen. The guest list will fill the society column for weeks."

"I hope I'm invited."

She gave him a teasing pinch. "You will not be invited. You'll be the groom. And it's going to be the best wedding in the world."

Chapter Thirty-One

*O*n the morning of the wedding, a dozen things went wrong.

Bixby snagged and ripped her veil.

George ate her flowers.

Chase and Ash wouldn't cease arguing over which of them was the "real" best man.

And now Aunt Caroline was nowhere to be found. They couldn't begin the ceremony without her. She'd agreed to walk Penny down the aisle.

Penny tapped her toes beneath the hem of her gown, trying not to betray her growing concern.

"There, I've done my best." Emma held up the hastily mended veil. "The damage shouldn't show too terribly."

"You're a miracle worker. I don't know what I'd do without you, Emma." Penny hugged her friend. For good measure, she hugged Alexandra and Nicola, too. "I don't know what I'd do without any of you. My three graces."

"Only two graces," Alex countered. "You know I'm not a duchess. Yet."

"Only one grace," Nicola said, subtracting herself from the total. "No matter what title I carry, I could never lay any claim to grace."

"I daresay you are the most gracious among us, Penny." Emma packed away her needle and thread. "Who could have guessed you'd be the last of us to make it to the altar?"

"However, if my aunt doesn't appear soon, I may never make it to the altar."

"She's still not here?" Gabriel stood at the vestry entrance, looking as impatient as he did handsome.

Penny took a moment to simply admire him. He cut a splendid figure in his morning suit, his broad shoulders stretching the slate-gray wool of his coat. His freshly clipped hair was a swoop of tamed black, and his clean-shaven face looked smooth as a baby's. Despite his civilized appearance this morning, however, she knew that come evening his jaw would be scratchy with dark whiskers, his hair would be thick, untamed waves—and that elegant morning coat? By then, she would have stripped it from those broad shoulders, revealing the beast beneath.

Everything about their wedding could go wrong, as long as this one thing went right. When they left this church, this magnificent man would be hers. All hers. That was all that mattered, really.

"I hate to interrupt," he said, "but there are flower girls and a ring bearer currently running footraces between the nave and back of the church."

"Oh, dear." Alexandra leaped into action. "Most of those are mine."

Emma followed. "Not all of them, unfortunately."

"None are my responsibility yet," Nicola said. "But I suppose I might need practice."

Once they were alone, Penny turned to Gabriel. "I can't imagine what's delaying Aunt Caroline. I'm worried about her."

"Whoever or whatever is delaying her, I'm worried for *it*."

Uneasiness knotted in her belly. "Do you think she's changed her mind?"

With her parents and Timothy overseas, and Bradford at a great distance in more ways than one, Aunt Caroline was her only close relation in Town. If even *she* didn't appear, Penny would feel rather abandoned.

"Your aunt has not changed her mind," Gabriel said stoutly. "Why would she? The woman adores me."

Penny arched an eyebrow in doubt.

"Very well. She doesn't adore me, but that's only because she isn't the adoring sort. Don't worry. She'll be here."

"Penny?"

She wheeled toward the familiar voice. "Bradford?"

Penny hadn't seen her eldest brother in a year. Not since that misty morning in St. James Park when she'd put the choice to him. He was her brother, and she loved him dearly—but as long as he maintained a relationship with his father-in-law, they couldn't be a part of each other's lives.

In the months since, they'd corresponded in stilted, impersonal fashion when necessary, and naturally she'd sent him notice of the wedding. When friends asked, it wasn't difficult to explain his absence. The excuses wrote themselves: too long a journey from Cumberland, another child on the way, and so forth.

And now . . . here he was, without warning.

She swallowed a lump in her throat. "I didn't know you were coming."

"To be fair, I wasn't certain, either. In the end, Aunt Caroline gave me a kick in the arse."

Gabriel made his presence known. "If you're here to object during the ceremony, I'll kick you in the arse myself. And I'm a fair bit stronger than Aunt Caroline."

"I'm not here to object to the wedding." He looked to Penny. "I'm hoping to be a part of it. Might I have the honor of walking you down the aisle?"

She couldn't speak.

"This past year, I haven't kept my distance out of anger or mistrust, but out of shame. I'm your older brother. I should have paid more attention. I should have . . . known somehow. I wasn't there when you needed me, and I know I can never make amends for the past. But if you'll allow me, I promise to be there from this day forward."

"You don't have to say yes, Penny," Gabriel said.

"I know."

She took her brother's hands in hers. The space between them couldn't be bridged in one morning. But if he'd taken the first step—several thousand first steps, considering the distance from Cumberland—she could make the next.

Before speaking, she paused to reflect. "Bradford, I'm glad you're here. So very glad. But I don't want you to walk me down the aisle this morning. I'm not yours to give away."

Bradford looked disappointed, but he took it well. "I understand. I'll fetch Aunt Caroline, then? She's just outside."

"I'm not Aunt Caroline's to give away, either. Or anyone's. I'm my own person, marrying the man of my choosing." She reached for Gabriel's hand and looked up at him. "Why don't we walk down the aisle together?"

"Rather a break with tradition," Bradford said. "But if it's what you want."

"It is."

"Then that's how it should be. I'm happy for you, Penny." Bradford kissed her on the cheek. On his way out, he leveled a finger at Gabriel. "You're not good enough for her."

"Neither are you," Gabriel returned.

Bradford nodded. "What do you know, we've already found some common ground."

When her brother had left, Penny turned to her groom and smiled. "I suppose we should go be married."

"No hedgehog in your pocket?"

She shook her head. "And no shilling in yours, I hope?"

His reply was strangely hesitant. "No."

Suspicious, Penny skimmed her hands over the silk of his waistcoat and the hard planes of his chest beneath. When her fingers encountered a hard, flat object in the region of his breast pocket, she gave a cry of displeasure. "Gabriel."

"What?"

"You know very well what." She worked her gloved hand

under the superfine wool of his lapel, delving into the concealed pocket.

He shied from her touch. "Brazen woman."

"You promised me."

"And I kept my promise."

"Truly?" She pinched the coin between her thumb and forefinger, wiggling it free of its satin-lined hiding place. "Then how do you explain this?"

"Spare change. Can't imagine how it got there."

She tipped her head in reproach.

He exhaled, sounding resigned. "It's not what you think."

She turned her hand palm-up between them, letting the coin serve as its own accusation. "I think I know a shilling when I see one."

"Look again."

She looked down at the coin in her gloved palm, where its embossed face stood out in sharp relief against white satin. Light glinted off the surface, revealing the color to be not the expected dull silver, but a coppery hue instead.

Oh.

A sharp pang of surprise caught her heart. He'd been telling the truth. It wasn't a shilling after all.

It was a penny.

A bright, newly minted penny. One he'd been keeping tucked in his breast pocket. Right next to his heart.

She drew a shaky breath. "Gabriel."

His hands went to her shoulders—but it was his low, husky voice that reached out and drew her close. "You know the squalor I was born to. And you know I promised myself I'd never be that barefoot, starving boy again."

She nodded.

"I have every luxury a man could desire. Hundreds of thousands of pounds in my accounts. I worked like hell to build a fortune, and yet . . ." His thumb met her cheek with a reverent caress. "Now I'd sell my soul for a Penny."

She stretched up on her toes and placed a soft, lingering kiss to his cheek, nuzzling as they drifted apart. They stared into each other's eyes for a time. She couldn't have guessed whether it lasted seconds or hours, but she knew it was a sliver of always.

He held out his hand. "I'll take that back, thank you."

She surrendered the coin gladly, tucking it back into his pocket before straightening his lapels and smoothing his coat flat. "I'm going to walk down the aisle with a reddened nose and watery eyes. I hope you're happy."

He replied simply, "I am."

Epilogue

Several years later

I love you," Penny said sweetly, as she did at least once an afternoon. "I *love* you."

"Pretty girl."

"I love you. I love you. I *love* you."

"MRS. ROBBINS!"

Penny sighed and offered the bird a bit of crumbled biscuit. "Oh, Delilah. I'm not giving up, you know. One of these days, we're going to get it right."

Over the past few years, Delilah's repertoire of phrases had indeed expanded, in many of the same ways that Penny's life had grown.

In the first year of their marriage, Delilah had learned to mimic Bixby's barking. She'd also mastered, *"No, George! No!"* which amused Gabriel no end.

By the following winter, Delilah had learned to imitate a newborn's wail with such startling accuracy that she'd drawn both of them out of bed on many an early morning, after many a sleepless night. Gabriel found this significantly less amusing.

A few months more, and Delilah could hum the first strains of a lullaby. She'd learned to call out "Mummy!" mere weeks after little Jacob did.

For whatever reason, however, Penny could never coax Delilah into repeating those three little words. She'd dangled every flavor of biscuit in Nicola's recipe book, to no avail. Surely the parrot was teasing her. She heard the phrase repeated often enough, and not only from Penny. This was a house full of love.

She decided to try one more time. "I *love* you. I l—"

"You're still trying to teach that bird?" Gabriel entered the drawing room.

"Of course I am. I never give up."

"Yes, about that." He tugged off his gloves and threw them onto a side table. "Mind telling me why there's a flock of sheep in the mews?"

"There are three sheep in the mews," she said. "Three sheep are not a 'flock.'"

"Flock or not, they are three more sheep than we had in the mews this morning."

"They're going to the farm, I promise." Under her breath, she added, "Just as soon as they're out of quarantine."

The farm was the first purchase Penny had made with Mr. Lambert's seized assets. They'd begun with a smallholding in Kent, but when a parcel of adjacent land had come available, she'd enlarged the place. They rebuilt the old farmhouse and added new barns.

The farm wasn't only a home for unwanted animals. During the summer, it was their home, as well. Emma, Alex, and Nicola brought their families to visit. Last year, they'd even welcomed Bradford and his boys for a few weeks, just before the Michaelmas school term began—and Gabriel was actually civil to her brother, for the most part.

Gabriel sat down on a bench to remove his boots. "Where's Jacob?"

"At the park, with Emma and Richmond."

"The baby?"

"Sleeping."

He dropped his boot to the floor and gave her a slow, wicked grin. "Is that so?"

"Yes, it is." She walked toward the bench, moving with a coquettish sway in her hips. He caught her by the waist and hauled her into his lap for a slow, deep kiss.

"I love you," he said. "You may never teach that damned parrot to say it, but you taught me. You'll never hear the end of it now, pretty girl. I love you." *Kiss.* "I love you." *Kiss.* "I love you."

Penny laced her arms about her husband's neck. "Fancy a fuck, love?"